The Big Q

D0432914

Also by Des Dillon

Me an Ma Gal
The Big Empty
Duck
Itchycooblue
Return of the Busby Babes

EdFest 2004

The Big Q

DES DILLON

To Duncan –

here's to philosophy

Des.

review

Copyright © 2001 Des Dillon

The right of Des Dillon to be identified as the Author
of the Work has been asserted by him in accordance with
the Copyright, Designs and Patents Act 1988.

First published in 2001
by REVIEW

An imprint of Headline Book Publishing

10 9 8 7 6 5 4 3 2 1

All rights reserved. No part of this publication may be
reproduced, stored in a retrieval system, or transmitted,
in any form or by any means without the prior written
permission of the publisher, nor be otherwise circulated
in any form of binding or cover other than that in which
it is published and without a similar condition being
imposed on the subsequent purchaser.

All characters in this publication are fictitious
and any resemblance to real persons, living or dead,
is purely coincidental.

ISBN 0 7472 7547 5

Designed by Ben Cracknell Studios and Des Dillon

Printed and bound in Great Britain by
Clays Ltd, St Ives plc

Headline Book Publishing
A division of Hodder Headline
338 Euston Road
London NW1 3BH

www.reviewbooks.co.uk
www.hodderheadline.com

For Davy – phone me when I'm not in!

And Brother Philip

A BIG SIMPLICITY OF STARS

See me? I believe in the magnificence of man.

I'll tell ye this for nothin – see yer nose? Smell? It's the most closely associated sense wi yer memory – smell. One whiff of disinfectant an ye're back on the Ward.

SNIFF!

It's handy yer nose.

SNIFF!

SNIFF!

I'm sniffin the air.

Spring chills laced wi the scent of summer. That's what Easter brings. It's not yer brain that works yer memories it's yer nose. Organ of memory. Olfactory memory factory. A truffle-huntin pig. Inside yer head it digs. Searchin through the darkness of soil. Tunnellin under roots. Searchin out faded love-letters. Uprootin the repressed pains of growin. Diggin up the things ye don't want to look at. Bloodhoundin things ye hoped were dead an gone.

SNIFF! Try it.

SNIFF! Try spring. Smell yellas an

greens. Smell the Easter snow fadin away leavin the grass lank an damp. That smell that almost squeaks.

SNIFF! Try summer. Smell shattered

light on rhododendron leaves. Their hunners of different angles reflectin the ordered day into splinters. They stab light out at angles from its parallel arrival.

On the Ward Jimmy Brogan was rememberin light. He was young. Standin in the darkness of this ordinary tree. Hidin from the world. He's ten. This ordinary tree disintegrates the daylight. He's dazzled. The whole world's in bits. He tries but he can't project order on the forest sun. So he stays mesmerised by the light. Enchanted by the dark.

When he was in that tree Jimmy Brogan was mesmerised by somethin else an all. It was the time his feelins were all separatin. Fragmentin. He told me all about it. What brung it about was a tune. Well two tunes really. Or mibbi three. I can't remember right what he sayed. But lookin back now it's easy to see that was the start – the very beginnin of his troubles.

'Rule Britannia'. That's what it was. The tune. They were doin Singin Together an this week the song was 'Rule Britannia'. It was:

John John John the grey goose is gone an the fox is off to his den oh, last week.

Jimmy Brogan liked that. An he liked 'Rule Britannia' an all. The whole class's singin away like true patriots.

Rule Britannia
Britannia rules the waves.
Britons never never ne – ver shall

                              be

                                    slaves.

He sung it. He drummed it out on the desk but Miss Boswell never bothered. He could drum away to his heart's content far as she was concerned. An she was usin her pencil as a baton. The whole class was singin. Jimmy Brogan says he felt tears in his eyes. It was good to be British. Rulin the waves an all that. Lettin no cunt mess. Don't fuck wi the Brits. Union Jack ya bass.

At playtime Donny O'Hare sayed that was a lot of pish what the teacher sayed cos we're Scottish. Jimmy Brogan an him sung Scotland The Brave. When we all went back in it was wi a totally different attitude. Totally different. Donny O'Hare an Jimmy Brogan sang it to the teacher. She thought it was good. Got them to sing it in front of the class. It was great to be Scottish. Fuckin brilliant!

The next Sunday he's been at mass Jimmy Brogan. An it was:

Hail glorious Saint Patrick
Dear saint of our isle
On us thy poor children
Bestow a sweet smile

And now thou art throned
In thy mansions above
On Erin's green valleys
On Erin's green valleys . . .

Then on to the Granny's. An in his Granny's wi her Irish
accent the schism came to him. He couldn't name it a
name in them days. He could only see it for what it was all
them years later in the Ward. But that was the exact time
his head started to go wrong. Right there in his Granny's.
That was when he knew. It was one word that done it.
OUR. That was the word. Goin through an through him.
Our Isle. That's what they all sung at mass. He thought
bein Scottish was all Hail Marys an shillelaghs an John F.
Kennedy an pictures of the Pope. But that was Irish. An he
was Scottish. But he was Irish. Erin is Our Isle. But on the
map he's Scottish. But the songs're Irish. All he remembers
is lookin at this shamrock-covered recipe on the wall
IRISH SODA BREAD. It all started spinnin. Next thing
he's wakin up in bed wi the doctor there.

SNIFF!   Autumn's a bit schizophrenic. Autumn deals in
absolute beauty an certain death. Somethin reaches its
peak of beauty just at the point ye realise it's goin to die.
Nothin's goin to be there forever Jimmy Brogan sayed. He
sayed it was Thanatos. That's a great word. Death.
Brrrrrrr!

SNIFF!   Winter. Snow. A philosophy of snow. It sounds
good. Right. Like a Pride of Lions. I can smell a
philosophy of snow. Sniff it in. I can look up an see the
flakes whirlin down. High speed – whoooooooooodoooosh
an birrrrrrriiiiiiiilllll. Micro-angels – that's what they are.
Holdin hands, some of them, in their wee white gowns.
Smilin mibbi. Aye – smilin. An then there's the lonesome
ones. All a spin an nothin to grab onto. But they're all
movin. They're all glidin in rumours an murmurs cos

13

that's the noise they make – rumours an murmurs
rumours an murmurs   rumours an murmurs

    rumours an murmurs rumours an murmurs

  rumours an murmurs   rumours an murmurs

rumours an murmurs

    rumours an

murmurs rumours an murmurs.

   murmurs rumours an murmurs rumours an

      murmurs

murmurs   rumours

               rumours an

An there's more if ye'd only sniff. Close yer eyes. Take a
sharp stab of winter. The snow's fallin. But there's a
paradox. A hypocrisy if ye like. It's a fallin paradise comin
from the low electric red of clouds. A fallin paradise fallin
over our fallen paradise. A coverin for the bad things.
Heavy. The trees twist under billions of micro-angels. An
envy of green branches strain under the weight of snow.
An above. Look up. Above. Up! Up for fucksakes! Into the
whirlin. The spinnin. Into the dizzy eternity that is white.
White. White. White.

White. White.   White.

   White. White.   White.

            White. White.

   White.

White. White.   White. White.

White.   White.   White.   White.

                                White.

White.   White.   White.   White.   White.

                        White.

                                        White.

      White. White. White.

White.

                        White.

                        White.

            White.

White.   White.

White.

                        White.

WHITE

Stick yer face out the door an suck hard. Close yer eyes. Smell the night an the blue haze of snow. Let the molecules scud the bobs an buffers inside of yer nose **Ding ding.** Yer head lights up like a pintable.

Ding donk thunk

Sexual repression's nothin compared wi nasal repression – that's the fella alright. So suck. Sniff long an hard. **Ziiiiiiiiiiiiiiiiiiiiiiiiiimg** go the signals to yer brain. Wee pictures. Feelins.

 emotions ye thought ye were incapable of. Fireworks in yer head. Bangers an rockets. Let it take ye. C'mon, don't fight it. Hand yer will over to it. The nose filters nothin. We do that. Ye're yer own censor.

Go wi it! A fairground in the rain. Browned out bodies. Umbrellas an hats.

Go wi it! Whirly faces smilin. Curly Baroque music. Big wheels an waltzers.

Go wi it! Crazy hats an candy.

Go wi it! Kiss me quick an feel me slow.

Watery ain't it? All out of focus in the cinema inside yer skull. That's yer past whirlin. Yer history. Its blade sharp in emotional precision. The pain on the world's finest blade. The pleasure.

Go wi it! Touch the stuff ye thought ye'd adulted out yer psyche.

Go wi it! The heavy thrum of loss hummin like pylon wires in yer heart. Ooh now that's sore. Sore as fuck.

Go wi it! The breathtakin

THRIZZZZZZZZZ

Of success.

Go wi it! The Gregorian chant of contentment movin like a fish in clear water. Plip! **Whoops** it's gone. Ye seen yer own shadow. Run. Run like fuck cos everythin's changin round about ye all the time. Change change change. Ye can run but ye can't keep up.

But what am I on about? Ma head's always takin a wander. I'm tryin to tell ye this story an I ends up bumpin ma gums about noses. **Sniff! Sniff! Sniffity Sniff!**

Back to the story. It's nearly Easter. I'm drivin at night. There's some snow on the moors still and it's dark blue. Every now an then there's headlights. Sometimes light can blind ye.

Every time I read a book I become a **That Book** maniac. Right evangelic. Top of the mountain stuff. Shoutin. Then it fades an I get back to the flat surface of normality. It's always flat normality. Normality absorbs abnormality in the end. Gravity draws the universe thegether. In The End there'll only be one gravity tuggin at nothin. That's the way it'll be. Endless peace an stillness.

I'm always puzzlin the universe. God? Me? Us? Planets? What's it all about Alfie? If there was a Big Bang everythin that makes up the universe theday must've came from there. That singularity. That wee ball of everythin. That means the atoms in us're the same atoms that were there at the beginnin of time. An the same fuckin atoms that'll be there at the end of time – if it ever comes. We're eternal for fucksakes! What the fuck're we worryin about? Everythin's goin to be alright. Everythin's goin to be fine.

Whoaaa! Whoa!

Whoa! Whoa! Hold on there bald eagle.

Don't shut

the book yet.

Pssst!

C'mere!

It's not about the meanin of life. It's about Me an Pat an Davy Doom. In Italy. In a monastery. OK sometimes I wander into the big

Q

Tell ye what – miss they bits out. See if I start goin on about lyin on the Piazza under the stars – I'm about to take a wander. Move on. I'm the same – I hate borin stories too. I can't help it. It's like I've been programmed. Tangent man they should call me. Fuckin Tangent man.

So I'm in the car this night. Drivin over to pick up Davy an Pat. Up through the sunroof there's a big simplicity of stars. Ever do that? Look at the most complicated things an feel the easy breath of simplicity? It's stars wi me. Some people it's poetry. Or maths. Davy likes maths. It's wood wi Pat. Pat likes wood. An sculptin. An paintin.

I'm usually makin simple things complicated. Like ma life.

Go wi the flow ya mad cunt, Davy always says when I start ma philosophisin. So I go wi the flow a wee while an then . . . then . . . mibbi a wee bird twitterin an another wee bird twitterin back sets me off again.

Sometimes I think the more ye know the better. So I read books all the time. But wi a zillion facts even the head of a pin can be awesome.

Q – How many angels can ye get on the head of a pin?

A – How many atoms in a grain of sand?

Complicated? I don't know!?

I'm goin wi Davy an Pat to Cucuruzzu. It's a village near Monte Cassino. I'm hopin me an Davy'll start gettin on the way we used to. I mean we're still great pals an the crack's good. But things've not been the same since I stole

21

his burd out Memory Lane. It was just after I got out. I think the freedom was makin me bold as fuck. I had no fear wi the wimmin. No fear at all. Davy fancied this wee thing behind the bar an he got me to chat her up. We done that for a month. Me an him'd go in an sit at the bar an grin at her. Turns out she thought it was me that fancied her. Davy always had the suspicion I shagged her. I never. When it came to the crunch this amazin black feelin went right into me and I couldn't do nothing. Not a thing. I remember runnin through the night to get away from it. Anyway I hope we get rid of that bad current flowin between us. That's what I hope for me an Davy.

Ye hope for things for people all the time. Years since Pat's been in a chapel. Weddins an funerals just. A monastery'll calm him down mibbi. He's got this thing in him that stops him relaxin. It's a gyroscope. It's turnin all the time an upsettin his gravity. It was a long time ago somebody tugged the string. He's spent his life containin it. He paints an sculpts. He's good. But he's tryin to get off the drink an this is as good an opportunity as any. The sunshine an the work. An the lazy way they do things in these countries – specially in a monastery. Pat thinks it'll be a cinch.

Mibbi stop it all thegether, he says, *the drink.*

His Maw died. I was on the Ward. It was spring. It was snowin an we kept losin thoughts in the snow. Ye could see them pushin out people's ears like icicles an then breakin off. Fallin in the snow. Makin a wee groove then fillin so ye'd never know there was anythin there. Smooth snow. Powder for miles. I was numb fumblin about for them.

Pat visited an sayed about his Maw dyin. Hardly affected me. I tried to bother. I think he wanted me to come out for the funeral. I mind there was this tear on his left eye. I was in it an the whole ward bent out of shape behind me. It sparked. Every time he turned his head the whole world wobbled inside it.

It was tryin to get me to say, *Right yar Pat. I'll be there. The wake an all. I'll be carryin the coffin.*

But I couldn't say nothin. An Pat – he's bitin his lip. After his millionth look round the place he goes, *How's the food? Is it good?*

Aye, I say. I want to say, *Aye Pat*, but I can't. There's too much stuff jammed in ma throat.

What about Jimmy Brogan? he says. An the thing is he's lookin in ma eyes like he's more concerned about Jimmy Brogan than me.

He's out in the snow. Thinkin.

The way I say it he knows it's the end of the visit. He looks out the windies. It's all white. He laughs a bit an goes, *I'll see if I can find him before I go.*

There's more tears on his face now. But I'm blank. All the drugs've made me not care. I want to say somethin that'll make him feel better but I can't. He doesn't turn back all the way up the corridor. I go to shout on him but the door opens an this cold breeze rushes at me. I wrap ma arms round maself. It's funny. They're that numb it feels like somebody else's cuddlin me.

We need to get the eleven o'clock bus to Manchester an a plane to Rome at seven in the mornin. Arrive in Rome half past twelve I think. We're due in Cassino at two or three. Train. The monk's goin to pick us up. We help build the monk's Hermitage an we get a holiday. Grub an a bed. That's the deal.

I arrive in Coatbridge. The Brig.

Yer home town. Ye're always comin home when ye drive through it. Homecomin. I decided to live somewhere else when I got out the Ward. But Christ! The amounts of times I've left. An it's not the leavin that was on ma mind. It's the homecomin. That's what's important. See how much distance – miles an hours – ye could put between leavin an comin home. The homecomin party never materialised. Ye weren't missed. No cunt commented on the void ye thought ye'd left behind. It was like ye went to the toilet an this's you comin back out zippin up yer strides.

Alright mate – get us a pint up eh?

Homecomins're the thing alright. We're always tryin to come home. That's another gravity.

Mibbi we got lost thousands of years ago. Lost but we still want to go home. But we wouldn't recognise home if it popped up out our cornflakes. Concentratin on wealth an technology's pushed everythin to the side. Like spirituality. I don't mean religion. I mean feelin good about existin. About just bein here. Humans bein. That blue sky feelin ye get lookin at the sky an suckin summer up yer nostrils.

But there I'm away again. Back to the story.

I pass the Pop Inn. That's where Jimmy Brogan drank. That's where I drank an all. Last week Pat was on the drink. First in six months. He always boaks when he's drunk. In his sleep. This day about a year ago he's scrapin hard sick off the sheets an I'm lookin out the veranda. Fourth floor. Cracked an bare. There's herds of young team about. This guy about eighteen staggers through them. He's got a wane an it's pink. Too soft for the place that surrounds it. I want to tell it.

Hey! – Wane! Get yerself to fuck out of this *while ye still can!*

But I can't do that. Its life's mapped out right there. The child is the father of the man. Read that on the Ward. An this wane's programmin the brain that'll grow the man from the drunks an scar-faced clowns that mill around it. It's wide open to the winds that blow through here. The winds that blow through here blow through the young team an through the wane's Da. I don't know if it's a boy

or a girl. The Da gets a slug of Buckie an cracks a laugh.
The baby's eyes're glintin an takin it all in – takin it all in –

TAKIN IT ALL IN

It's not even two. One an a half mibbi. At the most.
Carried through its early world like a rucksack. He lifts
the wane up onto his shoulders. It hovers over their heads
like a demented Jesus. The Da's shufflin along. It's all grim
to him. Except the drink an drugs an the handin the wane
back to its Maw. Burd got up the stick to get a house off
the Council. When he gets rid of it he's up the dancin for
another burd an the same oul wheels turn round an
round. Wheels within wheels.

John Doc goes by. He's drunk but his back's straight.
His shoulders're up. He'll banjo the first young cunt that
says anythin. Anythin except *Want a swally Doc?* The
garages're derelict. For a minute I think I sees Jimmy
Brogan lookin up at me. But I couldn't've. They got rid of
him. Long time ago now. We ended up like brothers in the
Ward. Inseparable sometimes. The doctors were always
tryin to drive a wedge between us. Always.

This scheme was built in the sixties. I mind movin in.
All the white houses an wee fences everywhere. An grass.
Grass like a golf course. Now it's shot down in flames.
Guts strewn on the slabs.

Daaa daa da da daaa daa daa. 'Greensleeves'. That's a
laugh. It's the van. A procession of wanes wi clinkin
bottles an fat-arsed Maws foldin their arms over their tits
stream out closes. Then there's wanes' faces pressed
against the glass of other rooms. Mibbi their Maw's skint.
Drank the giro mibbi or pissin it up an playin Trivial
Pursuit wi the neighbours. The last quid spent on a plastic
bottle of cider.

What's the coldest temperature ever recorded? Shug it's you.

25

Aye right. I remember that one. Is it two hunner an sixty odd?

Two hunner an sixty odd what?

Aw how the fuck do I know. Bananas?

Naw Kelvin. Two hunner an seventy-three degrees Kelvin. An it's fuckin minus anyway!

Are ye givin me it?

No way – ye've got to say exactly what's on the card.

Even the crows've aged. The pavements're a patchwork of tar.

UP THE PROVO'S DOCKLANDS HA HA

it says on the wall. That's what some cunt inherited from his Irish forefathers. An if there's injustices in Ireland it's hard to focus on here for drunks an junkies.

The tops of the flats're like the Amityville horror. The windies're dark eyes. The houses're sparse. Couch telly video microwave. The floors're warped. Nobody notices the uphill struggle to the door. Doors're nailed up an steel-shuttered. All electric. No heat. Too dear to turn on. Irish songs ring through the nights.

But they didn't say why Billy Reid had to die
But he died with a gun in his hand.
No they didn't say why Billy Reid had to die
But he died to free Ireland.

Father feeds them on to son. The doors breathe in one generation an breathe out another. An down below tracked an re-tracked wi wanderin feet that don't know where to go – the grass – even the grass struggles to stay green.

I drive up to Davy's close an pump the horn.

DOOM

I've parked ma car up. We're in Davy's Da's car. Daddy Doom's drivin us to the bus station. A good example of Daddy Doom is when I just got out. Me an Davy decided to take on the Munros for therapy. Clean air an wide open spaces. We bought the same boots. Mooren Ecosse. A hunner an fifty a pair. Davy takes them in an shows them to his Maw.

We're goin to do the Munros, he says.

What's a Munro, Daddy Doom says.

Mountains. Over three thousand feet.

Ye'll fall aff, goes Daddy Doom an flicks the paper up in front of his face.

Daddy Doom an Pat're in the front an me an Doom's in the back. But we're not goin to the bus station. We've turned round at Bargeddie lights. Davy's forgot his passport.

That's him all over the back, Daddy Doom says. He sees his chance to get the EEC/stray cats story in.

I got thirty tins of EEC beef an he fed two to the stray cats.

I ignores him. So does Davy. But Pat's interested so Doom Daddy tells him a story. It's the story about how Davy fed two perfectly good tins of EEC beef to the cats that lived under the back shed.

It's dark an yella streetlights're runnin over the surface of Pat's face. It's like mine his face. A pile of rocks.

Eleven the bus leaves, yees'll never make it, Daddy Doom Dooms.

We pull up at Davy's close again. Davy bolts past the young winos. They never say nothin when a car's there. Daddy Doom's still goin on about the cats.

Stuffed up wi beef they were. Couldn't even fit back under the shed once they'd scoffed the lot, he goes. An he's mad. But not about the cats. That's just a cover.

But what he's really mad at is Davy goin to a Catholic monastery.

Forgettin his passport! He's been like that all his life. Won't take a tellin. I don't know what yees're takin him for . . . what can he do? He's handless. I mean he's not even a Catholic.

Look at them, is all Pat says ignorin Daddy Doom. He's on about the young team that's drinkin the wine in Davy's close. Davy's light's goin on up in Amityville. Light out. Door slams. He clatters down the stairs. Out the close. Young Team act like he's not even there. It's all that cause an effect stuff. Davy's light goes on so I say – *Oho – that's Davy in his house.* There a pause where nothin much happens. So I go – *Oho there's Davy lookin for his passport.* The light goes out an I thinks – *Oho here's Davy comin back out wi the passport.* But for all I know one of the Young Team's waitin in his house an whacks him wi a baseball bat. Or Davy switches the light on an dies of a heart attack. Then after the while that I think he's been lookin for his passport the power card runs out. So then I think he's on his way out but he never arrives. It's alright the oul cause an effect. Most of the time we just assume what's happenin. Best guess – that's what it is. If we never done that we'd be runnin a million complications through our brain.

BANG!*!*! FIZZ!*!*!

We'd fuse in a week.

Buchanan Street Bus Station Da . . . shove that in Pat, says Davy an hands him a tape. Paganini.

One an two, he goes. *Ye should hear them. Sorry Pat – no Johnny Cash.*

So we allegro, adagio, allegro spirituoso all the way to Buchanan Street. But Daddy Doom can't take all the silence between us.

I don't know why ye're goin over there David – what's the Catholic Church ever done for you? Davy blanks him. Daddy Doom says it all over again like we never **heard it.**

I don't know why ye're goin over there David – what's the Catholic Church ever done for you? Then he says nothin the rest of the journey.

Buchanan Street. Daddy Doom lets us out. Says nothin an vrooms off wi gospel music evangelin out the windie.

♪ *What a friend we have in Jeeeee-sus . . .*

We wave like it's *The Sound of Music* an sing the Daddy Doom song.

♪ *Daddy Doom Daddy Doom. Doom Daddy Doom Daddy.*
Daddy Doom Daddy Doom.

When he skips a red light an turns the wrong way anyway we crease ourselfs. Buchanan Street Bus Station. The journey starts here.

A right full stop this is.

The journey stops here.
The ticket guy's noddin his head.
Your bus left twelve hours ago! Exactly nearly.
Not only that but he's sayin it in the way ye know he intends doin fuck all about it. He's wantin the buses away then he's goin for a kip the rest of the night. Snug in his wee bothy. Last thing he wants's trouble.

The bus leaves Glasgow at eleven at night to catch the seven in the mornin plane. The tickets say **11:00**

They should say **23:00**

Airdrie Journeys doesn't know its arse from its twenty-four-hour clock. The ticket guy's loadin other people an ignorin us now. Like that's the end of the matter. Like we're satisfied. Basically the bus we are booked for left twelve hours ago.

Pat's quiet as a volcano.

It's an omen, Doom goes, *we've not to go. It's a sign. The plane's goin to crash.*

Lava's comin out Pat's eyes. He's lookin about for somewhere to erupt. But it's not the Bus Station's fault. It's Airdrie Journeys'.

It's no use. Ma head's startin to go now. It's the only flights we could get. We've only got spendin money left. What a waste. What a fuckin waste. I'm volcanic now. Eruptive. Doom sees what's happenin an I sees him whisper in the ticket man's ear. The ticket man does nods an hands at the driver.

Next minute the driver says we can go on but we'll have to sit on the floor after Carlisle. Christ – we'd've went in the boot. On the roof. Inside the fuckin tyres. There's this long

Ye'd think it was the buses but it's me an Pat coolin down. Only Doom can hear it right. The lava in Pat's eyes turns redorangedark. It cracks an falls to the floor. But hardly makes a noise. It's just two wee clicks on the expanse of tiles. Two stones in an ocean.

So it's out the M8 an down the M74. I can see the Brig in the distance. It looks like it's got a hangover. **SNIFF!** Some cunt's wearin Brut. **SNIFF!** I fuckin hate that. Makes me sick. One whiff just. One whiff.

BLOODY SUNDAY

Jimmy Brogan was watchin the telly years ago. It was any other Sunday. His Da was still wi his Maw. He'd dogged mass an spent the plate money on Curly Wurlys. Three. Sat down the graveyard freezin. It's the second last day of January. He sayed a couple of Hail Marys about missin mass an watched the clouds. An read what was wrote on the stones. All the names. Harkins. Duffy. Riley. Dillon. Brennan. Cooney. Donnelley. O'Hare. Ryan. Conway. Conlin. Coady. Daley. Regan. Bonar. Doyle. Tolland. Straney. Nalty. Conroy. Foley. Fox. O'Neill. He licked his finger an rubbed some of them an wondered what it'd be like to be dead.

$\flat$ *John john john the grey goose is gone and the fox is off to his den oh . . .*

Jimmy Brogan sang through the tombs till it was time to go home. A crow flaps by. Jimmy Brogan wonders if ye really do go somewhere after ye die. Resurrection. He looks about at the stones. Must be some size heaven he's thinkin. An Hell. In the distance he can see the people streamin out of mass an shakin hands. He heads up the road.

It's later on he's watchin Bernie The Bolt. Up a bit. Down a bit. Left a bit. Left left left. Stop stop stop. Fire. Thunk. Ye had to break the thread. An sometimes all the

gold coins came out an sometimes they never. He couldn't
remember if the coins came out that day or not. But there's
somethin he did remember. The News. He sayed that was
where he took a wrong turn. That was the day that
changed everythin.

So Bernie The Bolt's finished an it's the News. He's on
his belly readin a *Topper* an swingin his feet in the air. An
things're good cos there's half a Curly Wurly planked
outside. The news man's rattlin on about fuck knows
what.

> A civil rights march in
> Londonderry turned into a
> shoot-out today when British
> Paratroopers fired on the
> demonstrators, killing
> thirteen and wounding another
> seventeen. Local politicians
> have dubbed the tragedy
> Bloody Sunday . . .

Jimmy Brogan's tryin to sneak out the door without his
Da noticin.

> . . .and attacked military
> handling of the march and its
> aftermath, although British
> Army chiefs maintained that
> the soldiers had begun firing
> in self-defence . . .

Hanna! Hanna c'mere quick an see this, his Da shouts. In
comes the Maw wipin her hands wi a towel. They're
lookin at the News. Jimmy Brogan peeks back round the
door.

> The violence erupted as
> Republican civil rights
> demonstrators tried to break

```
down a roadblock in the
city's Bogside area and the
troops began to open fire,
initially with rubber
bullets but then with live
rounds . . .
```

There's this Priest jumpin about wavin a hanky. It's only shinin in one eye the telly cos Jimmy Brogan's halfway out the door. He tilts back so his two eyes can see. The telly sucks his whole body back in. His Granny was always goin on about Ireland. Belfast Derry Donegal.

That's where ye want to go. Donegal. Get yerself over there when ye're big an get a nice Irish lassie, she sayed all the time. That's where yer Mother was born. Goats an Hawks she came from. Goats an Hawks Donegal. Jimmy Brogan laughed every time.

What in the name of Jesus're ye laughin at? That boy's touched so he is. Touched, she'd go. But he'd be on the floor wi all this mad stuff goin through his head.

Hello there ma name's Jimmy Brogan an I'm visitin these parts. Ye couldn't tell a fella how to get to Goats an Hawks could ye now? he went doin his Granny. Then he'd do some mad Donegaly.

Sure no I couldn't be tellin ye that — I'm from Pigs an Monkeys meself. Never heard of that place you're talkin about now. What would it be called now? Dogs an Cats?

No ya tattie howkin cunt. It's where ma Graaaaaaaany's from. It's Goats an Hawks.

But he's not laughin here. Not on Bloody Sunday. He's gettin sucked into the telly. It's the Paras.

```
Over a hundred rioters hurled
stones and missiles at the
soldiers. Eyewitness reports
said the first shot was in
fact fired by a Loyalist
Gunman . . .
```

They're shootin every cunt. Probably cunts from Goats an Hawks an all. Wanes. Priests. Oul Wimmin wi bags like yer Maw. But it's the Priest that gets etched into Jimmy Brogan. He's bent over wavin a black bit of cloth out at the front. Bent over like he's dodgin bricks goin over his head. But it's not bricks. It's bullets. That's how he's bent over. An there's four guys behind him. An they're just ordinary guys like what worked in Dundyvan. Or drank in Mackenzie's. Ordinary fellahs. This one's got a tie on an he's quite neat. Like he must have an office job. He's got the body by the ankles. Grabbin it by the trousers. An a wee guy like Garden Bobby down the lane. Exactly like him. Wee an baldy. He's lookin up an his arm's comin under the body an there's a white hanky in his hand. But even Jimmy Brogan can see the body's dead. They're carryin a dead body. An the wee guy's lookin up at the sky an his face is like he's holdin the body up to God for an explanation.

What the fuck're ye goin to do about this God? Eh? What the fuck're ye goin to do?

But Psheeew Psheew is all ye can hear an then Jimmy Brogan knows that fuck all's what God's goin to do. Not a fuckin thing. The next guy's a student. Like John Paul Brennan up the road. He's a student. He's got glasses an a long coat. He's got an arm under the body an another arm over the top grippin the lapel. It's that hand on the lapel that's stoppin the body floppin forwards onto the ground. The body's just a v shape wi the arse near trailin off the ground.

An Psheeew Psheew the bullets're goin. Psheeew Psheew. But there's another man. He looks like he's carryin the body but he's not. He's got a bunnit on an he's lookin at all the blood comin out the head. An his eyes're narrow. An his mouth's open but straight. Ye can tell he's goin to do somethin about it. By fuck he is. Ye can see it in his face. If any cunt's goin to do somethin he's yer man.

An Jimmy Brogan wants to be him. The man wi the
narrow eyes an the straight lips. The man that wants to do
somethin about it.

> There's thirteen dead, the
> Newsman said. And seventeen
> wounded.

It was the Paras that done it. The Paras. The Brits.

AIRPORT

Manchester Airport. Doom wanders about lookin for a bin to put an empty coke can in. He snifflin. Pat's away for a wander.

I've caught a cold. The air vent was jammed open – blowin on ma face all the way down, Doom goes.

I don't answer. It's just his feet squeakin over the polished floor an wanderin off into five in the mornin. I'm lyin on this padded bench but I can't sleep for echoes. I can't stop maself from lookin up. Agoraphobia keeps slidin under ma eyelids. Liftin them. The place's big an shiny. Squeaky clean like a morgue.

These two Security Guards're talkin about me. A man an a wummin. I still get paranoid. Even wi the pills. An not sleepin's no help. I can see their dog eyes zoomin the hunner yards over. I'm the only cunt here. They must be talkin about me.

I catch their eye an grin. Not a smile. I copy the inane grin Jig-a-Jig used on the Ward to frighten people away. He used to grin an the Doctors'd grin back. But he'd keep grinnin Jig-a-Jig. An the Doctors'd feel uneasy. And he'd grin more starin in their eyes. An they'd look away. An they'd walk away. That was the only power Jig-a-Jig had. He couldn't even speak far as I know.

I grin more. They look away. I gets the head down. I feel safe now. I hold ma bag like a teddy bear. I take **The Three**

Deep Breaths an try to concentrate on where the air comes in at the nostrils. Meditation. Thursday nights. Ward One.

In   and – out.

In   and – out.

In   and – out.

FFFUCK!

Davy comes back. He's stressed right out. The Security Guards're watchin him now.

Ye know there's not one fuckin bin in this whole airport?

I say nothin.

Not even out on the end of runway three.

He wants me to laugh. But I'm not laughin. If I laugh he'll assume me wakened. I don't move either.

I nearly got ran over wi a seven-four-seven on runway two. I think it was Babbington.

He says it to the vast space between us an the Security Guards cos he knows I'm not for laughin. That's when I notice the announcement that's been runnin over in a loop since we arrived.

It's warnin to be on the look out for terrorists. Don't leave yer case lyin about or they'll blow it to kingdom come just to see what's in it. I talks to Doom without even openin ma eyes.

They've took the bins out so ye can't plant bombs in them.

I hate the IRA, he goes.

He puts the can in his pocket an lies down on the next padded bench wi his head across from mine.

That's the holiday ruined. Can't even get a bin for IR fuckin A. They're all Fenians in Italy an all ain't they?

I say nothin.

Aye – they fuckin are, he answers for me. *Fuckin IRA!*

But then he shuts up. Like it's somethin he never wanted to say. Like I'm in the IRA or something. It doesn't bother me what he says about Catholics an the IRA an all that but sometimes he acts like it does. I don't give two fucks about it. Fuck the Provos.

Fuck off Doom. I'm tryin to sleep, I go.

Silence for a while.

Doom speaks,

I don't deserve that name by the way . . . Davy Doom. I'm a quite happy guy really. I'm never depressed – not as much as you ya cunt. I resent that name in fact. I don't want ye to call me it again. I want another name.

Silence for a while.

D'ye hear me?

I says nothin.

D'ye hear me I says?

I speaks,

I've got one.

He sees the grin on ma face an says nothin.

I've got a name for ye.

Nothin.

It's nothin doomy.

Silence for another while.

What?

No. I'm not tellin ye now, I goes.

C'mon – I'll give ye a crushed Coke can.

OK – It's Joyous Dave.

See! I knew ye'd rip the pish out me again.

Silence again. Just the whisperin of the guards in the distance. An every now an then a plane shudders up into the sky.

I speaks,

It's either that or Doctor Death . . . or we can just stick to Davy Doom!

Nothin. I rolls into sleepin position.

Goodnight Joyous Dave.

Nothin.

The can hits me on the head. The security guards run off chasin the echo throughout Manchester Airport. Ye can hear the click an twist of their shoes. Somewhere in the labyrinth there's footsteps. An they're tryin to find their way out of the darkness. To me – washed in the brilliant strip lights. A white light. The colour of God.

PLANE SAILIN

I'm next to this wee Italian guy about sixty. Forty years in Preston he's been. Waiter. Served an saved an got his own café. Nice but. Skinny an nervous. Can hardly talk English. Probably feels like an intruder still. Immigrants're never left to integrate. I couldn't give two fucks. I'm not his oppressor. I'm Scottish. Or Irish. I'm the same as him mibbi. But he's treatin me wi too much respect. I can't handle too much respect.

He's tryin to prove to me he's a worthwhile citizen. Ye'd think it was the war an I'm some high head chief bummer in the government tryin to stick him on the *Arandora Star*. Torpedo fodder. Floatin tomb. They got treated like shite durin the war the Tallies. But we don't mention it now. No no – as long as they're happy sellin the best ice-cream in the world in Largs that's OK old bean – what?

So the oul guy gets tore into Mussolini an Fascists in general. Then he slows down. He moderates. I gets the feelin his life's been one long compromise in Preston. He moves more into the middle of the bed. He's bein careful not to sound too left wing now in case I think he's a commie. I couldn't care if he was Mengele's cousin or Lenin's brother. He's just a wee Tally guy on his way home. How the fuck his nerves've took forty-odd years in Preston I don't know.

He's had that suit a long time. It's not tatty or dirty. Or worn or stained. It just says – suit of a long time. An his hat. Been on his lap since seatbelts an no smokin. He's turnin it in small arcs. Now an then he flaps it up an down. He flaps it up an down when he cracks a joke an he's hopin it's funny. There's somethin big on his mind. Sometimes he holds it tight. Like it'll keep him afloat if we crash into the sea. Like it'll keep him aflight if the plane blows up an we go meteoritin down into some Belgian field beside the bones of our ancestors. We're flyin over our history but I can't pinpoint it in the matrix of fields.

But I'm the same. We're the same. Me an Pat. An Joyous Dave. We're low in the oul self-esteem. We're immigrants too. Ye wouldn't know from our accents. We came over on the tattie boat. The Irish Famine. That's us. Up the Clyde on a tattie boat. 1846. That's how we got to Scotland. It's only a hunner an fifty-five years ago. We're no good. Worthless pieces of shit.

We're Irish wi Scottish accents. Some of us've stopped callin our kitchens sculleries. Ye'd think that'd be a good thing. Bein both Celtic people an all that. But it's not. Hugh MacDiarmid – I met him on the Ward – I think – he said, *Scottish steel tempered wi Irish fire, that's the weapon I desire.*

An he could've been right. How would England've liked a nation that sat beside her an on top of her? But Shuggie MacD forgot one wee thing. Bigotry. Right off the tattieless tattie boat. Irish in Scotland. Catholics in a Protestant country. Think about it. If I say I'm Italian-American that's OK. Irish-American – that's OK an all. Italian Scot? No problem. But soon as ye say ye're an Irish Scot they're on ye like a pack of hounds.

Ye were born in Scotland so ye're Scottish an that's that!

Soon as they see ye're a Tim ye're no good. *School'd ye go to?*

If it's saint anythin ye're fucked. That's the way it was. But I've never seen it. That's because I'm not lookin deep enough they say. It's there. Ye'll never get anywhere in this country if they find out ye're a Pape. But it's them that draws ye back. It's them that draws ye down. They're makin up their own excuses for gettin nowhere.

Sure it's there. It's in the Orange Walk an the Republican Flute Bands. But it still doesn't keep ye down if ye want to jump up. Doom's a proddie. The council painted the whole street but missed his house out. Everybody knows it's cos he's a proddie but the council says it was overlooked. They slurp their drinks in the Knights of St Columba club.

Ye've got to be positive. Think yer way out of it. I keep tellin Doom that but he shakes his head at positive. Joyous Dave was in Waterstone's this day. At the Positive Thinkin section. He's just stretchin out his hand to pick up

NINETY MILLION REASONS
TO BE POSI+IVE.

What fuckin good'll that do? he says an walks away. But we're all robots of self-destruction. Programmed. I've nearly self-destructed a few times. I've spoiled ma own chances while I was makin them. I've sat overflowin wi the Poor Me's. Starin in rivers. That's how I spent half ma time in the Ward. It was Jimmy Brogan that put me right there. Showed me how to think ma way out of depression.

 ve thinking – says Jimmy Brogan – *that's the thing for you alright.*

When our ancestors got off the tattie boat they couldn't speak the local dialect. Couldn't speak their own either or no cunt'd understand. So they used plain English. English words carried in Irish rhythms. Like tugboats on turning streams.

Hello me darlins top of the fuckin mornin to ye. None of that shite.

But there I'm rantin on again. What the fuck do you care about the infightin an bigotry in a parochial wee place like Coatbridge? What does the Brig matter to you? I mean all we are's particles of dust. Each in individual floatin space. We're gettin blew by winds of all kinds till we stick in love or lust. An two dots can't float. Too heavy. We sink an stay. That's how races're made.

The plane's comin in to land at Brussels.

Mind Babbington? He's drivin this plane, Joyous says. I hope he lands it alright after the last time.

Care for a sprout? goes Pat as the plane grinds onto the runway.

The wummin behind us's from Sheffield. She says trains're cheap in Italy. That's how she tours it every time. Doom's moanin about his flu now.

Pat says, *He's deaf an blind Babbington. If he doesn't get it off the ground this time he's gettin the sack.*

Christ! Ye should see this. Some people's easy fooled. Emperor's New Clothes right enough. Amazin how they determine first class. I'd never've believed ye.

Away an run up ma ribs, I'd've said. They slide this big board up an down the plane. If ye're in front of it ye pay forty quid more. An what ye get's an extra slice of ham an a wider seat. First Class. Ye pay for yer fat arse.

Us plebs might aspire to the banjo-sized arse or cello-sized arse brigade. Or the bass arse. Only the elite have double bass arses. They're that self-important they could fart on the way past an not bat an eyelid. *Sniff that up for*

me would you, they might say. To them all smaller arses –
pot an plate size – have lost significance. Everybody's got
their own perspective. But it's usually above everycunt
else. Except if ye suffer from immigrantitis.

I'm so small. I'm so insignificant.

The seats in front of the magic board're like accordions.
They get pulled out into the aisle concertina-fashion
becomin a couple of inches wider. So that's it. It's a
wonder the stewardesses can do it wi a straight face. Or
without a mask. Dick Turpin had the decency to wear a
mask when he robbed ye.

A lot of first classers get off. Brussels. I've not been on a
lot of planes. But they could be gettin off the Monday
mornin bus in Buchanan Street. They file out wi their faces
trippin them. Christ – they probably commute to work.
Manchester to Brussels. Weird. Imagine doin that in a
horse an cart? An that's just a hunner years ago. No
wonder the Tally's so nervous.

Fast fast fast that's the way it's all goin. Fast fast an
fuckin faster. Even I've noticed it an I'm only young. It's
this Millennium. It's been a race to get here. Ye notice it
drivin from Scotland to England. Cars're a hunner yards
apart on the A74 an two hours later at Birmingham
cunts're right up yer arse screamin the horn an flashin the
lights an no cunt'll let ye back in the middle lane. Stress
stress stress. Fast fast fast. Fuck them all but. We're off to a
monastery. Holy Joe. Here we go.

The stewardesses roll the big board forwards so only
the front three rows're first class. The plane's empty. I
moves forward an gets a windie seat. I'm where first class
used to be five minutes ago. The seats've been shoved in.
But I'm right on the same bristly fibres this Lady Penelope

Pitstop lookalike's arse caressed only minutes ago. It's still warm an ye can smell that expensive Japanese perfume. Kakyshakimakiwakifaki.

The stewardess goes by. Her face moves an I think she's goin to go – *Hoy you! Cunt – fuckin shift!*

I smile but it misses her an hits this sixty-year-oul soup dragon. That's her all the way to Rome. Smilin an settin me up in her headroom bedroom – a toy boy writhin about a leather-clad bed covered in baby oil. That's what she looks like she's thinkin. She keeps runnin her tongue over her wrinkly lips.

There's nothin good out the windie. Just other planes an pipes an wires. Even the stewardesses've stopped struttin about. So I take in the magazine. Designer this an that. No Hai Karate. No Splash it all over. Good underwear. Babes ye can only dream about.

Flight delay. I've even read the makeup section. The Sheffield wummin says we can get a train from Rome right down to Cassino.

You getta da ticketa afore ye go on a train, goes Café Preston.

It's sunny in Brussels. Feels warm. The plane doors're open an a foreign breeze's washin up the aisle. Planes're comin an goin. All them people interactin. All that communication. The wee guy's moved up to first class now. He's grinnin an lookin about. Feelin the seats. Turnin his hat. I lean over to talk to him. He's in the seat right behind me an swingin his head about. He looks like he hopes somebody he knows'll see him. Like mibbi an oul school pal. Or a relative that drummed it into him he'd come to nothin.

You'll a come a to a nothin a you good a for nothin insecta!

He doesn't see me leanin over the seat. He takes out a big cigar. It looks like an antique. Like he's been savin it all his life for somethin special. Somethin special's usually weddins an winnins an births an birthdays. But this's his. His first-class moment. It's the same as thousands of other moments in this airport. Millions of moments round the world. Sittin on a plane. But for Café it's the moment he's picked to crick the metal case of the cigar open. It's the moment he's choosin to unwrap the crepe paper that hides it. To bite a hole in the end an strike a match. He blows the smoke onto the windie an laughs. Not loud. He laughs for hissel. He doesn't want any of these strangers to get the joke. To see his moment. Sure they can see him sittin smokin a cigar. But they don't know what First Class means to him. He's not ignorin the no-smokin sign. He's oblivious to it. The stewardesses ignore him. I think it's out of respect. They've seen his story before. Heard it. Every week mibbi. Barmaids of the airways.

The doors close an the tarmac starts movin. Café leans back like he's never off planes. Like he's first class every other week to Rome. Good on the wee guy. Power to his elbow. May the road rise up to meet him an all that shite. I leave him to it.

But he did notice me. He talks through the sponge an plastic of the chair like he knows I'm tuned right into him.

The pace of a life is a gettin faster ana faster – goin a so fast I can't take it any more . . .

I leans up an turns round again, *I know I was just lookin at them planes an . . .*

But he talks right over me. Not loud. Not impolite. It's his moment. It's his wisdom that's floatin down the aisle. An it's not me he's sayin it to. He just sayin it. As if utterin the words'll get it out. Get it away. Lighten the load.

I can a never move back home. Never go back. The village where I a lived. In a my youth. My youth. It's tourist now. It's a bloody tourist. They made it a good. Come here they say. Come a here an see real Italia. Real Italia? What a is real? What is a not real? What is Italia? Eh! Rome? Napoli? Who cana tell. But they made it a tourist an . . .

He takes a couple of big puffs an stares out the windie. We're coastin up to the runway. He thinks I'm fed up listenin. I'm not but ye can see that's what he thinks.

Too fast, he goes, *too a bloody fasta.*

Mibbi that's where we took the wrong turn. Right where he's on about. Not the place but the concept. His village's gettin faster an faster. Acceleratin away from serenity. Simplicity – the hardest thing to find. The easiest thing to underestimate. Think of what ye'd have to give up to achieve the austere simplicity of a monk: Argos. Tesco. Petrol. Turbo. Diesel. Digital TV. BBC Choice. E-mail. World Wide Web. Shaggin anythin that moves. Fantastic plastic shopfront gods. McDonald's. Screamin an bawlin from fuckin cars. Low-profile tyres. High-profile greens an sick yellas. Yer career. Careerin row after row of nice teeth. Tooth after tooth of posh food. Food for thought an early learnin books. Books in bed an goodnight lights. Lights on little posts in gardens. Gardens bigger than every other cunt's. Cunts sayin *Hello–good-morning* in the rain. Rain skitin off the conservatory glass. Glass objects reflectin Italian suits an cocoa smells. Smells of pot-pourri everywhere an everywhere's not quite right. Right On – room for improvement. Recitin designer names, like the poetry of the misguided. Magic mushroom shootin stars of star-spangled crazy fire. Drink. Devil-may-care sex an vales of somebody else's tears. Quite a lot really.

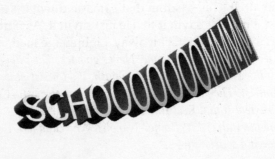

We take off.

Above the clouds over Brussels ye can see the world's round. It's a glassy dome. Ye could polish it wi a cloth. Blue. An the clouds're slippin downhill at every angle. An the sun. Relentless. I gets this feelin. God. That's the feelin. Fleetin. Buzzin like a star in ma chest an it's gone. Over an out. Ta ta buzzy star God feelin. It's like existential dread but instead of the dread it's Joy I feels. Existential Joy. That's the very fella.

Infinity. The sky goes on forever. Einstein. E = mc squared. They're always tryin to confuse ye wi that shite. Cunts that don't know what they're talkin about.

Oh yass infinitayyy. Yass that's a difficult one. Hummmm.

E equals M C squared. Yass it's rather difficult to explain.

You're talking **pause** *you're talking constants of immense proportion. Yass. How –* **longer pause** *– how –* **exasperated pause wi hands in the air an fingers all spread out –** *how can one explain the concept of infinity? E equals*

MC squared . . . an on an on they go. Be as well sayin E equals MC Hammer cos it's got fuck all to do wi infinity. Cunts've been tryin to bamboozle me all ma life wi shite just like it. Bandicoots. It's nothin to do wi infinity. It's to do wi mass changin into energy. An energy changin back into mass. Basically if ye turned the head of a pin into total energy it'd blow a small town away. Ye multiply the speed of light by itself an then ye multiply that wi the weight of the pinhead. The answer's the almighty size of the

BANG

ye'd get. An the converse is ye need hunners of energy to crush down into a pinhead. It's all about change. The universe is in constant change. Constant destruction an creation. Death an resurrection.

Anyway. Rome. That's the eternal city. That's where we'll be landin. That's where I'll be lookin for the eternal.

Death – that's eternal, Davy says. Every religion's into it. The oul death. Ubiquitous. It's a good startin point as any. I hardly think about it much now. Used to bug me. Terrified I was. I don't care one way or the other now. But it sneaks up sometimes. Like take-off. Nervous laughter at bad jokes. We could end up as new statistics. New front-page news.

PLANE GOES DOWN IN ALPS
PASSENGERS EAT EACH OTHER
DEATH SCOFFS

Things've been grim recently. I'm overjoyed. I never expected this. One minute I'm sittin there sharpenin my sickle next thing I get a call to hightail it to the Alps. It's a funny oul business death . . . oh yes a funny oul business. Oh well – it's a handy pick-me-up. Happy to say no survivors.

I'm not scared of dyin. I think death's a happy thing. Like a lullaby. A simple melody. A landscape of white an high bells ringin. The promise of eternal rest. Peace. An singin birds.

Ta ta Brussels hello fluffy clouds. Could be mountain valleys covered wi snow. A land of puffed-up arctic ice floes in everlastin seas.

Yum yum. We get a meal. I like plane food. An hospital food. I never took food for granted. A free meal's like Christmas. Jimmy Brogan was the same. He was a free dinner at school. Miss Nuel was an oul cunt. She hated Jimmy Brogan. She used to go:

Two shilliny dinners!

Some posh wanes'd walk out an pay.

One an sixpenny dinners!

Some not dead posh wanes'd walk out an pay.

Shilliny dinners!

Tenpenny dinners!

Sixpenny dinners!

Thruppeny dinners!

An after everybody'd paid she'd glare at Jimmy Brogan an go.

And **FREE** *dinners!*

She'd shout *free* an scan the rest of the class. If she had her way all free dinners'd be shot at birth. Jimmy Brogan'd walk out wi his head swingin like a kicked dog an get his dinner ticket. The two shilliny dinners laughed the loudest an the laugh diminished as the price went down.

The thruppeny dinners used to manage a smile as he walked back to his seat. He could remember the weeist things Jimmy Brogan. I don't know how he done it. There's big chunks of ma life I can't remember. Specially the end of the Ward. The year before I got out.

I'm scoffin away. The punters in front of the board've just got an extra tattie this time. The soup dragon smiles. She thinks I'm smilin at her. I am smilin. But it's not at her. It's at the calculations I'm doin. Ten tatties at forty quid each. Four hunner quid for a bag of spuds? Free enterprise. Maggie Thatcher lives on. Some people don't even spend forty quid on a week's messages. Kwik Save. Plain white wrappers. There's no gettin away from it – they make ye feel bad. Ye might be sayin *Oh aye right good value this!* But inside ye feel like shit. Like bein poor's yer own fault. Just like free dinners. Suburbia's families're eatin dinners we can only dream about.

Mad. The plane's got a sense of humour. Flyin over the border of Germany an France, the left hand's got Bratwurst an the right's got frogs' legs. I think that's what it is.

Doom! Doom! I goes, *there's a guy skiin down that mountain. Reebok trainers an a Joe Bloggs tee shirt. Smokin Marlboro fags.*

Buy me two submarines then, he says without openin his eyes or releasin his grimace.

Some of these mountains probably nobody's ever been to. I'm away wi it. Amazin. An there's all these towns along the steep valleys. Man's creepin up the wilderness like a virus.

37,000 feet. Passin over Lake Geneva. Babbington's bumpin his gums. He doesn't even know where he is. *We are now flying over Madrid,* he's sayin. Madrid? Fuckin Madrid?

Listen to that daft cunt, Pat goes, *Madrid!*

We cross the Alps a lot quicker than Hannibal.

The Tally's sayin there's people remember no electricity in his village. An the same people watched man land on the moon. Technology accelerates. What's the distance between a horse an cart on a rocky mountain road an the lunar module? Hannibal an Armstrong. An who took the best step for mankind? They'll be shootin satellites out the sky wi laser beams next. Mountain wars to Star Wars. The only thing changed's the location. The Tally hopes this millennium'll be better for the children.

That's twice the Captain's walked by Pat, Joyous goes.

Who's drivin this thing? Pat says.

This wummin like Mrs Brolly walks back from the toilet. A part of Jimmy Brogan's life pops up. He's always doin that. Appearin anywhere in ma head he likes. Like pop up targets on a shootin range. This time it's Jimmy Brogan in the seventies. Flares an Doc Marten boots. One minute he's an ordinary boy. Smokin an dossin about wi no particular aim – dodgin school. Dodgin mass. Next minute it's Bloody Sunday an he's fizzin. All of a sudden he's IRA daft. It's all Kevin Barry an Brits Out. An he's drawin shamrocks on Brolly's gable end.

It was a laugh he says. This day he sprays IRA on Brolly's wall. Wi a tin of black. He goes across the street an sits on the electric boxes to watch it. See if it's good. Mrs Brolly comes in from the shops. She goes mental. She doesn't think it's good. Not one bit. No sir. She drops her bags an turns this way an that flickin her hair about. Next thing she sees Jimmy Brogan the artist sittin on the electric boxes. She drills the eyes into him. He done a shamrock on Curry's last week. The whole block knows it's him. She looks at the IRA an turns an Black an Deckers him again. Jimmy Brogan looks left an right like he's waitin on some cunt. But no way he's waitin. Brolly's tryin to kill him wi big turnin masonry bits comin out her eyes. Like a cartoon.

But he just sits there swingin his legs an bumpin his Docs off the electric boxes. Brolly's got steam comin out her nostrils like two platinum rods. She picks up the bags an storms off at some speed into her house.

🎼 *There were men from Dublin and from Cork – Fermanagh and Tyrone . . .* he's goin an his rubber heels're doin a good impersonation of a bhodran.

Dum dum de dum dum dum de dum

Next thing Brolly comes out wi a tin of white paint. Gloss.

Dum dum de dum dum dum de dum

🎼 *Sean South of Garryowen . . .*

She opens the tin.

Dum dum de dum dum dum de dum

Brolly starts paintin over the

She's just gettin to the bottom right of the A when the Polis go by. One's starin at Jimmy Brogan but his pal's lookin at Brolly. He slams the brakes on. Jimmy Brogan remembers their Irn Bru jerkin off the windscreen an scooshin everywhere. The cork must've not been on right. It's funny the things some people remember. Specially when ye consider how much ye forget. All they see's this wummin paintin a big white

on the wall.

THUMP   THUMP

The cops get out the car. Brolly struggles like fuck when she's gettin lifted. She's shoutin an pointin at Jimmy Brogan.

It's him. That wee shite there! I'll be lettin your mother know.

Jimmy Brogan's sittin wi a lollipop in his mouth. *Hi Yi Mrs Brolly*, he's goin. *Nice paintin.*

They stuff her into the car. It's just her fat face an drill-bit eyes tryin to bore through the glass to get him. There's wee white circles in the glass Jimmy Brogan says – wee white circles where she's grindin the glass down. An the Polis slappin her on the head tryin to calm her down.

Bye Bye Mrs Brolly. Enjoy yer trip.

Dum dum de dum dum dum de dum

🎼 *Say hello to the Provos . . . say hello to the brave . . . say hello to the Provos . . . an Ireland will be saved . . .*

he's singin an dum dum dum go the heels an Mrs Brolly's just a wee shiny square of glass wi a red face. She's a mad paintin disappearin into the infinity of Old Monkland Road.

When she got home that night the

was black again. Jimmy Brogan? Nowhere to be seen.

ITALY

An here's a runnin commentary on that eejit Babbington landin the plane. Babbington misses the runway. We go flyin by Rome an out in a big circle over the Mediterranean. He's trailin the tip of the wing in the sea to turn better. Oho. He's straight now. He's goin to take a runner at Rome. He's goin to land in Rome main street – let the buildins rip the wings off. No. Hold on. He's seen the runway. In he goes.

An Babbington's takin another go at this runway an . . . hold on there the runway there . . . there it's there . . . what's he up to? He's missed it again.

Whoaa!! Looks like a belly flapper here. Flaps up an engines off. We're headin for a big field. Be ploughin up turnips for half an hour before we stop.

Oh. Thank Christ. He's found El Airporto. It's either an airport or a chicken factory.

Hoy! Babbington ye're supposed to glide it in not flap it!

He's tryin to flap the wings. Probably still got his provisional. An a word wi one of the customers.

It's got to be one of the worst landins ever Pat – what do ye say about that?

Absolutely brilliant. Well – it's gettin smoother now we're the right way up.

Oh! Oh! Babbington's all over the runway. I don't think he's goin to make it. I don't think he's goin to make it. We'll all end up in a cake shop on Rome main street. He's got the boot on the brake now – the oul Ferodo's squeezin into the disc. Oh man Jesus H Christ! Everythin's fell apart at the back – the engines're openin up like flowers. Big metal petals're foldin out from the engines. It's like pushin a giant silver tulip against the wind. Fuck we're all dead. Davy's tryin to get out the back door. His feet're scrapin off the runway. Well done Doom boy. Davy's brung it to a stop wi his Doc Marten's.

Ye should hear Babbington now. He's all chuffed. People're havin heart attacks in their seats.

Ladies an gentlemen welcome to Rome. He nearly fuckin killed us the cunt.

It was easier gettin into Rome durin the War, Pat says.

Doom goes, *Well ye've got to give Babbington his due – it's a bit windy out there.* Happy as an orange for a change. The prospect of a good tragedy cheers him right up. Every time.

No reason to nearly crash a plane, Pat says.

Look at the bright side Pat. Don't give the cunt a plane again. He'll probably crash into a phone box on the way to the terminal.

Quick as fuck we're off the plane an out the place. Onto the street right outside the airport.

C'mon lads I know what I'm doin! I goes.

I sees a bus outside the terminal. I decides it's the bus to the train station. It says somethin on the front in foreign. I can't make it out but I tell Pat an Doom it means Train Station. We hop on.

Italy here we come!

It doesn't take long to discover we're tourin all the major car parks near the airport. We're on the car-park bus. The driver finally clocks on an shouts his mates over to look at these daft cunts lookin for the train station. They laugh.

Doom an Pat don't.

After they're fed up laughin. When there's no more to be had from shoutin at us in Italian – *bastards stupido* an all this. They shrug an go away. Apart from that we don't understand a word. An that's good cos Pat's on the edge of his cliff. The driver takes us to where we can catch a train to Termini.

Termini. The Cassino train's about to leave. I asks this wee guy if it's OK to buy the tickets on the train. *Yes yes ees OK a train OK* . . . he goes an we jump on.

On the train it's the same guy we asked on the platform. He charges us double the normal fare. Says it's cos we never bought the ticket before we got on the train.

Ya wee cunt, Pat goes, *ya fuckin conman.* He's just about to rise out his seat when Doom pushes him back.

Leave it Pat, foreign country, Doom goes.

The Monk's pickin us up at Cassino.

CUCURUZZU

We phone up from Cassino. It looks like a South American
town. We have a doss about. All Fiats an motorbikes.
Every café's like a coffee advert. A couple of coffees an
Davy sees this wee dark blue Fiat micro minibus purrin
away at the Station. When we get there there's Francie
shiftin through the rosary beads at some rate.

Are you Francis from the monastery? I goes.

He nods an finishes off,

holymarymotherofgodprayforussinnersnowandatthehourof
ourdeathamen

Hello lads good to be meetin yees.

Turns out to be mad as fuck Francie. He's singin all the
way along the mountain roads. ♪ *Sweet Heart of Jesus*
... Fount of love and mercy ...

What the fuck've you got me into now's the look Davy
gives me. Pat's the same.

Cucuruzzu. Places're never the way ye imagined them.
Comin up the mountain road it's clingin onto the summit
of a hill. All these wee white houses wi red tiles. They look
like they're piled on top of each other. Like one shove an
they'll all come tumblin down. Housalanche. Roofslide.
An yella windies. Blue sometimes. Or red. Some people're
movin about slowly dressed in black. Wimmin in
doorways not talkin. The Chapel's at the top of the hill. Up

to the left there's a mountain. It's like a village out a paintin. We pass a guy strollin along wi a donkey. He nods at Francie.

We pull into the Piazza an there's the Parish House overlookin it. The Hermitage's up the top of the mountain. Francie says there's a lot of work to do in the house an the Blessed Lord's happy to have us there. Davy gives me a Do they know I'm a proddy? look. There's a couple of villagers smokin on a bench. They don't even seem to notice us except for a slight nod as we pass.

Francie takes us up. *Get the bags later, all in the Lord's good time,* he says. Joyous Dave blesses hissel wi his left hand. Francie smiles not noticin the mistake.

This's what the house's like. Ye walk up thirty steep steps into the wee bit of garden. The walls're ancient stone. Through the door an there's this big statue. It's a stone floor an white walls. Francie's on his knees givin it Hail Marys again. St Teresa of the Roses it is. Francie's favourite saint. That's who the statue is. To the right of the statue there's a stair goin up. To the right of the stair there's a cellar. To the right again's a room called the village office. To the left of oul Teresa – or young good-lookin Teresa I should say – to the left of her's three doors. A bedroom, a bathroom, an a chapel. A fat wummin comes out the chapel kissin her beads an noddin away at Teresa like they're best pals. An smilin at Francie. Adjacent to the chapel door's another door to the outside. It leads to the narrow streets that wind through Cucuruzzu an up to the chapel on the hill.

We go up the stairs to the right of the statue. At the top there's a big square hall. There's two couches, a stone floor, white walls an holy paintins. There's a room on the right. That's Francie's. There's a room to the left of that. There's another room to the right. That's the Monk's. There's a room straight ahead. That's got an electronic organ an books in it. There's a door just to the left – on the same wall as the one we just walked through. That's the kitchen.

The kitchen's massive. There's the sink on the left wi some units an cupboards. There's the cooker away in the right-hand corner. In the immediate right-hand corner there's shelfs wi all kinds of tins an stuff. The sink's on the left-hand wall. On the same wall as the sink's this door. Francie takes us out there. It's a flat roof. Ye can see the whole valley from there an into the yards an windies of the wee houses. There's a door in the wall into another buildin. That's our room.

Ye walk up three steps to our room. It's another stone floor. Ye need to put the light on cos there's only this wee windie at the left. There's a bed on the left. A bed on the right. An bunk beds just to the right as ye walk in. It's white walls again. I takes the bed to the left below the windie. Doom takes the bunks an Pat takes the bed to the right. Francie leaves us to it. We'll meet the Monk an the rest of the people after.

Padre Fabian's this fat Franciscan monk. He speaks good English but we've got to talk dead slow so he can understand us. Francie translates sometimes. From Scottish into Irish. The Monk's used to Irish. We get settled. Unpack the bags an we're on our way up to see the Hermitage.

It's only six portakabins perched on a mountain. While they're in an out discussin what work needs done I sit beneath this big cross an look out over the valley. A river far below.

Dinner. Met the usual kinda people ye meet in holy places. Hilda – fifty-odds and nervous as a shrew. Newcastle. This Mad Monk wi a ball an chain. Aye ye heard me right. He's got a ball an chain attached to his leg.

Dinner's soup wi big burnt lumpy bits in it. Yeuch. Pat

an Davy pour it down the sink. Ye can hear the rats chokin on it. That's followed by soggy rice – wi more lumpy bits.

If you like pasta you'll love this, says Suzanne in her posh accent. She's forty-odds. Not bad lookin. It's the worst thing I've ever tasted. The only cunt eatin's Mad Monk. Boggin he is. Smells like a ten-year-oul tin of cat food. Wi a ball an chain on. He loves it. Rasputin. Francie an Fabian've fucked off. Must've sampled Suzanne's cookin before. Just as we're thinkin she'll never beat the soggy rice she does. Special orange crumble.

Nobody lifts a spoon. Even Rasputin's content to fiddle wi the soggy rice an peer out his cowl. Davy takes the plunge. **Hup!** In it goes. **Chew chew munchity munch.** All eyes on Doom.

He slides a masticated bundle out an plops it back into the plate. *Excuse me that orange is a bit dominant is it not. I've tasted less bitterness at the Orange Walk,* he goes. Suzanne nods like it's a compliment an flings it down her neck. The worst meal I ever had. I'd rather eat haggis than that shite.

It's been a long shift from Glasgow. I'm tired now. I'm out on the flat roof an the stars're out over the valley. This's where the battle of Monte Cassino was. From here Monte Cassino's a massive white bird on the wind. Twenty monks, Francie says. Monks walk twenty long corridors. A corridor each. They're fadin away. I picture them walkin wi their hands stuffed up their sleeves. Shufflin along. Measurin out the last of monastic peace. But the buildin doesn't seem ready to give in yet. It's obstinate as the Pyramids. Scientists of serenity that's what they are. Benedictines're hot on the trail of peace – draggin the rest of the human race behind. Fishers draggin their nets. An us ignorant to what their game is. But now, in the valley, the lights of fast cars're buzzin like fireflies on a carcass too heavy for twenty monks to pull.

Pat an Davy's already in their beds. Above, the stars're movin on an out while we wait in our stagnant pool of space. An we're waitin for change. That's what it feels like. Like this millennium's goin to do somethin to us. The words of that Bowie song 'Changes' starts singin to itself inside ma head.

I'm in bed. Seems I've just nodded off an there's the bell. Ding a ling a ling it's goin. Ding a ling a ling.

🔔🔔🔔🔔🔔🔔🔔🔔🔔🔔🔔🔔🔔🔔🔔🔔🔔🔔🔔🔔🔔🔔🔔🔔🔔🔔🔔🔔🔔

What the fuck's that? says Pat. Davy leans out his bed an opens the door. There's the Monk standin ringin a bell. 🔔🔔🔔 *Mass ees in fifteen a minutes*, he says.

Right, says Davy an swings the door shut. It's half four in the mornin. *Fuckin mass?!* is the last thing I hears.

COCK A DOODLE DOO

First thing's the bell goin in the church an a voice through a megaphone. I'm half awake thinkin Fabian's callin the parishioners to mass.

O a kay a ya lazee a basterdos. Geta upa fora massa. You no geta up a Padre Fabiano a make a sure a you a sleep a wi a de fishes.

Turns out to be a van sellin eggs milk bread etc. One of them blue three wheelers they use in Italy.

An nearby some mad chicken's struttin its stuff.

COCK A DOODLE DOO!

Best I've heard. Ever. All over the world chickens scream like burst hi-fi speakers. But here's the true home of the cock a doodle doo. It's still dark in the room cos of the one wee windie. This warm light an air floods in when I open the door.

The weather's great. Blue skies, birds whistlin. Spring. It feels like love. I can see the Mediterranean as I look south-west towards North Africa an Spain. The hills're blurrin in the mornin haze. I suck in a tube of air. It's spring here but it's summer in ma head.

It might be warm now but we were shiverin like dogs in our beds last night. Davy's been moanin like fuck. Last night he got up, opened his case an put on socks an boots an jumpers an went back to bed. Moan moan moan he went all night.

Joyous's been doomin the food too. *How we goin to last out here wi food like that!!??*

We'll have to persuade Suzanne that we'll do

some of the cookin. Some = All

Suzanne's got this perfect accent. It's like havin a newsreader in the scullery. I make the breakfast. Coffee made in these wee lunar module coffee pots. An fresh cut bread fried in olive oil. It's great. Francie showed me it last night. Ye can mibbi stick a wee bit of garlic in the fat first. If ye like.

Pat's away down to measure up for cabinets in the village office. That's the empty room immediate right ye enter the Parish House. For storin the Parish Records.

I spend the day on the Mountain. Sometimes I think there's somebody else there. But when I turn there's nothin. Nothin at all. I decides I'm goin to run up here every day. Get fit. Run past the last barkin dog in the raggle taggle village. Up into the emptiness of the . . . what the fuck's that . . . ? Nothin. Only me an a stiff neck. I'm goin to stop doin that. It's only paranoia. It's only ma own brain tryin to talk to me. Trickin me into thinkin there's somebody else up the Mountain wi me.

It's night. Davy Doom's makin the dinner. Suzanne's layin the table. Oul Father Ball an Chain's still eatin the bowl of soggy rice when we tuck into a Joyous Dave omelette wi everythin on it an big tore-off chunks of bread.

The Monk starts talkin about visitin holy places. Suzanne an Hilda're right into it.

Oh yes Father we'd love to go. Wouldn't we Hilda?

Eey wai, goes Hilda, *sounds leek a great day oot.*

Simply superb, says Suzanne, clappin like a wee lassie. I catch Doom smilin when she does that. First I've seen him smilin since his granny got her tits caught in the wringer.

Rasputin grunts into his bowl of rice. The iron ball's clunked on the table beside him. The Monk counts him in. Francie beams his Irish zealot smile an the Monk figures out his battle plan. He's got his side thegether. Them an us. Holy cunts versus me an Doom an Pat. Them that's not been to mass yet – that's how Fabian sees us.

We're rubber earin the Monk. Fuck this holy stuff. It's three heads munchin. One silver one brown an one shiny. Suzanne's got a programme. The Monk gave her it. When to work, when to pray, when to shit. Her an Hilda're studyin it like it's a map into the next world. They're readin it out loud so's we can hear.

Mass *OPTIONAL* *five in the mornin.*

Work half past five until seven.

Mass *OPTIONAL* *seven o'clock*

I glance up an I can see Padre Fabian's approvin eyes shinin above folded arms, above hangin dewlaps. His eyebrows're down. If they could sing they'd be baritone. But we're still three heads munchin an Mary Poppins's trippin the list off her tongue like a poem. Hilda's noddin wi her arms up her sleeves like a chinaman. Rockin back an forwards in her chair. Francie's sawin a pile of bread an the olive oil's spittin in the pan. Spittin in the pan an hissin like snakes. Oul Ball an Chain's makin a meal of one grain of rice. He's movin it about the stumps of his rotten teeth wi his razor-blade tongue. His breath's like sulphur. I get

up while Poppins an Hilda're still expoundin the joys of
Franciscan dictatorship. I'm careful to have no eye contact.
Francie's shovin slices of bread around the pan. I know his
ploy'll be, *D'ye want some fried bread lads?* an then Fabian'll
be right in there wi, *How's about some optional mass at five in
the mornin?*

I sneak out onto the flat roof. The click of the door
separates me from them in the kitchen. From the roof I can
see the sun shinin on valley Gargliano. Hard to believe a
war happened here. It's like the backdrop to a Bellini
paintin. Jimmy Brogan learnt me about art on the Ward.
The Great Artists. He got it every fortnight. Sleepy village
after village among vineyards an pastel shades of green an
yella an blue. Behind the closest mountains giant snowy
peaks rise into the sky. The air's clear an fresh. I feel alive.
Hard to believe it was ablaze once. The War. In Monte
Cassino Nazi officers made hoors of girls from Cassino.
An Cucuruzzu probably. This red an yella butterfly
spindles by on the breeze. It gets between ma vision an the
Chapel on top of the hill makin it glare pure white. Pure
white it's blazin.

Last night at the Hermitage Francie pointed out Monte
Cassino. Contrast. These six portakabins donated by the
government. They were used in the earthquakes of the
eighties for temporary housin. Austere. They face the
Benedictine opulence of Monte Cassino ten miles across
the valley. Sentries guardin the vow of poverty.

Allied troops were stationed uphill from the village.
They took Cucuruzzu from the Germans. The officers
were billeted in this actual buildin. From the Chapel on
the top of the hill the Allies viewed the Gargliano an
directed the final assault on Cassino. We've landed right in
the middle of our own history. This village was the turnin
point of the War in Southern Italy.

But the valley theday, smoke risin from the odd house,
is peace itself. There's a smell all the time of burnin wood.

Sniff! Sniff! A sweet smell. Makes ye feel at home. Like the river windin slow through the valley.

We go to collect a bed from an Italian wummin. She's fat an dressed in black. She makes us a powerful coffee an points at her tartan skirt askin Fabian if all Scotsmen wear kilts. I'm scoffin her cakes. I don't know if ye're meant to tuck right in or nibble away. She stares an I nod ma appreciation. She's happy wi that. She leaves us to it an goes out into the garden.

Fabian leans back pattin his belly. He starts tellin this story. Me an Davy's dumbfounded. Francie's glowin away behind a big slice of Italian cake. Here's the story.

Eet was a years ago. Een a convent a. Thees a nun she a she a was very holy. Very holy.

Francie nods like he knew her. Fabian goes on.

Five a hundred years ago. She used to a say to the other a nuns. I've got a the cross of a Jesus in a my a heart a.

Me an Davy's listenin out of politeness an scoffin cakes.

So a when a she die they a cut a her open a . . .

Ma mouth falls open to a sludge of cake. Fabian looks at me puzzlin. Then he sees what it is. He waves ma unspoken objection away an goes . . .

I see. I see. Eet is OK – In a those a days they a had a a a . . . ?

Autopsy, says Francie.

A otsopy . . . they had a those in a far a way a times a. Well. The nun she die. And they a open a her up a and there eet ees. A cross. A metal a cross a. Een her a heart a!

We're supposed to look astounded here. Ye can tell that's the way we're supposed to look. But just in case we don't know there's mad Francie at the other end doin astounded so's we can copy if we're not sure. But we are astounded. We're astounded cos he thinks we believe all this shite. Fabian's beamin at our faces. He takes in a long breath that sounds like three medium breaths cos he's so excited he's found some people wi the unshakable faith he's got.

Eet is steel in a the church a you can a see eet. We might go Francis?

Only three hundred miles away Father, says Francie wi joyous teeth.

But Davy can't take it any more. The cakes're finished. He slurps down some lunar module coffee.

What sort of metal is the cross made out of Father?

Eh? goes Fabian. Francie can't believe it.

What's it made out of – gold?

Fabian's like a computer wi the wrong programme.

What a metal? I no know. Eet ees in a the church in a glass a a a . . .

Box Father, goes Francie.

Een a glass a box a. You can a see for yourself . . .

But what kind of metal is it Father? asks Doom again.

Fabian an Francie get up thegether an it's time to go.

BERNIE THE MONK

The Monk's early mornin bell. 🔔🔔🔔 No cunt flinches.
🔔🔔🔔

There's a bunch of oul Italians down in the square. More
like a circle really. The Piazza. We're in an Italian version
of *Last of the Summer Wine*. They're watchin everythin.
Puzzlin. Laughin. Discussin. Oul cunts.

Above the Mountain the sun moves into the mist an
turns red. It's got definite edges ye can look at. An the
ragged mountains're ripped paper across the sky. There's
this wummin bent over in a field. She's workin slow in a
white dress. There's a black shawl over her. Behind her a
Charollais bull wi muck for wellies chews on some vines.
She straightens up an rubs her back. She turns at the
chewin bull. I'm expectin mayhem but all she does's
chucks a wee dod of dirt an the bull moves on. Back she
goes to the plantin. An oul man wi a black hat lights a fag
on a bench. He's watchin her too. Mibbi it's his sister. I
don't know. He's slow an deliberate. He sucks the fag into
life an blows out smoke. Like it's the first an last trail of
smoke he'll blow up the purple sky.

Still the odd star's pushin its light against the sunrise.
The sun'll always go an stars'll always come back but this
mornin the stars're pushin. They want more time in the
sky. It's spring an their time's gettin shorter. They don't

want the change. The sun's winnin. There's a strange
thrum under the soil. The terraced fields an dry plants're
burstin wi the pressure of spring pushin down. Pushin
down from the sun.

The early-mornin inversions along the valley're softenin
the ground for life pushin up from the roots, rocks an
rivers. A distant thunder underground drums out a
rhythm we've forgotten but can't forget.

The usual oul guys come into the Piazza. They're
photogenic the oul cunts. The black hats. The black jackets
an enough clothes on for winter. They sit hour after hour in
the sun. Sometimes one disappears through streets windin
through narrow alleys. Spreadin out in all directions an
elevations on Cucuruzzu's steep hillside. I've been runnin
up the Mountain an back. Four miles. But the first two're
up the Mountain. An they're hard.

We pass by Monte Cassino on the way home from the
wood yard. Perched away up on a hill wi its light cream
stonework against a Mediterranean blue sky. Fabian says
walkin one corridor six times's a mile. It's so high up yer
awe's magnified when ye crane yer neck to see it.
Megafuckinlithic. Encasin the colossal irony of only
twenty monks. Pax to them says I. Benedictine cunts.
Franciscans rule. An talk to the birds.

The irony of the empty monastery's furthered by some
facts from Christianity – supplied by Padre Fabian as the
dark blue ex Polis Fiat micro-bus tears along dusty roads
at incredible speeds. I hope there is a God. I hope he likes
monks. An mad Irishmen. An me.

This's where St Benedict's buried. His monastic rule –
Regula Monachorum – moved out from here to all over
Europe. But eventually all across Europe the monks fell
into disarray an disarrangement – wine wimmin song an
politics. *An organisation wi a no a discipline turns on itselfa*,
says Fabian. Christian monastic life went into decline. It

was St Bernard that brung the monasteries back into order. Here's his story.

BERNIE'S DA WAS A KNIGHT. TESCELIN. HIS MAW WAS ALETH. RIGHT RICH CUNTS. I'M TALKIN ABOUT 1090 HERE. THE LAST MILLENNIUM. BIG CHANGES WERE NEEDED. THEY LIVED AT CHATEAU OF FONTAINES NEAR DIJON. GUY, GERARD, HUMBELINE, ANDREW, BARTHOLOMEW AN NIVARD WERE THE NAMES OF HER WANES. BERNIE WAS THE THIRD OLDEST.

IT WAS HIS MAW THAT TAUGHT HIM READIN AN WRITIN AN ALL THAT. BUT HOLY BOOKS. THEN – THE USUAL – BERNARD HAS A VISION. WELL – WHAT'D'YE EXPECT? HOW D'YE EXPECT A SAINT TO GET ON WI NO VISIONS ? HE WAS SEVEN. HE SEEN JESUS. BABY VERSION. NOT MUCH REALLY FAR AS VISIONS GO.

SO BERNIE GETS STUCK RIGHT IN AT SCHOOL. LATIN, THE BIBLE, POETRY, OVID AN ALL THAT MOB. FORE HE KNOWS IT HE'S SIXTEEN.

HIS MAW DIES. ALL HER WANES AN THE DA CARRY THE COFFIN TO THIS ABBEY NEARBY. THAT WAS THE FIRST TIME MOST OF THEM'D BEEN IN AN ABBEY. IMAGINE THEIR FACES IF YE TELT THEM THEY'D ALL DIE IN A CLOISTER?

YEARGHGH!!

THAT'S WHAT YOU'D BE SAYIN WHEN THEY STUCK YE OLDE SPEAR IN YER RIBS. BUT THAT'S WHAT HAPPENED. WEE BERNIE WAS HEARTBROKE. HE PRAYED AN PRAYED BUT THE HOLE IN HIS HEART WAS LETTIN THE WIND BLOW THROUGH.

HE COULD'VE DONE ANYTHIN. HE WAS A LORD. BY THIS TIME BERNIE'S BROTHERS WERE LAYIN SIEGE TO CASTLES ALL OVER THE PLACE. A RIGHT BUNCH OF WILD CUNTS THEY WERE. BERNIE GOES OFF TO JOIN THEM. BUT HE STOPS FOR A WEE PRAYER BREAK IN A CHAPEL AN

WHAM!!

THAT WAS HIM. ALL DECIDED. HE ROUNDED UP HIS BROTHERS AN OFF THEY GO TO JOIN CITEAUX MONASTERY. A BUNCH OF OTHER SOLDIERS THOUGHT THEY'RE AS WELL GOIN TOO. THIRTY OF THEM JOINED THE MONASTERY. THIS PLACE WAS RIGHT INTO THE HARD STYLE OF MONKERY.

SO TIME GOES BY AN IT'S 1115. BERNIE'S SENT OUT TO START A NEW MONASTERY WI HIS REAL BROTHERS. MIBBI THEY WERE TRYIN TO GET RID OF THEM – WHO KNOWS. BUT OFF THEY WENT AN BUILT A MONASTERY. HIS DA AN HIS WEE BROTHER JOINED UP AN THAT WAS THEM ALL IN. CLAIRVAUX IT WAS CALLED. SOON IT WAS MOBBED. BERNIE SENT MONKS OUT FROM THERE TO BUILD TROIS, FONTAINES, FONTENAY AN FOIGNY.

THEY WERE CALLED CISTERCIANS. AN IF THERE WAS SOMETHIN THE CISTERCIANS NEVER LIKED IT WAS THE WINE WIMMIN AN SONG OF THE SO-CALLED MONKS AT CLUNY. CLUNY WAS ONE LONG PARTY. BERNIE PUT THE VERBAL BOOT IN THERE EVERY CHANCE HE GOT. WHY SHOULD THEY BE LIVIN ON A GRAIN OF RICE BETWEEN THOUSANDS AN FREEZE IN THEIR STONE BEDS WHILE THE CLUNY DUDES RAVED IT UP ALL NIGHT?

YE'D EXPECT THE CLUNY MONKS TO COME ROUND TEAM-HANDED AN KICK BERNIE'S CUNT IN, THE THINGS HE WAS SAYIN ABOUT THEM. BUT THEY NEVER. COS AUL BERNIE BOY HAD A FEW TRICKS UP HIS SLEEVE. MIRACLES. HE WAS A DAB HAND AT THE AUL MIRACLES. PEOPLE CAME FROM FAR AN WIDE TO SEE HIM. AN THEY BRUNG MONEY AN GIFTS. IN 1130 THERE WERE THIRTY CISTERCIAN MONASTERIES. BY 1140 THERE WAS A HUNNER AN FORTY-THREE. BERNIE HAD WENT PLATINUM ALL OVER EUROPE. CISTERCIAN MONASTERIES WERE ALL THE RAGE. EVERYBODY WANTED ONE.

SO BERNIE STARTS GOIN ABOUT LIKE JESUS. MEETIN WI THE POOR AN SAYIN STUFF LIKE,

If your neighbour does not have enough time to prepare his meal, bring him a portion of your own.

SAME TIME THE CLUNY LOONIES'RE SAYIN, If yer neighbour's not got enough time to prepare his own meal well tuff titty neighbour SCOFF SCOFF MMM this is a good roast chicken.

HE WAS FLY AN ALL BERNIE. GOT RICH WIMMIN TO SEND MONEY FOR PRAYERS AN FAVOURS IN HEAVEN. JUST LIKE FORTUNE TELLERS,

Ye're goin to meet a man wi a Monday Book of his own an live happy ever after in a sea of super lager an club king size.

YEE HA! SAYS THE FORTUNE TOLDER AN ZIPS OUT THE DOOR.

BUT BACK TO BERNIE. NEXT THING THERE'S TWO POPES. BAD ENOUGH WI ONE BUT THERE'S ANACLETUS AN INNOCENT. THEY CAN'T SORT IT OUT. IT'S POWDER PUFFS AT DAWN AN THEY SEND FOR BIG BERNIE TO SORT IT OUT.

Next thing there's another crusade. Bernie's enlisted for his patter an he riles up all the soldiers. Off they go to take Jerusalem in the name of God. It was Louis the Seventh. This day he's sittin wi fuck all to do an he says – I know what to do – in order to atone for my sins (an he had plenty of them the cunt) I want to go to Jerusalem. I am ready to take arms.

But dul Louis got fucked. Got the shit kicked out him. So at the siege of Damascus he's havin a wee glass of wine an he goes – Oh well, fuck it, this is borin the french knickers off me, I've seen Jerusalem anyway so let's all go home.

An off they went back home wi their arms hangin off.

But for all that Bernie wasn't daft. No sir. He wrote a wee book. On Consideration it's called. Ye can't read it an stay high an mighty for long. Here's his patter.

Look at yourself, apply your whole bein to the search for truth.

That's what I'm tryin to do all the time. But Bernie was much better at it than me. I'm an amateur compared to him. An he wasn't slow in tellin the popes where to get off.

First look at yourself.

The Pope is high in status. There is no one so distinguished on earth.

Strip off your robes and you are naked and as lowly as dust.

Look again to higher things. See the well beloved. Who is this God? He is length, breadth, height, depth. Marvel at his eternity, love his charity, fear his might, embrace his wisdom.

On the twentieth of August 1153, at nine in the mornin Bernie died. The bells of Clairvaux sounded the knell. An that was the end of Bernie O.

Seek not for whom the bell tolls eh? What makes people want to be monks? It's hard to understand. But ye must've searched out solitude in yer life. At least once. That's part of the attraction. Only the monks keep at it day in an day out for years. I've got to admit I feel somethin strange in monasteries. A compression of serenity an peace. Mibbi it's permeated into the stone.

For all we know monks might've achieved as much for the human race as technological progress. Scientists of serenity. PhDs of peace. An achievement neither advertised nor self-announcin.

Don't mistake spirituality wi Religion, Davy says.
Religion's the politics of spirituality.

Olympic athletes take the physical towards its absolute limits. Mibbi monks're athletes of the souls. Stretchin theirselfs spiritually – takin what it is to be spiritually human towards its absolute limit. If there is a God monks're draggin us in a big net like prehistoric fish. Their sacrifice's numbin. While we twist round bends in fast cars an outdo each other in stock markets an playin fields these navvies're layin the tarmac to the golden gates. If there's a road they'll find it. They'll keep it open. But the way's narrowin. How long can they go on? They want the pollution of hedonism to dissipate. So there might be clean skies of clarity.

Monks've had the job of pullin the weight of the unaware human race into spirituality. The mass of us gets

heavier; the mass of the monks get lighter an their
momentum diminishes. Mibbi we're destined to take

one

        last

                wrong

                        turn.

THE BATTLE OF
THE SALAMI

There's a mist settlin on the village now. Monte Cassino's fadin on its mountaintop. The odd drone of a car travels up the milky sky from the Gargliano floor. I can hear the cars but I don't know where they are.

Theday we got salami.

Sniff! Sniff! What the fuck's that? Sniff! Sniff! goes Davy.

It's a salami a, says Fabian all proud. As a Scotsman might be of haggis.

It's mingin! Davy goes.

Fabian gives Davy the eyebrows.

What ees thees meengin?

The Monk can't understand. Davy sniffs it again. He's got a way of bringin things down, the bold Doctor Death Davy Doom Joyous guy.

That ham's off Monkypoos.

Off? Gone? What ees you a sayin?

He keeps shovin it up the Monk's nose.

Smell it! It's offa. Boggin a, Davy goes.

Fabian leans back wi his hands folded on his belly an smiles lowerin his eyebrows. He's not sure. He thinks he finds us amusin. Next thing's the **thump** of the salami landin in the sink. The Monk raises his eyebrow. Ball an Chain scrapes his chair out. He lifts his iron ball an the chain's clickin off his massive rosary beads. He rescues the salami out the sink.

Clink clink goes the chain. **Thump thump** goes the ball. I feels a song comin on but I thinks better about it. The tension's buildin. The Monk's not too sure if he finds us amusin now. Not too sure at all. Hilda's got her head hung that much her hair's a curtain. Or the cloth ye pull round the tabernacle in chapel. Her eyes're behind it like two wee boys hidin in a hedge. Suzanne's suckin her cheeks thegether that much they must be touchin inside her mouth. Lemon suckin mode.

Doom's a tatties an mince man. I can usually eat anythin. I gives it a sniff an we starts to eat it. Big slices wi bread. Pat's horsin through the loaf wi a bread knife like a sandvik saw. Hard point. ZZZ ZZZ ZZZ. I'm slllllllllllllllicin the salami. All of a sudden Fabian jumps up.

Stop.

Stop eet.
    Stop eet just now please.
        Just now please.

He's got his palms facin us like he's pushin a bus. His eyes're lookin to the sky.

Mibbi he feels a wee miracle comin on, Pat says. I thought we'd forgot to say grace.

Eet ees Friday! he goes, like that explains it all. I knew what he was on about but it looked like Hilda never cos she's peekin out a partin in her curtains an twistin her eyes into a question mark. The more she twists the more her head tilts to the side. It's nearly touchin her shoulder. Doom's shoulders're at his ears. He's not got a clue. Francie pipes up.

We don't eat meat on Fridays.
Who? goes Davy.
Catholics – we don't eat meat on Fridays.
That's OK – I'm a proddie, says Davy.

The whole place goes silent. Even the birds outside stop whistlin.

Eh? What ees thees proddie? goes the Monk really confused now. Francie leans in an murmurs what a proddie is. **Ting ting ting** the bells of the Angelus're goin off in oul Fabian's bonce. Francie leans back an bows his humble head. The Monk glares at Davy.

What!!? What!!? Doom goes, *I only sayed yer salami was mingin.*

87

NO EATA!!!

It's the bit in the films when Clint walks in an the whole place stops.

We're paused wi bits of meat an bread hangin out our mouths like rabid dogs' tongues. Except Ball an Chain – he's nibblin another grain of rice. His fifth this week – greedy cunt.

I'm wonderin why they're all starin at me. I soon finds out. Unbeknown to me ma hands've started workin on their own. Like there's somebody else inside ma head workin them. They're cuttin into a lump of salami wi a knife an fork. Ma eyes're flabbergasted. The only sound's the wind blowin the mist about outside. It's like Windowlene on the glass. Ma knife starts again. The kitchen's lit up horrible yella an this holy red candle's flickerin crazy patterns on the wall. An there's dark shadows. Dark shadows like hell. It's like the last supper. All eyes're on me. The knife's through to the squeaky surface of the plate. The red flame shimmers across Fabian's eyes. Francie starts murmurin Hail Marys. His rosary beads're clickin off the chair. Hilda shuts her curtains. Suzanne sucks her eyes shut. Dooms face's wide wi delight. Pat's liftin his knife an fork. It feels like the Apocalypse.

I push a bit of salami through the silence to ma mouth. Quick survey.

It's like bunjee-jumpin – I'm up there so I'll have to go for it now.

In it pops. The room gasps so hard the mist's sucked in under the door an through cracks in the windie frames where the light beams in. Next thing every cunt starts wolfin in.

The Monk stands up an him an Francie shuffle off. Somewhere in the outer darkness I can hear gnashin teeth. But it's teeth on meat that's gnashin here.

Some people's minds're that closed there's no peekin in even. People like the Monk that's right set in his ways. I can deal wi it but. I become things in ma head. It's easier to become things than think concepts. It helps me understand what ma mind's sayin to me. Instead of gettin angry at them I become a waterfall. I cascade over the top of them. Round about them. They turn into rocks. I become a movin enclosure over minds of stone. That's how I get round them. It's a picture. I don't need words for it. I don't know if there is any. He's the rock. I'm the waterfall. That's all.

Turns out things were worse before we came. That was the talk over the relieved dinner table. Ball an Chain helps hissel to three grains of rice, leans back an nearly smiles. Mary Poppins's sayin they've been livin on bread, coffee an rice since two weeks ago. The Monk says it's a Franciscan house so everybody'll live like Franciscans.

Like fuck we will! says Pat – *no grub – no work.*

I tells them all about the slap-up feed we got in the wummin that gave us the bed's house. Fabian must be gettin nosh mornin noon an night from the parishioners. Cunt. Fat cunt in fact. An he's been feedin this lot on scraps.

An he spent five zillion gadgets theday. About five hunner quid that is. On the wood for the parish office. For cabinets. To keep documents in.

But even wi the battle of the salami I'm gettin some peace here. Mibbi just windin down from the buzzzzzzzzzzzzzzzzzzzzzzzzzzzzzzzzzzzzzzzzzzzzzzzzzzzzzzzzz of the world. No. That's not it. Not just that. I'm gettin peace over an above windin down. A wee glow in ma chest. An sometimes a rush – like a fish thrummin in the chambers of ma heart.

I was in the van theday wi Dublin Francis. Once the work in the Parish House's finished Francie's goin to be a hermit up the mountain wi Padre Fabian. He used to be a scientist. His wife got AIDS. She got it from a blood transfusion. So what does he do? Only gets battered right in there tryin to find a cure for AIDS. But it beats him. Tears him apart. When she dies he gives up an goes all religious.

But he's not doom an gloom. No sir. He's a bit of a singer's Francis. So we get talkin about songs. Loves opera. Can sing it too. We're windin along a mountain road talkin about songs.

It's about measure an value, Francie, I goes.

He turns an smiles. I points at the road. He's got this wee habit of grinnin inanely at ye has Francis. That's OK. But he's usually eighty miles an hour when he does it.

It's about measure is it? he goes, *love songs?* He starts singin.

𝄞 *Annd I lovvve you sssso . . .*

Ye can tell if they're true love songs by singin them to God.

HOW????

If ye can sing it to God – or yer Maw or yer Da without embarrassment. That makes it a true love song.

Hmm hmm . . . says Francie treadin a bit close to blasphemy for comfort.

It's the separation of love from lust.

Is it? he goes.

Well – I could sing this to God an not be embarrassed:

𝄞 *I cried a tear you wiped it dry . . .*

Francie starts blastin it out.

See see Francie . . . It's like an AA punter. Imagine he's got off the drink an things were goin well. He might look back an sing that as a hymn instead of Faith of our Fathers an all that shite.

Francie agrees but ye can tell he doesn't like the swearin. I starts singin this Meat Loaf number, somethin about lipstick and dyin for a taste.

See that! That's not a love song really. It looks like a love song when ye first hear it but it's about lust.

Who sings that . . . I don't know that one.

Meat Loaf.

I don't like dat very much.

He bursts into song in case I sing any more of it.

♪ *Soulll of my Saaaviour sanctify my breast . . .*

But they've got another song on the same album, Meat Loaf – Bat out of Hell. *'Crying Out Loud', it's called.*

But Francie's had enough of Meat Loaf for the day. So he carries on singin. Tryin to not listen to a word I'm sayin.

No Francie. It's good. It's like 'Amazin Grace'.

'Amazin Grace'?

Aye.

Meat Loaf ye say?

Aye.

Bat out of . . .

Hell. Aye.

So I starts singin it. 'Crying Out Loud'. An I'm still singin it as we bump an wind along the banks of the Gargliano river. Out of the side of my eye I can see Francie startin to listen.

The micro mini ex police bus zooooooooooooms on.

As the river winds down the Gargliano the snowy mountains melt in the springtime sun. Francie the Irish monk an me talk of love an the measure of a true love song bein if ye can sing it to yer God an leave nothin out. Francie cried when he first heard Aled Jones singin *'Pia Jesu'*. The mystery of God's voice on a Coke-swiggin tongue. When I asked him why he cried he gave me four reasons:

1. Man's obvious sorrow at himself.
2. God's lullaby sweetenin him.
3. An innocence dimly remembered.
4. The mad futility of existential dread.

Later back at the Parish House somebody's singin an Italian song in the windin lane below. I think he's drunk. It's an oul guy wi a bunnit an a parka. Sweat'd be pourin out him if he was Scottish. I don't know what makes me shout it. It just comes out. I feel all happy inside. I leans over the edge an shouts down.

Buonasera!

Sera, he shouts. An carries on singin. I'm wonderin what the song's all about.

Serendipity dictates it must be a love song. Even if it isn't. This moment points to an otherness. Somethin bigger than the sense spectrums we swear by. Not light or sound or taste or touch or smell. Like there's another conscious bein inside me that watches ma every move. Watches over me an keeps me from harm. Guidin me to where I need to be.

There's this Persian Fairytale – The Three Princes of Serendip. The three heroes possess the gift of makin fortunate discoveries by accident. Happens to me all the time.

An I think Davy's made a fortunate discovery comin here an all. Suzanne. Ever since Jean he's been funny wi wimmin. He's not fancied any burds since that. Except the Memory Lane burd. He was in love wi this burd back in the Brig. Years ago it was. Been goin out for years. Just got engaged. Anyway life's trundlin along at the same oul pace. Work all week – drink all weekend. The Barnyard. That's where they'd go Friday an Saturday night.

They were like any other couple him an Jean. Every now an then they'd have this amazin fight on the drink an fall out for a few days or even a couple of weeks.

So this time they've been fell out for a week. Davy's not botherin his arse cos it gives him a chance to go on a bender wi the boys. He's off work all week an right into it. The Friday comes an he's in the Barnyard. In comes Jean. She ignores him. He ignores her straight back. The place's crowded. Davy's mates jeer him an fill him wi more drink. These guys're well past the fallin out wi their burd stage. No burds've came near them for years. Drink's the thing wi them. First an last. Beginnin an end.

The place is jumpin. Lights clinkin glasses smoke sweat perfume bleached hair narrow-eyed young team. Jean gets up an moonies wi this young good-lookin bastard. As they spin in each other's arms Davy's mates say nothin. They know how far ye can take these things. Jean smiles at Davy an bumps the gums right on the guy. Davy's watchin them come round again. It's 'Power Of Love' that's on. Jennifer Rush.

♪ *A whisper in the mornin*
Of lovers sleepin tight . . .

They're like planets. Round they come again in the shadows of other dancers. She opens her eyes still stuck to the young guy's lips like a sink plunger. An she turns the half-turn needed to have her back to him.

That's when Davy cracks.

He runs right across the dance-floor an

STICKS

the head right on the back of her head. There's an almighty crack. The guy's stunned. Staggerin about in the strobe lights like every second heatbeat's been edited out his life. His front teeth're fallin off his bottom lip. When they hit the floor Jean looks up. Her lip's bust an she's got a couple of teeth missin too. She falls from the guy's arms an thuds on the floor. The guy goes for Davy an a battle breaks out. The alkies're right in there. They don't give a fuck. It's tumblers smashin everywhere an the DJ screamin an the bouncers an sirens an the emergency doors flung open an blue lights. Davy escapes through the haze of spinnin blue. Like underwater – he strides out for the darkness.

Next thing he remembers is bein halfway through the night an halfway to Jean's house. An he'll do anythin to get her back. He'll forget about the guy. He'll take the whispers from his mates. The humiliation. He'll take that an all. Just to cancel out the night. To stop the horror of seein her wi another guy again.

He gets to the door an who answers but the guy wi just his boxers on. He grins like a gravedigger. Jean's behind him shoutin abuse. Her lip's all swol up. Black an blue. She's buttonin up her blouse. The guy makes a big mistake. He says *Fuck off mate if ye don't want a doin.* Davy's talkin over him to Jean. *C'mon Jean. I just want to talk.*

The guy steps down one step repeatin the same threats. Jean's got the folded arms. Davy's eyes're glintin wi tears. The guy's only young. He knows nothin about this game – other men's wimmin an all that. How out of his league it is. He's probably just used to givin some poor bastard a kickin on the street. Team-handed. Probably never been on the bad end of a good dig. That's how he thought he was in control. That's how he thought it was OK to put his hand on Davy's shoulder.

Davy came to in the cells. The guy lay in the Southern General for three months. Davy done three years.

But here's him an Suzanne laughin an tuggin each other over a bag of flour. Davy sprinkles some in her hair. She throws this glass of water over him. He chases her out through the stream of her own laughter onto the flat roof. Into the sun. An ye can't tell what's the brightest. The sunlight or them laughin.

That night in bed I'm kiddin Davy on about Poppins. He's not for sayin nothin. Instead he tells Pat about the story the Monk told us about the cross of Jesus. There's laughter for a bit an then some silence. I can't sleep. Just when I think they two are sleepin Doom pipes in wi his own story.

Years ago right. There's this nun. Five hunner years ago actually. The time when they invented autopsies. This nun. Sister Battleship. She went about sayin I've got a fully operational aircraft carrier in ma heart. Well none of the other nuns believed her. But when she dies they cut her open an there it was. Jets an helicopters the lot. A fully operational type three aircraft carrier.

Hallelujah, says Pat.

Praise the Lud, I goes.

Thanks be to God goodnight, says Doom.

An I'm lyin there thinkin about how can this Monk an Francie believe such shite when it comes to me. The true story. The nun was probably gettin on all the other nuns' tits sayin about the cross of Jesus in her heart an all that. So when she dies the first thing they want to do is cut her open. But not to find the cross – to prove there's no cross there. But even nuns that get right on other nuns' tits've got pals. So just as they're sloshin around there in her slit-open heart her wee pal shoves her hand in an pulls out this metal cross.

She holds it up. Wiggles it about. Her hand's half covered in blood. Immersed in a shaft of sunlight comin streamin in the window. *Praise the Lord,* she shouts. *Praise be to God for all things!*

An all the other nuns look up an see this cross glintin in the light an drippin wi blood. Down they go onto their knees. Blessin an prayin an mutterin an thumpin their chests. An the wee nun grimaces cos she's just took over the nunnery really. From a nobody to top dog. Up it goes in a glass case an that's it – a miracle. No cunt thinks of sayin to the wee pal nun, *Eh Bessie any chance of a wee look at yer rosary beads just to see if ye've whipped the cross off an shoved it in that heart yerself?*

It's not a case of Divine intervention at all. It's a case of resentment an revenge.

TAKIN ON THE MOUNTAIN

The Monk's early mornin bell. 🔔🔔🔔 Nothin. Polite chap on the door. Nothin. The bell. 🔔🔔🔔 *Fuck off Monkypoos*, says Doom.

Saturday. Four o'clock. I'm takin fifteen minutes' snooze before ma jog up the Mountain. I'm lyin in a deck chair an the breeze's flowin over ma skin. The sun's warmin ma muscles an lubricatin ma joints.

It's birds whistlin an the odd shout far away fallin into the hillside stones. Waterfallin down into the dust. Next thing a full-throated Italian motorbike surfaces in the square. It's like it rose out the marble. I can feel the oul men in black surgin backwards an the red lights of their pipes glarin an dyin out. The noise gets close to ma comfort. Even though I'm up the stairs I've almost opened ma eyes when it turns an fades outwards. I catch ma breath but ma heart's thumpin like I'm a new bird on still waters an a dangerous fish stalks the deep. Its mad purr strings along the valley lookin for other squares to reverberate. An we return to peace an sweet Italian voices. An the bike was black. I never opened ma eyes but the bike was black. Definitely black. An the rider? I think I know who the rider was. It looks like Jimmy Brogan.

Leavin the Piazza's easy. There's always an audience squintin under the rims of their hats or starin through thick Italian whispers. Or movin in dark windie spaces. An the Jeans Factory girls' giggling. All that an the freshness of ma muscles skim me across the Piazza's flat surface like a skater.

I'm out into the street in no time. The oul men hardly see me an I'm gone. Chariots of Fire ya bas. There's another sparse audience here an there at windies leanin against trees or sittin in the sun. They help me. Any jogger'll tell ye they always put a show on for an audience.

Climbin the early incline's hard physically but easy psychologically because it's lined wi allsorts crookity houses – an if there's nobody watchin, there could be. Ma strides're long here but losin the spring of the Piazza already. Eight hunner metres up this twenty-degree incline the road sweeps to the right an rises another five degrees. This's the side of the Mountain for real. Ma aim's to be able to do the whole run without stoppin. Sweat's started runnin out ma forehead into ma eyebrows. I'm leavin the village. The psychological push's gone. There's nobody watchin now save the odd black smudge straightenin up in the warm fields. I feel like stoppin an walkin. I feel like stoppin an walkin. I feel like stoppin an walkin. But I don't for three reasons:

1. I can still be seen from the village an don't want to look like a wimp.
2. There's another house uphill on the bend that leads towards the path up the Mountain an I don't want them to think I'm a wimp.
3. I don't want to think I'm a wimp.

So the torture goes on. Ma breathin's like two carrier bags inflatin an deflatin. To the house on the bend I'm obviously strugglin. But strugglin's good. Strugglin's perseverance an indomitable spirit. Strugglin's searchin for somethin stronger inside. Strugglin's what it is to be alive. When ye stop strugglin forwards ye start goin backwards. Ye're against the current all the time.

Soon I'm leavin the house an the bend behind. It's only the barkin dog theday. I seen a long curly burd two days ago. She smiled. That knocked a few seconds off ma time. Now, in the high valley there's only me, the breezeless Italian springtime an the raspin of ma breath. I can smell the vegetation. The road almost levels out for a mile.

A car accelerates into the next bend an toots a friendly horn. It passes an this auburn babe smiles. She's got black rosary beads clickin off the windscreen. I'm gettin ma breath back a bit. I've stopped showin off so I can go at a steady pace. There's only a crooked man an wife workin land miles from any houses.

The next house's got ten-feet fences round it. It's on the top of a hill. There's black dogs everywhere an in the distance it looks like men wi guns. That sends a shiver up an down me. A darkness. But I'm probably imaginin the guns. It's mibbi only men in black wanderin about the place.

Sera, comes at me through the clean air an I gasp one back. There's one of the men right at the fence. No gun but. I don't take a spurt. I keep goin at the same steady rhythm. It's always slow an ponderous uphill. Hard an heavy. It's me an the runnin. The veneer of egotism's cracked an fell off. I'm movin into the meditation of physical stress. It's easy if ye get a rhythmic mantra in yer head. Take in the colour. Take in the colour. Take in the colour.

Pogo on the Ward used to paint. Watercolours. He was brilliant. Said nothin in reality was Burnt Umber as he streaked it across a sheet of white paper. But here it is.

Burnt Umber. Real as the smudge of his brush. Some fields're green an some's rust an olive trees grow in rows.

Here's workers now dressed in black. They straighten up to watch me runnin by then sink back to work. They don't smile an they don't frown. I'm a break. A wee downhill in their day.

No wonder these landscapes inspired painters. I thought they idealised an stylised the world they saw. They didn't. William Empson sayed the job of an artist is to put the feelin inside the artist's head inside somebody else's head. That's a measure of the value of a work. An indication of how successful it is. These landscapes're draggin up feelins inside ma head put there by allsorts painters. They've done their job. An they've done it right. It's not far now. There's a track. On the left-hand side. Could run right by it. Leads up the Mountain. Winds. Twists. Winds again. Steep. Really steep.

First few feet's OK cos there's still a good rhythm in ma feet. Accentuated by crunchin into the stones. White an red stones an clouds of dust. The track bends into its inclines. Ye're just comin up a steep hill an ye're into a bend. Exhausted. Breathin like a Christmas tree's draggin up an down yer throat. Ye turn into the bend hopin the incline'll go down five mibbi ten degrees. Anythin. Any lessenin of the pain. But that's not what happens. It rises. Five or ten. Sometimes more. Where'd'ye get it? The extra to keep goin? There's no way I'm goin to walk. There's no way I'm goin to walk. There's no way I'm goin to walk.

I'm down to puttin one foot in front of the other. The heel of ma right foot lands at the toe of ma left. The left lifts an lands at the toe of the right. An this's the way I move imperceptibly up the hill. I round the bends at a crawl. But I'm runnin still. I'm not walkin. I'm runnin.

It's sometimes forty degrees slope. I think of things to keep me goin. Things I've done. People. The Ward. I get into a mode of thinkin that won't allow me to stop an walk. I'm like Ball an Chain. I'm just like that mad cunt eatin a bowl of rice a month. The Mountain's ma Ball an Chain. I gets to thinkin I don't deserve this landscape. The Mountain. The black bodies bendin down in the fields. The olive trees scratchin their scribbles in the blue sky. Aerials to God that's what they look like from ma puffed-up red face. Communicatin the peace of the hillsides.

Bleep bleep. Trees to God. Trees to God. Over.

✝ *Eh. God here. Come in trees. Over* ✝

It's all alright here big yin. Everythin's OK. We're tendin the fields an the sheep're goin about their business. But there's a man chained to the Mountain wi the invisible links of guilt. An he's movin. He's a pink dot. An like a bubble from the depths of the ocean he's pushin through fathoms an pressure.

As I go up an up the trees're less an less. Like aerials're no longer needed. Like on the Mountain we might talk direct to God. Kneel before him an confess all our sins an be lifted. Lifted. Freed from the body that rots wi creepin things. I've got to think of other things. I've got to think of other things. I've got to think of other things.

Steps the length of ma feet. One at a time. Climbin. Keepin goin. I'm tryin to suck oxygen through the impassable surface of plastic bags. Tryin to push up the Mountain. It's like drownin. It's me an the Mountain. The open country below's watchin. Its neck's cricked watchin the pink dot makin its way to the top.

For what reason? say the fields.

Why? whispers the grass.

He always comes back down with nothin! sing the wires of the fences.

Mibbi he's tryin to soar like us!? say the hoverin birds. An the eagle that swings round in big circles says nothin. It swings an watches.

Swings

an watches

an says nothin. Its only whisperin rushin over the thick frontal curve of its wings. Ghosts talkin.

Up the Mountain the air's clear. The air's blue. God's blue. That's what colour he is. The colour of the sky. The pain's fizzin out now. It's goin. The feet're crunch crunchin but the pain's leavin.

Endorphins. They're floodin into the bloodstream.

AHHHHHHHHHHHHHHHHHHHHHH!

I'm meldin wi the Mountain now. Every day this point comes a bit higher up the track. The trees an the hills're not a passive audience no more. They encourage. *C'mon son c'mon you can do it. You can do it!*

Jimmy Brogan ran the Glasgow Marathon. 1982. Came in 800th an somethin. Out twelve thousand. Everybody thought it was great but they never knew what made him run. They never knew what made him keep runnin. An wimmin were handin out sweeties an men were slappin his back cos he was fucked. Absolutely fucked. He hit the wall at Bellahuston park but the sweeties an the slaps kept him goin. An the wee lassie. That's right. That's what kept him goin. This wee lassie was skippin on this street near Bellahuston park. She had shoes on too big for her an a long grey dress. Thick. Heavy. Like the stuff the Monk's gear's made out of. She's taken wi it all an she hitches up her dress an starts runnin. Never go wi strangers an here's the wee lassie in grey away wi twelve thousand. But she finished. Jimmy Brogan saw her crossin the line as he turned an winced every step of the way through Glasgow Green. He saw her get her medal an then look about. Lost in the crowd. She sat down an started cryin. He never knew if she was cryin cos she was lost or cos she done it. She made it. Jimmy Brogan said *Hi Yi Hen!* as the men wrapped him in silver foil. She smiled. That's what he remembered most. She smiled at him.

Up

Up

Up

Every step the trees say, *Up*

The hill's suddenly bearable. It should be harder. The incline's much steeper – the air's thinner. Ma muscles're burnin in lactic acid. But it's gettin easier. The wee lassie in grey's runnin in ma head. The whole world's tilted so the hill's actually flat. An all over the rest of the world crazy steps an angles confuse people's steps. They suddenly lurch sideways or forwards in subways – into the arms of lovers – out of the arms of lovers – into the awkward arms of strangers – towards the grave – away from the grave. The whole world doesn't know where to put its feet.

If yer spirit can leave yer body I'm nearly there. Ma body's thrummin wi pain. Swishin an vibratin like violin strings. But I'm painless an separate. Severed an free. An the landscape's free. We merge. We meld. I'm washin out in all directions. An ma body trudges its way up the Mountain. Trudges its way up the Mountain.

Just before the top the incline drops to five. In the distance I see the big wooden cross. Ten feet high. Padre Fabian carried it up in procession wi the villagers snakin behind. But now the place's empty. Except there's me reformin beside the cross. I'm waitin on maself so I can unmeld from the land. When ma body stops at the cross I rejoin it. Ma breath chases itself round ma lungs slowin them down slowin them down slowin them down.

I kneel an say an Our Father an a Hail Mary. They're scored into ma head. I used to be a chaser of spiritual highs. No bones about that. A nun warned me about it. That's not where IT is she sayed. That's how I remember cos she sayed that's not where IT is. Like she knew what I was lookin for. An she knew I was lookin in the wrong places. But I can't help it. I'm the same wi drink an drugs. Every cunt was into speed an coke an what not on the

Ward. Or dope. They all wanted to get high or low. Up or down. But me? I wanted to go sideways all the time. I wanted to be out this world. Not slowin it down or speedin it up. Relaxin it or pzaaaazin it. I wanted to see other things. Things no cunt's ever seen before. Sideways into heaven. Sideways into hell. It never bothered me what one.

Doctor Fegan asked me what I think of ma addiction to chasin extremes. But that's not what I chase. It's differences I chase. Different experiences. I've got to keep fillin ma head wi new things. Fill it till it's burstin an fill it again. I never sayed nothin to Fegan I just let him believe what he wanted. Things've got to stay the same for doctors or they can't say what's wrong. An if a doctor can't say what's wrong what use's he? So I nodded an sayed, *That's right Doctor right ye are there Doc – the highs an the extremes – I'm yer man for them alright.*

An all the time I'm lookin out the windie at the magic mushrooms in rows like little soldiers leadin me into Legobucketrumpelstiltskinland through the October mist.

On the Ward the Voice told me we all carry our history inside us. I told Buzz. But I shouldn't've. Ye can never tell how somecunt's goin to react to their own history. Once he found his history inside him – Buzz thought there was some cunt inside him wi a chainsaw. Tryin to cut their way out. His history was terrible. His history had melted into pain an then re-formed into the harsh metal roarin of a chainsaw. Cuttin his guts. Every cunt on the Ward was there cos they carried their history inside them. Every cunt. Even the doctors an nurses an the big body builders they hire to hold ye down. They're there cos they carry their history in their heart's pouch like broken bottles.

Jimmy Brogan told me he was goin to get rid of his history. He was goin to get rid of his history an get out the Ward. An once he got out he was never goin back. He said he'd mibbi take me wi him.

I finish the prayers. I feel good for doin it. The rest

lowers ma pulse an soothes ma breathin. Ma body heat's tropical. Rainforest steam's comin off me.

Round the hill a bit's a derelict house. Blasted by the roots of trees an tin opened by storms an relentless sun. It's dried to white weakness. Francie told me a story about it. Two young German soldiers got shot by the advancin Allies. It's hard to believe any cunt died here. Wherever they turned was beauty. Then – birds strangely silent. A thought of movement. Bumps in the shadows where there was none before. The illusion of breathin? Twigs crackin. Feet in the fields. More movement. Figures in the distance. The thump of footsteps. The run. The shout. The grunt. The crashin in of the door. An all the time surrounded by beauty. All the time – beauty.

They'd always thought the tree's rustle could never allow them to die. So far away from their girls. No no. Not here. It could never happen here. Not wi the rocky outcrop at the summit where – if ye stare hard enough – ye can see the form of Our Lady holdin a baby. She's watchin over. Nights of fags an cards an stories an songs sung low. But this one night. The door's been crashed in an the guttural voice of a Glaswegian mibbi shouts an as they move through fear they're sprayed. Sprayed far from home an the things they knew. Bullets fired as casual as a spray painter might spray a room an move on to the next. There's work to be done. Money to be made.

Even the Mountain's shaped by its history. Even the Mountain.

I bless maself once for me an twice for the two boys. The route back down takes me by the Portakabins an down a grassy path. I'm a gazelle jumpin an boundin. Too steep to run up this path but it's a muscle-shudderin pleasure to bounce down it. Like a mobile massage.

Down

        down

                down

                        it goes

bendin an windin an dippin again. It's eyes to the ground. I'm goin so fast every step could be a broke ankle. But the ground's soft an before I know it it's levellin into Cucuruzzu.

By the village I'm refreshed an flyin. I step the pace up an the slap slap of ma feet on the ground attracts attention an I'm acceleratin to insane speeds into the Piazza. They probably think I've ran that speed up the Mountain an all. That's what I want them to think. But that's not it. They'd need to be daft to think that – this's their mountain an I'm a runner from a faraway land. As I approach the Parish House there's Pat an Davy leanin over the railin in the evenin sun.

THE HEARTBEAT
OF GOD

After dinner the Monk tries the winkin eyes of the dead
nun story. There's this nun an she lives miles away. Well
she's a dead nun really. She died five hunner year ago an
was a saint for fuck knows what. But the thing is she's
sat up on this altar all rotted away to brown paper an
wispy hair. An her eyes're closed. Closed that is except if
ye're one of the special people. One of the chosen few.
Only three people's seen the dead nun's sparkly blue
eyes all this time she's been dead. Stiff an propped up wi
sticks. But Father Fabian goes there this day. He's very
sceptical. Very a scepticalli. But fuck me is he not sat
there prayin an he looks up at the lump of rotten
cardboard an there's these two celestine eyes radiatin
love an goodwill right at him. So he looks round an tugs
this other nun. He asks her if she can see the eyes. *Some a
see her eyes some a don't*, says the nun an falls back into a
warm nun smile.

   He looks at us when he's finished. It's makin our
shoulders vibrate. He doesn't know what to make of us.
We don't like miracles, relics, mass, confession or livin on
bread an water. But we're good workers.

I'm out tryin to find the pub. The village's quiet. Barkin
dogs, two or three passin cars. It's pretty chilly. I keep
forgettin we're high in the mountains. The pub's nowhere
to be seen. I go home an onto the flat roof. There's no one
else about.

I'm lyin lookin at the stars. See if ye want de-stressed
instantly – look out at a dark blue sky spattered wi stars.
It'll draw the tension out ye like clear water's bein sucked
through yer body. Ye become part of the beautiful chill of
the universe.

A crescent moon's slidin into position over Cucuruzzu.
It's weird to think there's goin to be people livin on it.
When they melt the ice caps they've found. Fuck it's like
that film – *Total Recall*. They'll probably shove big rods
into the ice an the steam'll come whooshin up. Might
create the atmosphere needed for life. The night's
swallowin up the valley an the mountains're bein erased
by mist. Cats push through dust like little roadsweepers –
their engine purrs drivin through layers of fallen cherry
blossoms shimmerin in the light of streetlamps. Each
petal's a pink microgram of beauty – rockin on its own arc.
Darker an darker it's gettin. Darker an darker an more
holy by the minute.

Soon it'll be dark shapes against stars. An black-ridged
hills spattered wi distant lights an a thin line of snowy
summit. Deliniatin heaven an earth. A dog barks who
knows how far away. A lamb bleats. A pretty Italian girl
smiles as she closes the windie shutters an a wummin's
heels click out across the square.

Another night has come to Cucuruzzu. All's calm. But
for now any point of light will do to believe there're others
out there like me – lookin too. An listenin mibbi. Listenin
to the voices night brings to poets an mad folks. It's a clear
night. The stars're bright. Sometimes they look like they're
sizzlin out there. I've got a bath towel under ma back
against the cold concrete. I hope I see a shootin star.

Shootin stars're good luck. One's sure to come along –
scorin across the sky. Try it. Five whole minutes an I bet ye
see one. It's just that we never spend five minutes lookin
at the sky. Ye'll be amazed how long five minutes is. Ye'll
be amazed how relaxed ye feel. Ye'll be amazed at the
sense of awe. The feelin inside the Star Maker's head's
puttin itself inside ma head. God's not out there in the
stars. He's everywhere. There an here. Outside an in.
Inside an out. Davy Pat an all them's in there drinkin wine
an tearin big lumps off loafs.

zzzzzzzzzzzzzzzzzzzzzzzzzzzzzzzzzzzzz🔔 🔔🔔
zzzzzzzzzzzzzzzzzzzz🔔 🔔zz🔔🔔🔔z🔔🔔🔔🔔
🔔🔔zzzzzzz🔔🔔🔔🔔🔔🔔🔔

Must've fell asleep. The bells're ringin for midnight. The
notes're pourin downwards from the hilltop chapel. The
resonance of every new peal moves up through the rocks
an stones an through ma bath towel into ma body. Ma
body alone on a patio. The stars singin krishna krishna in
multi spectra light language an the words of John Donne
spinnin in ma head.

No man is an island entire of itself;

every man is a piece of the

Continent, a part of the main . . .

Any man's death diminishes me

because I'm involved in Mankind;

an therefore never send to know for

whom the bell tolls; it tolls for thee.

Des Dillon

So it's me an the stars. They're coverin the earth. They're not *out there.* That's the way I always think of them. They're everywhere. It's us an our wee minds that's *in here.* The stars wrap round the world. They're a sparkly blanket. We're the wane. The wane that can't see nothin but its egocentric perspective. We're just one wee ball of stuff an we're movin through space at incredible rates cradled in the magnetic shawl of the surroundin galaxies. Insignificant. Magnificent. Magnificence is ubiquitous in the universe.

We've managed to part an partition the planet. Continents. Countries. Cities. People. An some people have managed to split theirselfs into two. An the atom. An we've started on out there now. Vacuum volume by vacuum volume. Satellites tracking into the holy sanctity of space. One day we'll be sellin it on the stock market. That's a laugh. How can ye sell the stars?

That's when Chief Seattle's speech comes into ma head. This guy in the Ward thought he was Chief Bromden out *One Flew Over The Cuckoo's Nest.* But he even managed to get that wrong. He thought he was Chief Bromden alright. But he's in the Ward he said for refusin to sell America to the white man. So the situation was – Billy Higgins from the Whifflet thought he was Big Chief Bromden. Big Chief Bromden thought he was Chief Seattle. He never spoke. No that's wrong. He never communicated wi anybody else. No that's wrong. He never tried to communicate wi anybody else. He went about all day repeatin the Chief Seattle speech. I've never seen it on a bit of paper but Higgins/Bromden/Seattle woke up sayin it an went to sleep sayin it. An for a long time I was strapped to a bed same ward as him. It's printed tippity tappity on the inside of ma skull. If I close ma eyes I can see the words carved out on the slimy bone. But it's good, though, it gets ye thinkin.

Everythin's connected. So says Big Chief whatever his

name is. Under these stars it's easy to see all things're connected. But at some stage we level our eyes to the earth an don't look up the rest of our lifes. An that's when the connections snap. The hawsers that tow the world through the cosmos prang an the jolt's felt as a ripple movin out through infinity.

I'm lookin out to these stars takin deep gasps of infinity. Stars an mountains an land an seascapes give me awe. I can leap from that to a God. No problemo. Right now God's the thing that holds all the lights an darkness thegether.

How can ye look at the stars an back to words scattered on a page an treat them as the be all an end all of life? If God writes surely the stars're full stops an the writin's somewhere in between them?

Holy writin – a human's attempt at communicatin their awe of man's consciousness to another human bein. Nothin wrong wi that. Poets do it all the time. But they're like monks. No cunt gives a fuck any more about poetry. It's when people start usin Holy writin as a rule book it all goes haywire. I'm in favour of the four gospels of:

Look at the Stars.

Look at the Mountains.

Look at the Sea.

Look at the Landscape.

Lookin an lookin an lookin. An when yer mind wanders lookin an lookin an lookin again. At one thing. The head of a pin or the black line where the grey of the sea meets the blue of the sky. Lookin an lookin an lookin so that line's the only thing. No other thoughts attached. It's only the line that exists. Suddenly – an for a fleetin second ye'll've shook off the veils of human language. No images, metaphors or similes. No language. No feelins. Except this immense cleanliness an clarity. The pristine crispness of bein.

The Monk says do as he does to see what he sees.

No a books, he says. *No a good. Pray for seein. For a God.*

An I do. Every day on the Mountain.

I can hear Davy an Pat in the room laughin their heads off – probably at me lyin out here talkin to a tape recorder.

It's a lot later when Padre Fabian comes out. Says nothin. Sees me but. He gazes along the Milky Way. Brought up in a monastery. An asylum without labels. Who's madder than a monk? There's a trace of a smile on his lips. I think we're different from his usual bunch of rosary swingers. Another smile flickers along his lips an he goes in, shuttin the door lightly.

I'm fallin in love wi the place. Really fallin in love. I'm comin over all calm. Peace. PAX for fucksakes.

A SHOOTIN STAR

Yes! Right in the middle of peace. Smack in the centre of pax.

I'm feelin very relaxed. Mibbi I'll try an learn some Italian while I'm here. Aye that's it. It's a wonder we can communicate at all wi all the different languages in the world. I went for three bags of sand the other day an they delivered three ton of chips. That's when I decided it'd be a good idea to concrete the cellar floor.

STAYIN FLOATIN

The Monk's early mornin bell. 🔔🔔🔔 Loud as fuck. Davy
rolls over an farts.
　Mass. Mass. Optional mass, goes fat but holy. We're silento.

Padre Fabian's still tryin to convince us to go to some holy
places. *This one we'll be in the micro-bus for six hours*, Francie
says like it's somethin good.
　Fabian's countin us wi his other hand restin on his belly.
　There's a eight a goin, says Fabian.
　No there's only seven, says Pat.
　Suzanne and Hilda gasp. But Fabian thinks it's a
mistake in the countin Pat's pointin out. He counts again.
Suzanne coughs an Hilda scurries away to make the tea.
　But Fabian counts an there's only seven countin Pat. He
smiles an says, *Oh you a are a correct Pat. Thanks you. Seven.*
He's rubbin his hands thegether an bowin forwards still
seated. He always does that before he leaves the table. He
shoves his chair out. Pat's countin one two three four five
six seven. Fabian stands smiles an nods wi these wide
eyes. But Pat's on the ball.
　No – ye mean six – I'm not goin, he says. The Monk tries
to talk over him. Hilda pours a shaky cup of tea all over
the saucer an tablecloth.
　I'm not goin either, Davy says. Suzanne chokes on a bit of
fried bread.

The Monk an Francie leave before any more call off. I'm tryin it but my neck's too stiff an he's gone before I can wet ma lips.

They've got a great clock in Cucuruzzu. Davy knows it inside out. He can't sleep. That's his war cry. Says he's never slept since he was born. He lies in bed wi all his clothes on listenin to the chimes. It fascinates him. He's got it sussed he says. It chimes six times for six o'clock an ten times for ten o'clock. Nothin wrong wi that. It chimes once for quarter past, twice for half past an three times for quarter to. Nothin wrong wi that either. But there's problems Davy says. Big problems.

1. Take ten o'clock for instance. It chimes ten times. But it chimes ten times an gongs once for quarter past. It chimes ten times an gongs twice for half past an it chimes ten times an gongs three times for quarter to eleven.

It does the same routine for every hour on the clock.

An the other big problem is:

2. It's right outside our room.

The whole room shakes an vibrates. Jackets fall to the ground. Cups smash on the floor if ye don't grab them. Twelve o'clock's an earthquake. Davy the Joyous says they turn the volume up as it goes through the night. One o'clock's like a bell in a spire across the valley but it gets louder every quarter of an hour till ye can't bear it. By the time six an seven come it'd take a good man to keep sleepin. Doom blames the Catholics. The clock's in the chapel spire. God runs Cucuruzzu's clock.

Got talkin to Suzanne theday. Divorced wi a lassie about eighteen an a boy. Her man's been married three times.

Split up wi his third last year. He's livin wi a twenty-year-oul now.

Same every holy place ye go. Breakdown city. Nervousville. Neurosis Outer Bumblefuck. Grief. You an the world. You an the rest of your life. When ye've nothin to hold onto ye search yer history for meanin. Ye'll not find any. It's just this flat expanse of grey sea. It's not hot an it's not cold. It's the same temperature as you so it doesn't feel ye when ye plunge into it. An you don't feel it. It's existential dread multiplied by the size of the sun. An ye search an ye search. Every direction there's nothin. Silence. Space.

Ye stop splashin about. Yer ripples move out an leave ye joined perfectly to the glassy surface. Ye wait.

An ye wait.

An ye wait.

Then the surface's broke by a barrel. It bobs up wi white water fallin off it. For that moment ye're happy as Christmas. Happy at seein somethin. Anythin. An ye start swimmin to get to it. It's like a mountain head. Ye're always gettin closer but it's always movin away.

The barrel's somethin ye could hold onto if only ye could get there. If only ye could wrap yer arms round it an hold. Hold tight. Close yer eyes. Sigh. Hold tighter. Then at least ye'd have somethin. Somethin to keep ye afloat. Ye could float an float. One day the sea'll get colder – or hotter. At least ye'll be able to feel again. Somethin. But for now ye'll hold on till somethin happens. But ye can't get there. It's too far away so ye swim an ye swim.

An ye swim.

An ye swim.

Nobody ever reaches the barrel. But after a while they realise it's not the barrel that keeps them floatin but the swimmin. All that useless energy's useful after all. The prayers an the diggin away at holy books. The days. The weeks. The months in monasteries an convents. An the holy people who gave ye no answers only hospitality. Then one day ye're wonderin why they don't have answers. Why it's only handshakes an cups of tea an long walks. Then ye realise mibbi in the head of a flower or the sight of a bird in the dark valley. In that moment ye see YOUR question could only ever be fitted by YOUR answer.

That's when the sea heats up. That's when the sea gets colder. That's when ye start to feel. When ye come alive again.

I always remember what Jimmy Brogan used to say. *Aye*, he'd go, *Aye, dyin's bad enough but the worst thing's dyin when ye're still alive.*

An that stuck in ma head. I run it over an over.

He said the Cherokee Indians believed yer soul could die an yer body could live on. Junkies, alkies an loonies he sayed. By the look in his eye I realised he must've swam at the barrel too. Jimmy Brogan. Lost at sea.

Suzanne an Hilda're keepin afloat wi the Catholic thing. Ball an Chain's found hissel an anvil instead of a barrel. Certain to sink every time. Me an Pat an Davy've got our own barrels too I suppose. We've all got one. That's how

ye've got to respect everycunt that's tryin. Everycunt's
had tragedy. Broke hearts. Somecunt's goldfish dyin might
affect them as much as your Maw dyin. Aye! Ye've got to
respect anybody that's tryin.

A man that expects respect doesn't deserve respect, is what
Jimmy Brogan used to say. But he heard it off his Da.
Father Boyle came round about whoever was paintin IRA
on the walls. Mrs Brolly was right in wi him. Never out
the chapel. His Maw runs away an gets Father Boyle a
chair. A wooden school chair. She puts it down in the
scullery for Father Boyle. He's a big redheaded boghopper
of an Irishman.

A hard chair for a hard man, says the priest.

Jimmy Brogan's Da stands up an tugs the chair off him
before he can sit in it. He nearly falls on his arse the priest.

There's only one hard man in this house, he goes.

An that's it. Boyle's away out an the Maw's all
embarrassed.

But ye're as hard as yer life's tough. Everybody. Or ye
wouldn't be here. We're all as tough as the mountain's
steep.

UNIVERSITY CHALLENGE

🔔 The Monk's early mornin bell. Louder. 🔔🔔 Louder. 🔔🔔🔔 The Monk tries the handle. Door's locked. The Monk's bell. 🔔 Nothin. The Monk's heel diggin into the door. Pat flings a shoe. The Monk's bell. 🔔 No cunt flinches. The Monk's bell. 🔔 Zzzzz.

Later I'm runnin up the Mountain.

The sky's fresh. Clear. The run's hard thenight. I stop longer than usual at the cross. I pray an meditate. But I can't get the German soldier out ma head. Them runnin in. The muzzle of the gun. The whole world reduced to the muzzle of a gun. Flung against the white walls. No pain. One's flung like he's been picked up. He hits the wall an he's starin at the tight eyes of the gunman. He slides down the wall dyin in a bliss of painlessness. He probably thought about his girl. Or his Maw. Or mibbi just walkin down the street. Walkin down the street in spring. Blue skies. Not a care in the world. Mibbi it's his birthday. His birthday an he's on his way to meet his girl. Eighteen he is. An singin. Some German song. A song that's the same as 'Wild Mountain Thyme' mibbi. I can see him now. Far from the War. Before war was a thought on his mind. He's movin down the street – a happy point in the universe. I wonder if his girl was thinkin about him when he died. Or was she doin somethin. Workin in a munitions factory mibbi. Hypnotised by the whirr of the machines. An later on. When she's walkin home. That's when she thinks of him. An she smiles. She remembers somethin he said. But by now he's dead. He's gone. There's been immense change in her world an she doesn't know yet. Not yet.

Runnin

down

the Mountain

I'm cryin. I don't know why but the tears're streamin down ma cheeks.

After a shower an fresh clothes ma skin's glowin red. I feel warm from the inside out.

Because of Mary Poppins's first-night meal fiasco I've been cookin most nights. Tonight it's garlic an ginger chucked in a pot wi mushrooms, various vegetables, pasta etc. I'm gettin to quite like this cookin lark. All them years institutionalised reduces ye to beans an toast.

DINNER! I shouts.

Shit. Soon as Pat comes in I know he's been drinkin. I know he's been drinkin cos he's got his

He's like that cheezy pepperami on the telly. Or Chris Evans. No – Tony Blair – that's it. That's who he looks like. If anybody could find a pub he could. Pat's the man for that.

He takes up position at the fireplace. There's no fireplace but if there was that's where he'd be standin. Elbow on it. Tilted to one side. Mibbi drinkin from a wee glass of whisky. Or a big glass. Tells us all about it. He's been meetin the locals so he has.

ITALY MEETS PAT   WI A DRINK IN HIM

JEEESUS H CHRIST. He's been in the pub. Talkin about the War probably. Aye. The War. He's tellin the Monk an Francie all about it. They sit wi cheezies as broad. Only theirs're cos they can't understand a word he's sayin. But I can. I'm kiddin on I'm not listenin. I'm choppin onions an tomatoes.

He's met this millionaire. But he's not Italian. He's in the pokiest wee village in Italy. In a bar that's hard to find. I've not found it yet. But he's American.

But the only thing about this American's his broad Italian accent, Pat says, *that broad it's dead hard to understand a word he's sayin.*

So Pat uses a universal male language. Arm wrestlin. He challenges the guy to some fuckin arm wrestlin. He's not that broad Pat. I'm a lot broader than him. But he's wiry an he's strong as fuck. They're all round about him he says.

Hoy hu Hoy hu Hoy hu Hoy hu Hoy hu Hoy hu Hoy hu Hoy hu

They're shoutin an bangin glasses on the table. The American wi the Italian accent's about ten years older than Pat. But twice the size. That's why he's shocked when Pat crashes his hand onto the lit candle. The guy's that impressed he lets Pat beat him another six times left an right. By this time the whole bar's pished. They're all at it.

123

An arm wrestlin epidemic.

Ye can see it startin to dawn on the Monk who the Italian American is. Pat's tellin the story about how he built a physique from nothin usin dynamic tension an a picture of Steve Reeves.

He builds motorways in America the Italian. Lives in a sprawlin house halfway up the Mountain.

Francie nods at the Monk. It is who they thought it was. They look at Pat wi even more awe now. Pat's demonstratin the ins an outs of dynamic tension. This is the guy that's payin to have the road up the Mountain tarred. The road I run up. Ye're talkin millions of gadgets – or whatever shekels they use in Italy.

The house's frightenin. Steel fence eight feet high. I've told ye about the black dogs wanderin the grounds. Video cameras scannin their evil convex eyes over the Gargliano valley. I thought I saw men wi guns. Remember? Like them in the Sicily bit of *The Godfather*. Black polo necks. If ye wanted to take this place out ye'd need a stealth bomber. An there's somethin else ye'd need an all. A new identity. The Monk an Francie probably think Pat's daft. Like he never knew who it was that built every road in America an usually came from Italy.

And here's your starter for ten Pat – who builds all the roads in America and fills them up with the odd body?

The IRA?

No.

The PLO?

No. I'll have to hurry you.

Is it . . .? Is it . . .?

I'm going to have to push you for an answer.

The Mafia?

Correct – and now for your bonus question.

Why the fuck did you humiliate the guy in his home village when he might just as well have you dropped slowly onto the rotor blades of his helicopter an fed your meat to the black dogs?

Merlin Merlin where are you goin so early in the mornin wi your black dog?

Pardon? Is that your answer?

Pat shrugs his shoulders.

Another question. Did you not know this man was Mafia?

Yes.

Yes you did or yes you never.

Bamber Gascoigne raises his eyebrows. But Pat's got an answer. He knew after seconds who the guy was. That's why he asked him to arm wrestle for fucksakes. Anybody knows Pat knows that. That's the exact reason he asked him.

Push you for an answer on this one Pat . . .

I don't give two fucks.

Sorry can you clarify Coatbridge Uni. You don't give two fucks about the question or is – I don't give two fucks – your actual answer?

It's ma answer Bamber.

Pause for dramatic effect.

And you are correct.

Applause.

In case ye're wonderin – the pub's in a back room behind the pasta at the local supermarket – which is only a corner shop really. I'm just hopin he's not goin to drink all night. I slope off an leave him posin like a demented bodybuilder. The Monk an Francie're amazed. Pat thinks they're amazed at his pecs but they're amazed he's been arm wrestlin wi the American.

ITALIAN MARIGOLDS

🔔 The Monk's bell 🔔🔔🔔 *Shut fuckin up*, shouts Doom, *we're not goin to mass. I'm a fuckin proddy.* Ting 🔔 ting 🔔 ting 🔔 Silence. Footsteps.

At breakfast Fabian keeps goin on about Santa Maria Goretti. She's top of the pops far as saints're concerned. She got raped an stabbed when she was fourteen. Workin in the fields. She never died for four days. But she forgave the rapist. On her deathbed. She got sainted an now she lies in a glass coffin like Snow White. It's some chapel miles to the north. An when Francie says miles he means miles. A lot. Like hunners.

Only time I ever heard about Santa Maria Goretti was Jimmy Brogan. He had a wee picture of her above his bed. An sometimes he prayed to it. When I asked him about it he just sayed, *Every little thing helps. Ye've got to try everythin.*

The work went well theday. Me an Davy shuttered two steps leadin into the cellar. All ye really do's make a box that's strong enough to hold the weight of concrete. A square foot of concrete weighs a hunnerweight. Ye fill the space up wi oul bits of steel an iron an pour the concrete in. When it's set ye take the box off. It's only three sides in case ye think how the fuck do we get the side off that's

concreted in. We're goin all the way down into the cellar.
We'll concrete the floor an plaster the walls. It's thick wi
dust. We've been sprayin the place down all day so we can
breathe. Dust that must be hunners of years oul. It gets
ingrained right in. Draws lines on yer skin.

I ran up the Mountain sweatin black rivulets. When I came
zoooooooomin out from the holy bit at the top this oul
wummin sees me. She gives it the quick bless an kisses the
beads. Must've thought it was blood.

    I gets

               down

                     fast

                                  theday.

Even wi ma lungs caked in soot. I get a good shower
but still at the dinner table there's dust on ma arms an up
ma nostrils. Breathin out's deposited two blunt triangles
above ma top lip. Davy's the same.

    I made the dinner theday. We're just finished an we're
out in the big lobby, me an Doom. I'm stretched out on one
couch an he's stretched out on the other one. Mary
Poppins's sat beside him.

    I'm just thinkin about how to bring the subject up. Davy
an Poppins. How to get some laughs out it when all this
laughin comes up the stairs. Millions of wanes burst in.
Catechism classes. It's great. Crazy. They all stop laughin
one at a time comin through the door. They gape at me an
Doom an Poppins. The wanes at the back're bumpin into
the ones at the front an soon this wee crowd of Italian
wanes's wonderin who the fuck're we.

    The Monk starts usherin them past wi a grin an a shake
of the head. They can't take their eyes off us. Foreign.
Milky white an different. An wi two strange-lookin black
bits comin out our noses. Mad Mustachios. They start
talkin an laughin again. *Lia la la la ma la mal mal lamla,*
they're sayin. Goin on an on. I goes out onto the roof again.

People're wanderin up an down the narrow alleys. The sun's on the side of ma face. It feels good. It feels really good. Down below two little girls go by. Two little girls wi marigolds pressed against them. The sun's shinin on the rustic houses an, high on the hill the churchbell rings out the crazed time signal. It's all for the good. The sun likes it. The two little girls like it. Squintin in the sunrays, they smile up; their eyes're narrow an blessed by the evenin breeze. The mountains rise up behind the village. Behind them, blue skies exaggerate the orange of the marigolds. The flower heads become the benign eyes of God strollin beside two girls.

Buongiorno, they say in small voices not shy or afraid.

Buongiorno, I say. They smile at me. At my Italian. They return to investigatin the orange petals. In the hazy distance a man cobbles along on a horse goin nowhere in particular. On a lazy bench two oul men lace the sky above their black hats wi warm smoke from slow pipes. Cucuruzzu settles for evenin sun.

CONCRETE AN CLAY

🔔 The Monk's bell. Bed springs. *Are ye goin to mass Davy?*
Pat says. Doom opens the door. *No mass theday thank you,*
he goes. The Monk looks blank. *No massypoos!* Davy says
an shuts the door. There's a limp little ring 🔔 an then ye
can hear his sandals shufflin away.

We're runnin out of cement. We're mixin the concrete out
the front of the house an carryin it to the cellar in buckets
to pour into the shuttered step. Ye've got to walk down all
the steps to the Piazza to get the sand an cement in buckets. The men on the square watch yer every step. But
there's no venom in their eyes like back home. They're just
watchin. They ain't criticisin. There's no cynicism. They're
watchin. They're only watchin.

To make a good step ye need a cage of reinforcin steel
bar inside the concrete. Usually. But this's Franciscan
Monk land. So we've got bits of allsorts metal instead. Oul
irons. Bits of oul metal fences. Rusted locks. Keys. A fryin
pan. An oul set of cutlery. A hobnailed boot sole. Nails – a
variety. Hinges. Tractor bits. An the Monk's early mornin
bell. Sittin in the middle all shone up an no place to go. It
looks like a Holy Relic among all the rusted paraphernalia.
Me an Doom's faces're smilin round its brass mirror. It's
all extra strength but. Every bit helps.

It's me then Davy for a bucket. We're sweatin like fuck.

Ye'd never think one step could take so many buckets. On the buildin sites it comes out a big lorry. An we've got two steps. Worst thing's havin to pour some one day an some the next. There's a big join in the concrete that nobody can see. But it's there. The rain an water seeps through it an eventually it cracks open. That's how so many bridges on the motorways're fucked. Two pours. The water goes in in autumn. It freezes in the winter an the expandin ice shoves the crack apart. Next autumn the bigger crack fills up wi more rain. Winter expands it more. On an on it goes. Till what was one object suddenly becomes two. If ye knew what went on in the construction game ye'd drive over fuck all bridges.

We're runnin out of cement.
Shovel shovel sweat sweat.
We're runnin out of cement.
Shovel shovel sweat sweat.
We've ran out of cement.

Francie went to get some but it's not open an we need five bags. We spend the rest of the day carryin sand an chips up from the Piazza a bucket at a time. I go

down.
Fill the bucket wi sand or chips.

                                                                          stairs

                                    the

                      up

          it

carry

Dump it on the pile.

Fling   the bucket to Davy.

He repeats the process an gives the bucket to me. On an on we go all day – sweatin like dogs.

Daniele turns up. He's fourteen. First day he goes,

He-lllllo.

Hello, I says back.

But that's all he knows so he comes away wi all this Italian stuff an we stand there wi our bags lookin at him. He looks like somebody off the Ward. He's got that look. The look when ye're tryin to communicate. Ye're makin plenty sense to yerself. But nocunt understands.

He comes back an hour later wi a phrase book. I'm leanin on the railin overlookin the Piazza wonderin is there any wimmin about. He comes right up to me wi the book open like I'm a learnin opportunity not to be missed.

He lets rip.

How olld arrre yuo?

Very old.

He's lookin up the numbers section for young.

Tventy? He goes.

He brings wee things for us. Magazines, cakes, fruit. Then he practises on us as we work.

But this day he annoys us too much so we get him an sellotape him all up. Three rolls we use. An when he's mummified we carry him out an dump him in the hedges at the side of the Piazza. The oul men on the bench tilt their head. I think they're goin to say somethin but they don't. They clap. That's what they do. Me an Doom bow an get back to work. All ye can hear is Daniele gruntin an the tape cracklin an the twigs snappin.

HAPPY HOOVERS

No Monk. No bell this mornin.

Father Baldy likes to practise English too. Davy calls him
Gary Baldy. He's turned up recently. Helpin out about the
house. Makes us lunch. Good thing is he tells us a lot
about Fabian. Turns out Padre Fabian's on a mission from
his monastery in the north. He's to get the Hermitage up
an runnin by September. If he fails he's bombed back to
the monastery. He'll be just another monk there father
Baldy says. But no matter how much I ask him he'll tell
me nothin about Ball an Chain. He shies away when I ask
any questions about that fella. Just makes a wee O wi his
lips, sucks air, looks up through his eyebrows an shakes
his head side to side.

Padre Fabian a beeg cheekin in Cucuruzzu. In a all a Italee,
says Father Gary.

Baldy comes away wi all this stuff about *Thee Ho-lee
Father.*

Turns out Fabian's got permission off the Pope to revive
the Old Rule of St Francis of Assisi. *Muchee stricter than a
the rule they a use todaya*, says Baldy.

But that's a laugh. Fabian's hardly adherin to the new
rule – never mind the oul stuff.

He couldn't spell poverty, Pat says.

Bedtime. Laughtime. Pat pulls his cover back an this cat hisses across the room spittin. He falls on his arse tryin to kick it. Me an Davy's on the floor creasin ourselfs. I pull ma cover back an Hiiiiiiiisssssssssssssssssssssssssssssssssssssssssss there's a black one slidin across the room. Its eyes're two green lights. They two cunts laugh at me now. As they're standin laughin their heads're gapin black holes an rows of teeth I sink into a dream.

This bit in the Ward comes back. It's Jimmy Brogan. He meets me in a corridor an he's got this bit of paper. He's happy. He's got that look ye get on people's faces when they've just discovered somethin. It's Samuel Beckett.

He writes plays, Jimmy Brogan says. Then he reads out what's on the paper. An the reason it sticks in ma head's the rest of the Ward's watchin *The Full Monty* in the big room. An they're laughin like fuck. An the laughin whirlpools into ma ears.

Jimmy Brogan says, *The tears of the world are a constant quality. For each one who begins to weep, somewhere else another stops. The same is true of the laugh.*

In the Ward that kept me goin. It kept surfacin when I needed it. I knew if I was feelin down somebody else was feelin up. When I was right down I used to imagine some cunt in Japan laughin. They'd be standin wi their burd silhouetted against a big green wave. An the sea'd be crashin in an stoppin just before their feet. They'd be walkin an laughin. I'd think of the same guy every time. I grew to love him. Hyundai Mitsubishi I called him. An his burd was Toyota Daewoo. An through lovin him an his burd I grew to love other cunts. I could love everybody sometimes. Even Fegan. There's only so much happy in the world mibbi an we've got to share it. Jimmy Brogan says the loony bins're full cos all them cunts out there on drink an drugs an other roller coasters're usin all the happy up. Happy hoovers he says. So we get it sucked out us an end up in the Ward. Brain Surgeons he called the happy hoovers sometimes. A surge in their brains's all they're after. A hit or a high rush.

Funny thing was wi me an Jimmy Brogan. After that I starts noticin this pattern. Sometimes when I was down he was up. If I laughed he cried. When we were in the middle we were exactly the same.

ALESSANDRA

I'm out an about. I wind down one of the streets an come
out at the graveyard where they're buried above the
ground. In boxes. Marble. I lie down under two lemon
trees an snooze for a couple of hours. A deep relaxed
snooze. I wake up infused wi oranges an lemons. Great.
When I get to the house Davy's goin wi Francie to get a
big order of cement, glue, nails, an all sorts of stuff. He's
rantin about the cats. This big black fucker's pissed in the
room. He's tryin to catch it to kill it. It passes an he swings
a kick. But the cat gives him the slinky slip an hisses as it
leaves the room. Its wide jaw an white teeth remind me of
a snake.

Pat's at the big wooden table wi a drawin. We've to
knock a hole in the wall in our room to fit a big stove.
Wood-burnin. Great.

I go out on the flat roof an talk to Suzanne. Sounds
stuck up wi the Mary Poppins accent an all that. But she's
brand new. Top of the pops wee Mary. Top of the Poppins.
Her wanes – a girl an a boy went to stay wi the rich Da for
a month. They never came back. Preferred the Da to the
Maw. Money to the love. Done her head in. Textbook case.
Cries for a few weeks. Drinks for a couple more an then
becomes a born-again Christian. But she ditches that for
the Catholic church.

A born-again Catholic, says Doom.

It's cos the Catholic Churches're more ornamental an intricate. Mystical. More nooks an crannies than ye could shake a stick at. Yer search could last forever wi only one wrong turn. An that's good. Cos yer hope's stretched like elastic. Searchin'll keep ye alive till yer whirlpools stop turnin.

She's in the sea we were talkin about before, Suzanne. An she's swimmin for the barrel. But she sees what she thinks's a better barrel. A raft. A boat. A ship. A cruiser. A whole fuckin love boat scenario for fucksakes. She falls in love wi the Priest.

Fall in love wi some cunt close to God an ye're fallin in love wi some cunt close to perfect. That's what she done. But he's just a screen where she projects her image of perfect love. No sex. That's even better. No plantin seeds of sexual jealousy. The celibacy helps wi her pristine image of love. Four years it goes on for. Up to three months ago. Now we know why she's here.

It's me an her an the birds. We're leanin on the ledge an lookin out over the streets. I can't think of nothin to say. I think she's alright wi that but ye can never be sure. I like that bit in *Men In Black* where the black guy asks his partner who the wummin is on the screen. He ignores him.

So the black guy thinks he's cool. Thinks he's got it all sussed. Knows it's his partner's ex-wife. He goes *Better to've loved and lost than never to've loved at all.*

His partner turns an goes **Try it.** That's it. Shuts the cunt up. So that's how I don't say nothin to Poppins. I just stand there. Sometimes it's good to have somebody standin there. Somebody in yer magnetic field.

Davy shouts on me anyway. I thought he was away. I just touch her on the shoulder an leave her cryin. Her tears're little silver planets droppin to the gravity of the street an the Mountain an village're reflected in them an they're smashin onto the ground in little

B   i   t   s.

I look for them as me an Davy an Francie's off in the micro-bus to get supplies. But it's only dust.

In the builder's we meet Alessandra. Stunnin. Looks Peruvian. She's married to the owner Francie says. Fuck it says I. She's a babe. So we get the stuff an leave. But her smile's that big an bright we're drivin along it for miles before we get to any road. Davy nudges me. *Don't even think about it ya mad cunt!* he says. An I know what he means. I know exactly what he means.

An another thing, he says, *Suzanne's mine – I get the burd this time!*

AIDS

It's night. Me an Francie's in the micro-bus comin back
from Alessandra's. Pickin up cement. She left it outside for
us. He starts on about the AIDS research he was doin. I
love science an stuff. That's mostly what I read on the
Ward. An poems. I like thinkin. He's keepin it ma level.
Not blitzin me wi mumbo jumbo. He's a metaphor man.
That's good so it is. What do I know about AIDS? Fuck
all – but that's what I'm sayin.

   Francie – Mibbi a brickie'd find an answer easier?
   Is dat right now? he goes.
   He thinks I'm thick. But he's wantin to talk.

   To highlight what I'm on about wi the bricklayer I tells
him this story about Jimmy Brogan. Jimmy Brogan was
thick as fuck at school. So the teachers sayed. Anyway, he
was doggin it this day. Last year at the primary. He's up
the Whiffiet an there's this lorry jammed under the
railway bridge. Its top's crushed into the girders. The
driver's scratchin his belly an the Polis're keepin the
crowd back. It's oul wimmin wi brown leather shoppin
bags mostly. Jimmy Brogan sits on the kerb an lights a fag.
A big tow truck arrives, hooks up an tugs.

   An **TUGS**

An **TUGS** like fuck but the only thing happenin's screechin tyres on the tow truck. Some of the oul wimmin get behind the lorry an shove.

A right pisser, Jimmy Brogan says, *yer granny shovin a forty-footer in her wee furry boots.*

Nothin happens. Stuck solid so it is. The Polis've got their hats off their heads. The wimmin're rubbin their bones talkin about liniment.

Jimmy Brogan flicks his fag away an walks right over to this big Polis.

The Polis waves him out the road. So Jimmy goes to the tow truck driver who's on the other kerb smokin. He sits down an lights a fag. The driver says somethin about smokin at his age an rubs his hair.

Let the tyres down mister, Jimmy Brogan goes.

What good'll that do wee man they'll still screech?

Jimmy Brogan sighs an shakes his head.

No. Not the tyres on the tow truck – the tyres on the lorry.

The guy gives it puzzlin eyebrows.

Flatten them an the top'll clear the girders. Drive it out an blow them up again.

The guy looks at Jimmy Brogan, looks at the tyres, looks at Jimmy Brogan, drops his fag an bolts over to the Polis.

So they let the tyres down an drive the lorry out an that's that. Ye'd expect him to steal the credit. Not the tow truck driver. An by this time the papers an the telly's there. Askin how he got the idea. Ye can see he's about to lie. *Scotland Today* it was on. He's about to lie but he just points to Jimmy Brogan. Jimmy Brogan realises the cameras're on him. Nips the fag an shoves it in his pocket. Over they go an there's Jimmy Brogan on the six o'clock news. *News at Ten* an all. He was the wee happy bit at the end. The *AN FINALLY SOMETHIN TO CRACK A SMILE ON YER MISERABLE FACE,* bit. Jimmy Brogan. Toast of the land.

That's done the trick a bit. Francie's not so patronisin now. He starts tellin me how he sees it.

. . .see di virus mutates n changes so rapid dat it outpaces any attempt bi di body to attack it, but, an dis is more of a problem, it mutates so rapid dat it outpaces any advances in medicine.

Like chasin a train? I says. He thinks for a bit.

No . . . not chasin a train . . . more . . . more like . . . it's more like – imagine you're standin in a tennis court . . .

Wimbledon?

He laughs.

Wimbledon if you like. You're lookin up an a ball falls.

I'm noddin away. I'm interested. I'm really interested. An the cars on the other side of the road're speedin by. Lines of white light tipped wi red. An every one might be an idea missed. A solution that's passed.

You move about di court anticipatin where it'll land. You catch it an put it in a box. Then two fall. You manage to catch dem as well. Den three. Den four. Eventually you have balls rain in down everywhere an your attempts to catch dem are futile. Dat's di problem.

The   bus bussssssssssssssssssssssssssssssssssssssssssssssssssssssses along for a while. But I'm not there. I'm miles away. In this tennis court. It's not Wimbledon but. It's a big fancy house I sneaked into when I done a runner from the Ward. I sat for hours openin their letters all about banks an holidays in the sun. Tryin to imagine what it'd be like to change into them. To change into somebody else an disappear. Next thing the guy comes in. I bolts out the door an across the garden. I remember runnin across the tennis court an jumpin the net to get away. Lightnin I was. Fast as fuck. The guy had no chance. I thinks of Superman. That's when it comes to me. Oul Soups in his red an blue suit blurrin about the place catchin all the balls.

Superman! I goes, nudgin Francie.

Eh? I think he was sleepin.

Superman. He could catch all the balls. Whiz whiz whiz.
Faster the better far as he's concerned.

He gives me question marks.

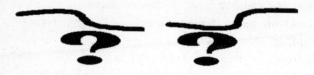

AIDS, I says. *If ye put somethin in their body that can move*
fast as Superman all the mutant teenage hero virus's'd be
sweeped up.

I'm thinkin he's goin to laugh.

!?!?!?!?!?!AHA!

He's interested. He's that interested he looks up at the
stars. I've read about that on the Ward. Not the stars.
Papers Doctor Fegan left lyin about. He used it to tell what
we were thinkin. That's why I kept hidin ma thoughts. I
kept ideas an dreams planked in trees an under bushes so
he couldn't find them. Sometimes they were perched on
trees like birds. Whistlin. Sometimes they moved over the
grass an they were butterflies. It wasn't just me. The whole
ward done it. But when the snow came it was no use. We
were all lost.

Neuro Linguistic Programmin it's called. That's what
Fegan was up to. I read all his stuff. Jimmy Brogan stole it.
The fact that Francie's lookin up an to the left shows he's
got a visual mind. He's a metaphor man. Visual.

I knew it. **I knew it. YEEEEEEEEE! HAAAAAAA!**

I like metaphor men. I can really get into what's it all about Alfie wi them. Right into it. Ma heart's pintablein about. Boom boom. Pstoom. Shoom. Ting. But I keep ma face straight in case he thinks I'm fallin in love wi him. He puts his hand up in front. His fingers're all stretched out an up like sea anemones.

I used too simple a model dere, he goes. It's not tennis balls all di time. It's tennis balls at first but after two or three it's spikes an den all sorts of shapes an sizes dat Superman couldn't catch. Shapes we can only dream about. Di virus mutates all di time. Randomly.

He drums on his knee scannin for good metaphors. His eyes're to the right – that means he's constructin a visual image. He calls them models but it's metaphors he really means. He's got his eyes to the left an down now. The Neuro Linguistic Programmin stuff says he's havin an internal conversation wi hissel. A bit daft really. I mean – ye'd hardly have an internal dialogue wi somebody else. Unless ye're a Schizophrenic. Two people livin in the one head.

I gets ma eyes up where the best visual metaphors are. Try it. Next time ye find yerself puzzlin somethin out check where yer eyes are. If it's upper left ye're a visual person. If it's middle left it's sound ye're rememberin – an if it's lower left it's the internal conversation stuff. If ye look to the right an level ye're buildin somethin out of sound. If ye look down to the right ye're buildin somethin out of feelins. This guy's the same as me but. Uses the upper left an right the most.

But there I'm away again. By this time I've got Superman changin at the speed of light into dogs, cats, budgies, rocks, umbrellas, lampshades, sea, toenails, comprehensive schools, atoms, by-passes, rubber ducks, buttons, islands, the head of a pin, photographs, holograms, ropes, palates, fairies, trees . . . He's changin that fast he's a buzzin blob of energy.

Could be a mutant Superman, I goes.

Changin?

Aye – change that fast that the balls an spikes an lumps of strange jelly'd've no chance.

Francie gets somethin.

But he'd need to see what it was an mutate so as to be able to catch it.

Aye.

But dat's impossible.

How?

We can't give an anti-virus intelligence. Dat's a whole other ball game.

So we're fucked again. Francie bursts into 'Bind Us Together Lord' as we buzz our way towards Cucuruzzu.

♪ *Bind us together Lord*
Bind us together
With cords that cannot
Be bro-O-ken . . .

The mountainside's white in the headlights. White. An the glitterin eyes of animals peer now an then from the darkness.

ASINO BRUTTO

Sunday. Went to mass. Because of the salami war an our complainin about the food Padre Fabian announced that Scottish're helpin to rebuild the Parish House an build the Hermitage on the Mountain. Will they provide us wi food. The parishioners.

But the mass was all in Italian. First I know's the word

Eccosse. The whole chapel turns an smiles at me. I'm redder than the sanctuary light. On the way out I'm that nervous I starts to have these nightmare feelins at the altar to Our Lady of the Poor. No pictures just horrible black feelins. Like God just opened a new universe inside me. Big. Empty. Dark. Cold.

I staggered out into the warm sun. The doors slam an open. There's somethin about church doors slammin that gives me the creeps. Everybody thought I was drunk an laughed. The Italian men stubbed out their fags an walked downhill wi their wifes. They don't go into mass.

I can't get away quick enough. They're all talkin to me in Italian; tellin me they'll bring food.

I gli porterà cibo

An they're bickerin about who's bringin what on what day. It's Daniele that's translatin staccato bits of it so I can

149

make it out. He's latched onto me for some practice. Comin on great his teacher says. The horrible feelin leaves me when I walk through a shadow. It stays there an I walk out into the light. I glance back an I see a pair of yella eyes like the night animals on the Mountain. Wild dog eyes starin. They're mad that I've gave them the slip. Soon it's just me an Daniele walkin along the sides of white buildins. Wild. Now I feel happy. Glad to be alive.

Daniele's helpin me wi Italian insults for Davy. Like **BRUTTO ASINO** – Ugly donkey. To say it right ye have to pronounce the R an the U in Brut an the I in Asino. **BRUTTO ASINO**.

Davy's new name. **BRUTTO ASINO**. He's good Daniele.

Baldy! he's sayin to Doom. Daniele points to his head an laughs. He does what must be a Davy Doom walk. Arms hangin – head hangin down an eyes up through the eyebrows.

BRUTTO ASINO. BRUTTO ASINO. BRUTTO ASINO. BRUTTO ASINO . . . he keeps sayin over an over all the way down the street. An laughin. An I'm laughin. I don't know what's so funny but I can't stop laughin. Specially after the episode at the Our Lady of the Poor altar.

When I get in there's this wummin like the back of her out the Tom an Jerry cartoons. Giovanna. Seventy-odds. But when she turns she's got the most beautiful blue eyes. She's cookin dinner. Usin her own stuff. It looks bare an simple but tastes great. Local spaghetti dish. Dig in wolf wolf me an Doom love it the most. Even Ball an Chain takes a saucerful. Fabian an Francie're beamin. Holy lines of light's comin out their faces. They've been prayin since yon time this mornin.

It's hot theday. Seventy-odds. I'm feelin not right again. I keep liftin ma shoulders up an droppin them but I can't relax. I'm bothered about somethin. Like there's somethin lurkin just below the surface of the world. I can't shake it off.

ABSOLUTION ZERO

Francie wants to be a Hermit of the Old Order of St Francis. Tell ye this – his eyes're always clear an blue. His face's always white an pink. Movements're slow an easy. Bein a monk's always been his ambition. Says marriage was a vocation too. Now that that chapter of his life's over he's free to be wi God. First time ye see him he looks fragile. He'd not last a minute tryin to live the kind of life ye're forced to live down where Doom lives. But that's just one way of lookin at it. That's lookin at it like life's a constant fight an a dangerous place to exist. But when ye get to know Francie a bit ye see how strong he is. His core's a metal unknown to man. Sharp but not offensive. Solid but not hard. It's just there. An he roots his every thought an movement in it. It's God. That's who's at the centre of Francie. Francie's God. God of mercy and compassion – that's one of his favourites. Sings it all the time.

An he says some interestin stuff does Francie. I'm on about the Troubles this day. Thinkin he's bound to be a Republican. He drives crouched over the wheel for a while. Ye can tell he's thinkin. But he's not thinkin from his Francie-from-Dublin viewpoint. He's moved into the core that is God an that's where he's speakin from. He comes away wi all this stuff.

To fight for justice is to fight for balance.

Long   drivin   pause.

If you take a step back an look from another planet. Say for talkin's sake you're on Venus lookin at the goins on on eart.

Drivin drivin drivin.

It's a final balance dat God's lookin for.

Drivin.

A final balance.

Drivin.

He wants di comin to rest of all conflict in di human condition.

Drivin.

He wants di physical stuff gone. Dat's obvious. Di bombs an di guns an di knifes an di fists.

Drivin.

But he wants di words gone too. Di fancy names an phrases.

Drivin.

An finally he wants conflict in every individual's mind to be gone too.

Drivin.

Peace. Absolute peace.

Woah. Hold on there crazy horse. Francie boy's right in there somewhere. He's talkin about absolute peace. I'm thinkin about absolute zero. Minus two hunner an seventy degrees Kelvin. Ye can't get any colder in the universe. But it's not the cold that interests me. It's the fact of what cold actually is. It's when everythin stops movin. I don't mean big things like stars an planets. I'm on about molecules. Atoms. Neutrons. Everythin stops vibratin. At that temperature absolute silence's reached. Absolute peace. An if Francie's anythin to go by – absolute God. If ye mixed the two concepts thegether – Absolution Zero.

Unlike Father Feed Yer Face Francie radiates what ye expect a monk to radiate. No name for it. Sometimes ye meet a monk an ye're not impressed. Mibbi they've got no understandin of spirituality. Too religious. But Francie? By fuck he's in tune wi whatever it is ye've got to be in tune wi.

Then ye look at Ball an Chain. What's goin through his head when he clunks the oul cannon ball on the table at meals? Pat asks him this night what he's wearin it for. In sign language that is cos we know hardly any Italian. I mean, *Scoozy but a what are a you a wearin a the ball an a chain a for a?* isn't the first phrase ye come across in *ITALIAN FOR TOURISTS.* Anyway he just dropped his head an sat there like a comma. Like shame.

Mibbi whatever he done the guilt's rotted him to this. Ye could speculate all day what he done. There's no measured amounts of guilt. Accidentally killed a mouse or raped an murdered his sister. Who knows? An I'm thinkin how loopy this cunt is this night when it comes to me. We've got somethin in common. All of us I mean. The whole human race. An that allows me a wedge to peek in an see it from his point of view for a minute. Everybody's got a threshold of guilt.

Matt Talbot wrapped hissel in chains for fucksakes an no cunt knew till he died. *Get the kit off him,* says the undertaker – *Fucksake Paddy would ye look at dis – dis cunt's been stealin chains from his work!*

Sometimes guilt'll make ye turn violent or ye might turn to drink. It's all the same. It's all the same slow suicide. It's all the same death wish.

The Ball an Chain's only the physical manifestation of things that most cunts hide. Things ye usually keep in yer head. Depression. Or mibbi your Ball an Chain's drink an drugs. Mibbi ye want to die of worthlessness. Have ye been there? Have ye? I know. I know. Ball an Chain's not so mad after all. Mibbi it keeps him from feelin the big dark hole inside him. Every time he clunks it on the table or clicks it off the ground the current of dread an fear buzz out his body an into the earth. Down into the earth. Discharged. But his memory generates electricity an his soul's a capacitor. He charges up again wi terrible voltage.

Holy places seem full of mad cunts at first. But if ye look in yerself ye can find a connection – the mad cunt that lives inside ye. They're over the edge you're standin on.

But that doesn't stop me an Davy nailin his Ball an Chain to the floor this night. He thought we were fixin the floorboards. Tries movin an chink. The chain's tight. His leg's stretched behind him like a skater. Says nothin. Just sits back down. An he was still there at breakfast the next day. We never had the heart to leave him any longer so we pulled the nail. But Doom painted the ball bright yella wi black stripes like a bumble bee. Ball an Chain scrubbed it off wi a toothbrush. Took days.

An what about Francie compared to Feed Yer Face? Fabian comes in the kitchen this day. He eats eight slices of bread. I'm countin. Then a big chunk of cake, two bananas an an apple. Francie sees what I'm thinkin an waves me away wi a there's more to the man than that look.

There's a crash downstairs. Then some manic laughter. Pat's drunk again an that's bad news. Unpredictable. Me an Doom moved crates an crates of wine out the cellar. He's been drinkin it all day. I starts spottin half-finished bottles everywhere. In the bog. In the kitchen. Two. In the lobby. Halfway up the stairs. An in the room. Six. It's not lookin good for a relaxed night. Not lookin good at all. No sir. So I go a walk up the Mountain an sit in starlight thinkin. An I'm thinkin about guilt. I can feel an immense pressure inside me. But it's like an oil-field trapped under pressin rock and seabed. Weighed on by fathoms of water. An I'm the rig tryin to find it. It's there. Ma head keeps goin back to the Ward. It's in there somewhere. That's where it is. The stars're krishna'd across the sky. They're bleepin out their sad binary code. Blip blip, they're goin. Blip blip. An the sky's dark blue. Definitely dark blue. An the stars are shinin. Definitely shinin.

TALKER WITH BIRDS

Next mornin I wake up on the Mountain. I'm wet all over wi dew. Allsorts birds're whistlin an hoppin over me.

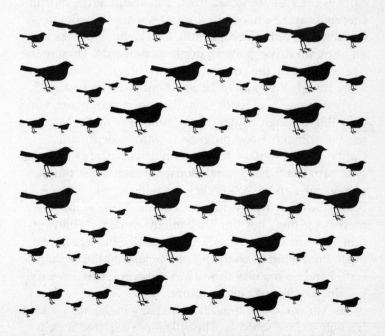

Hello wee birdies. Tweet tweet. I'm freezin. I gets up an starts stampin about. A burst of birds flutters a few feet away wi every stamp. Closin in again when I stop. I look down to Cucuruzzu. It's a paintin. It could be a hunner years ago. Two hunner even. Behind the village an inversion's lyin on the Gargliano valley. A sea of white mist. From Cucuruzzu to Cassino everythin's milky. Monte Cassino bursts up out into the blue sky like a fairy tale. I could swim over. Swallows're flyin about never takin the same path twice.

I walk slow down the hillside. I'm up wi the locals. Christ I never knew they got up that early. *Buongiorno . . . giorno . . . giorno . . .* is all I hear an now I'm part of the whole thing. Part of ancient Italy. The one that survived the Romans an all the wars.

An old woman, squintin, feeds her chickens. Her smile catches the sun. It catches the whole feelin of the mornin. *Giorno,* I say. She nods but doesn't say anythin. Below houses hold onto the rocky hill. On the dusty tracks men an wimmin drive goats an donkeys onwards. They're the ones missed by the shrapnel of technological revolution. They travel slowly an in an out them birds fly unafraid.

Way above them roads from the snowy mountains wind downhill through winter into summer. I'm on the tarmac road now makin good progress towards Cucuruzzu. Cars're startin to pass. Mad Italian drivers. Cars that hang wi rosary beads head miraculously at each other. But they always miss an the beads click the windscreen wi the ABS brakes. An they throw dust back at me. None of the drivers see me. They don't see me the same way they don't see any of the locals. Drive past like I'm a rock or a bush. I'm meltin in wi the place. I'm just another Italian farm hand on ma way to work as the cars speed towards Cassino an the buzz of the future.

The snow-capped mountains're hazy in the distance. It's goin to be a scorcher. The villagers've started movin about. Wimmin're carryin heavy bundles on their heads. Sticks for the fire. Stuff from their patches of land. Oranges an lemons. The loads're balanced on their heads on a rolled-up hanky or neckscarf for paddin. Their poise'd put catwalk supermodels to shame. Balance an grace. Their land can be as much as two miles from their houses Francie says.

As I come round the last bend into the village an oul wummin's comin down the steps that lead up to the chapel. She starts walkin along this narrow wall hangin out her washin in the mornin air. There's a fifteen-foot drop at the other end. I take a breath. Somethin in me believes she's goin to fall. But then I look again. She's solid an balanced. She's seventy if she's a day. Some people's born wi balance.

The sun's really gettin up now. There's sweat on ma forehead. There's somethin about the village comin to life. It's like a language underpins it all. The language lies under the surface of wakin up for another day. The people, buildins an things that move in the mornin're letters, words an paragraphs. Mibbi this's the Word Jesus was on about. An the Word from these streets's the stalkin cats that can almost talk

MEAWW   MEE   MEE
MEEAAAAA wo wo wo they're goin

an rubbin across ma leg. An the Word's the click of sticks bein sorted for fires. But the click reverberates down the ages. The click includes layin out of the bones of ancestors. Bones of ancestors that this village picked on its way to theday. Bones we all picked on our way to theday. Remember we're all made out of the same atoms that formed the universe. The pickin of bones's what our evolution's built on. I've picked bones to be walkin down this steep road into the village. Bones an bones an bones.

The heavy smoke of a damp fire spirals up out the middle of a field. A fat wummin in black brings it to life wi a straw hat. Wavin back an fro. Pausin. Wavin it up an down. The smoke's gettin thinner. She pauses again. The flames burst orange an yella. In France there's a cave an the ashes're twenty-odd feet deep on the floor. Prehistoric man kept the fire goin after he stole it from nature. Kept it lit. An we've kept it lit ever since. An this wee wummin's keepin it lit. An she's picked at the bones of her ancestors. There's always bones an fire in places like this. Fires're always needed in winter villages an summer fields.

I'm in the village now. I know Pat's snorin it off an Davy's makin plans to keep his head from gettin him theday. To keep the bones he's picked at bay. Away down in the valley the river's stopped. It looks like it's not movin – a bit of tinfoil glued to a watercolour. The sun's angle's low. The light blinds off it an lasers in wide sheets up here shatterin on buildin's edges an fillin dark gaps wi light. The river's silver's silver. Too bright. Its reflection pins oul wimmin to the shady walls of houses. They stay there glad of the damp walls behind their backs. An, wi their hands fumblin behind their backs they gossip about the sky, the river an the holy church. Sometimes they sweep an arm over the bricks an buildins that cover the Word that lies below.

They stop gatherin what's new in the nets of what the whole village knows. The nets of what the whole village has known for a long long time. An they take life as the moment. An wi the risin temperature they're once again at ease. The imperceptible tension's been noted an allowed to pass them on into another day.

Now the sweet smell of burnin wood wafts through the streets. **Sniff! Sniff!** I love that smell. I fuckin love it. I could click ma heels for it. But it's not the time or place for clickin heels. Mibbi later on. Late afternoon. But not here in the mornin. The wummin finishes hangin her high-wire washin. She waves some children up to breakfast. Watched by big fat mammas an yammerin cats. Some men walk in funeral precision down onto the Piazza to sit all day. The Word's in them too. The iron hammer in the cappella clock tower hammers out the message that time is God's. But the people move no faster. No slower. One lights a pipe. Their Gargliano shuffle'll have none of the knockin bell. Aye! they go to mass. Aye! they say their prayers. But that's a masque coverin the immense power of the Word. An the oul men an wimmin step out a rhythm older than iron; slower than time. The framework of livin can hardly contain them. In an out them the children buzz like summer bees blown by a warm but gentle breeze.

I'm fillin ma brain wi great memories. So's I'll have good things to think about. Whenever ma head starts to wander off to the bad things I'll just think of Cucuruzzu. That's what Jimmy Brogan was up to. When he stole Doctor Fegan's stuff. The Neuro Linguistic Programming stuff. He was right into it. He could make bad memories disappear. He called it the swish pattern. What ye do is ye get a good memory. A good picture of yerself an ye put it on the big cinema inside yer head. Get it as big an bright an colourful as ye can. Ye look at it all. What ye look like. Where ye are. Who ye're wi. Feel how ye feel. Feel great. Change the picture till it's just the best thing ever. Make it up if ye have to but make sure ye feel great when ye look at it. Once ye've got the picture ye want . . . It can be a short film if ye like. Mibbi winnin an Oscar or somethin. But once ye've got it ye shrink it till it's just a wee white dot buzzin away there. A star. Then ye get the bad memory up there on yer cinema. Ye look at it. Feel how bad it makes ye feel. Then ye summon the white dot of goodness.

Ye let it grow fast as fuck an swiiiiiiiiiiiiiiiiiiiiiish

it obliterates the bad memory. Ye keep doin that procedure till ye can think of the bad memory without gettin any of the bad feelins that go wi it. Ye're supposed to use this to make bad memories disappear. But Jimmy Brogan was makin good an bad memories disappear. He was loadin other things into his head an all. A made-up world. A set of memories an thoughts that weren't his. He was puttin new memories into his brain. Lies in sound an vision. Another history.

ASPARAGUS DALEKS

Finished work. I'm goin up the Mountain. We got chips for the concrete delivered. Shovellin it off the lorry's hard work. Driver's a lazy cunt. Stops. Tells ye the stuff's there. Hands ye a shovel. Lights a fag an sits wi the Piazza men. Smokin an watchin. Davy's down. Pat's got a hangover. Poppins's woe is her. An to cap all that Hilda's got the flu. She's in bed depressed.

Good thing is – ever since Feed Yer Face requested grub for us at the chapel, a stream of wimmin's came up wi dishes an loafs an tins an dinners ye could only dream about. I'm gettin fit wi good eatin an every day runnin up the Mountain.

Up the Mountain theday I met this wee guy wi asparagus tips. A carrier bag full. He picks them off the side of the Mountain an sells them. Gets a lot of money for them. Tells me all this in sign language. I'm tryin hard to make out what he's sayin. But then somethin happens. I notices he looks like wee Dalek. A fuckin ringer in fact. Only older. A lot older. He's still talkin away an rollin asparagus tips across his rucky hands. Like logs on a hillside. But his voice fades an becomes the background. The leaves in the trees flick in the light. There's a picture an then it's hidden in the edges of the leaves but – flick –

an there's Jimmy Brogan's face again.

Duffy an Jimmy Brogan got sent to sort out wee Dalek this time. It was an order Duffy says. Right from the top. *Toichfaidh ar la,* says Jimmy Brogan.

Dalek'd started sellin smack. They turned a blind eye to dope an speed an acid. But smack? That's another kettle of fish. The Polis'd get any amounts of information from a junkie. An there's safe houses right around where Dalek's sellin his stuff. An a lot of the local team's been buyin smack.

He's just a wee gringo guy Dalek. A rat wi a moustache. An a bit of a grass an all. An he's got no back-up. He's a loner. Keepin his own habit goin. So Duffy an Jimmy Brogan's on their own wi two baseball bats.

They head along the railway. Railways go nearly everywhere in the Brig. The dark arteries where no cunt can see ye. But you can see them beneath the sodium lamps.

They stop for a fag under the oul viaduct. That's where Duffy shows Jimmy Brogan the shotgun. It's in a pouch in Duffy's long leather coat. The coat's catchin the townlight an creakin like a wild animal – tense wi the springs of violence. Jimmy Brogan kids on he's not bothered.

Good man Duffy, he says, *is it loaded?*

Loaded? I'll blow the wee rat's legs off if he tries any of his shite.

The rest of the walk was different. Duffy's a fuckin loony. Ye could kill Dalek wi a wet tea biscuit. What the fuck d'ye need a shotgun for? It's the first time Jimmy Brogan's ever seen a shotgun. All he can think of all along's if it's goin to go off in Duffy's coat an blow both their feet off.

Soon as Dalek answers the door Jimmy Brogan shoves him on his arse an sets about the place. Smashin the phone an bootin in the eggshell doors. Dalek pleads wi them all along but they smash the whole place to splinters.

BOOSH – the glass ball light.

BOOSH – the toilet pan. A big vee in the front an the water waterfallin out onto the linoleum.

BOOSH – the Marantz hi fi. 🎼 *Buffalo soldier* That's its last words before a symphony of sparks and blue flashes.

Every now an then Jimmy Brogan cracks Dalek on the back wi the bat an sends him flyin. He's wishin Dalek'd stay down. Hopin he's done enough damage to stop Duffy gettin the shotgun out. But the wee cunt keeps gettin up an showin his palms wi his head tilted to the side.

C'mon lads – for fucksakes, he's sayin, *right right – I get the message.*

He's standin there like a question. Or a Jesus. Jimmy Brogan fucks him a dull yin in the guts wi the blunt end of the bat.

But it's no use. Jimmy Brogan's frenzy's not enough. Duffy's shut all the curtains. Jimmy Brogan's sat exhausted smokin on the ripped couch. The telly's smoulderin away an Duffy shoves the loaded shotgun in Dalek's mouth.

Now you've been a bad boy Dalek.

Dalek's eyes're shoutin **don't**.

I've been talkin to the birdies Dalek. You've been sellin smack the birdies're sayin.

Dalek's eyes deny it for a second. Duffy forces the barrel harder. There's blood comin out Dalek's bottom lip. Dalek's eyes admit it.

Tweet tweet – some wee rat's sellin heroin, says Duffy smilin at Jimmy Brogan.

There's this quiet bit. A splinter of TV glass falls. Duffy holds the stash up.

Tut tut ratboy, he goes, *you need sortin out.*

He shoves Dalek back onto the floor wi the gun still in his mouth. These white foamy slabbers're runnin down the barrel. The blood's makin some of it pink.

Close yer fuckin eyes ratchild!

Dalek screws his eyes up.

Cover his face! Jimmy Brogan hesitates.

Shove that fuckin cushion on his face Jimmy!

Jimmy Brogan still doesn't move.

The fuckin cushion!

Dalek's rattlin like fuck. Whimperin.

Duffy draws the gun out Dalek's mouth an Jimmy Brogan covers his face wi the cushion. Stars an moons it is. Gold on a dark blue background.

Duffy opens the gun an clicks the cartridges out an in. One two. Shlock they go. Slick shlock. He reaches in his leather animal an gets the bit that's sawed off. Jimmy Brogan's just wonderin what the fuck he's got that for when Duffy bends the cushion up an forces the sawed-off bit in Dalek's mouth. He breaks one of Dalek's front teeth in the process. He points the shotgun at the floor right next to Dalek's head an fires.

BANG
BANG

Dalek pishes hissel. The smell of shite starts fillin the room. Dalek's crying and vibratin on the carpet.

As they left Jimmy Brogan looked back. The house looked like an extension of what was goin on in Dalek's head.

TOOTHACHE

They're all still a bit down theday. I'm not that bothered
but. I can get lost in trains of thought. I can disappear
when I'm still here. Anyway it just takes somebody to start
clickin up the gears an they'll pull us all out. That's the
way it is. Birds of a feather affect each other.

Quite a cool mornin. Misted over. The sun'll come
through later mibbi. There's a warm buzz inside ma skin.
I'm not lettin on but. I'm not even smilin. If ye keep yer
good mood in yer voltage goes up. It turns into a mini
nuclear fission just under where yer heart is. I think I
know what's gettin them down. They're gettin wrapped
up in this wee world.

We're over here to stretch our lifes. Make them bigger.
Experience things. But now we're gettin sucked in. Fabian
wants to wrap us up like a loaf in his cupboard of a world.
The things outside the village're disappearin. Fallin off the
edge of the known world. But the Mountain's made me
immune. Ma brain's racin. High speed gas. Out there on
the rocky edges yer brain gets washed. Fresh an clean. I
can see for miles. Out beyond the edges of oppression. All
the way to the Mediterranean sea.

Every night after dinner's the same. Padre Fabian
repeats what he wants us to do. Mass, prayers, devotion,
this saint an that saint – includin or not includin Santa
Maria Goretti. Then it's the rota for work an housekeepin.

As much as he repeats it we nod *aye aye aye* an carry on doin what we want. Holdin in the laughin – that's what we end up doin. He ignores it. Francie puts the head down. I swear I seen his shoulders goin up an down the other night. Can't be sure but. Can't be sure.

I think the Monk put a curse on me this mornin, cos one minute I'm laughin an the next thing this

starts pulsin in ma jaw. When I look up everybody's normal. But Fabian's leanin back in his chair an smilin. He's lookin up at the ceilin. But he's smilin at me. His face's like a Picasso. There's nothin in the right place. Not a thing. Francie takes me to a chemist in San Rocco. I'm in fuckin agony. I could stand up an burst through the tinny roof in the van. Francie gets faster an faster. The pain throbs an throbs.

It's like a bank robbery the way we march in there an get the right stuff. Ye can't get this in Scotland. No sir. Best fuckin stuff ever. It's a wee round plastic bottle like an accordion. But it's got this big long snout comin out it like a hummin bird.

Ye use that to inject it into the cavity.

Suddenly the birds're whistlin again.

It's only once in the middle of the night I get up an put some in. There's Davy an Pat sleepin away that innocent. They don't know somebody's creepin about the room. I'm tryin to think of some good practical jokes. But there's none in the air. I inject the stuff. Lies down. Next thing it's the crazy mixed-up bells ringin out fuck knows what time. So I gets up. I leave Sleepin Beauty an **BRUT** ASINO. It's not light yet. I cross the flat roof into the kitchen for water. Fuck me – I shite massel! There's Francie an Fabian. An the look of guilt's like rabbits caught in headlights. They're drinkin coffee an a big pile of fried bread's on the table. Fabian's got one stickin out his mouth. But he's stopped chewin so it's like a thick crinkly tongue. Francie starts munchin to break the ice.

I'm laughin as I stuff coffee in a lunar module. Most monks get up at half three or four in the mornin to pray. The Hours it's called. That must be what they're up to. An

I'm thinkin Feed Yer Face's doin the prayin bit right even if he's not strict on poverty. I decides to give him a chance to boast a bit. To show me just how holy he is.

Do ye do the hours Father?

He crinkles his eyes at Francie. Our accents're harder first thing in the mornin. Like a cow's tongue's been transplanted in ma head. Francie fills him in on what I'm sayin.

Yes. Yes we a do. Franciscans a do a the hours eh Francis? Yes we do dat Father. We do.

I'm not tryin to catch him out. It's only chit chat as I reach for a bit of bread to make them feel more at ease wi their feast.

Must be hard wi a busy schedule – the Parish an the Hermitage?

A Yes yes. We a do Francis eh?

Yes Father we do.

Fabian leans back proud. He sweeps a take some grub hand over the table. That's when I see the salami an cold meats laid out behind the bread. I stuff a bit in ma mouth. That's when he speaks again.

A once a last October an a once in a January, he says.

I near choked for fucksakes! Three hunner an sixty-five days in the year an they've only turned up for two early-mornin sessions. God must be fuckin ragin. It's that absurd I can't laugh even. I keep chewin ma piece an smilin. Smilin an chewin. Chewin an smilin.

They shuffle out the room.

In a monastery ye'd have to do the hours. But down here Fabian's the boss. Fabian. Super Monk. Eats all the food he can get. Tries not to share it. Takes your share if he can get away wi it. Stays in bed for mornin prayers. He's a hoot. A right fuckin hoot.

Later on at breakfast he's askin about Santa Maria Goretti – who wants to go. I tell him I don't fancy the five million hours in the micro-bus there an back.

A bit of a sacrifice. He says, *you a know . . . if you a want sometheeng good you a must a put in a sacrifice a . . . suffer a . . .*

Davy's in quick, *What about stickin forks in ma thighs for about three weeks?*

Fabian does his question look.

Then I could go an see a good film, goes Doom.

Eh? says the Monk. He hasn't got a scooby what Davy's on about.

The film'll be all the better after all that forkin.

Fabian looks at Francie.

Nothin, says Francie, *it's nothin Father. Nothin at all.*

Fabian looks at Doom again. Doom goes, *OK OK I'll sacrifice like yer good self Father.*

They smile same as two con men at The Barras when they've caught each other out.

The electricity went out theday. Me an Davy had to work in the cellar by candlelight. I thought, *Shit! This's goin to be a bummer.* Can't see a thing. But it's only a different light. An wi a different light ye see different things. Turns out quite good. Really good in fact. Holy. No kiddin. Me an Davy's shadows're stretchin all over the place an the sputterin flame's searchin nooks an crannies an settlin down. Then goin out for another search. We're transported. A wee dark world of our own. Any time. Any place. Worldwide candles're associated wi religion an spirituality.

Reminds us we're gettin closer to our end constantly, Davy says. Mibbi he's right. Remindin us we burn down an die.

It's not time that passes year by year but men – I read that in the Ward. I used to look at them all. Heathcliff. Jig-a-Jig. Byzantine. The Chief an Jimmy Brogan an schuck this wee light'd appear on their heads. An their heads'd start meltin like wax. They'd not notice. But I seen it.

They were the men that were passin. An the clock said a big grinnin ten to two. Or sometimes a big smilin ten past ten. They were the only two times it said. But the rest of them in the Ward burnt down an down an the clock stayed still. I ran in an shoved ma head down the pan an kept flushin an flushin. The nurses, daft cunts, *He's tryin to kill hissel!* an all this shite they're goin. Shovin ma arms up ma back an tyin me to the bed.

So then I'm on Strict Obs an big Frank's askin me what the fuck I was tryin to do drownin massel in a lavvy pan? It'd be a first if I succeeded he says. He thought I was mad when I kept tellin him I was tryin to keep massel alive. Frank just shook his head an carried on wi the *Beano*. Out loud an showin me the pictures. It was the story where Plug fell in love. He was alright big Frank. Really alright. But I still never sayed nothin about the flames in their heads. I never sayed nothin about that. When I looked up over Plug an the Bash Street Kids the clock had spun back to the right time. Ye'd think I'd've heard it whizzin or clickin or somethin but nothin. Just the silence of Strict Obs an Frank laughin at the comic.

I beat ma time by one an a half minutes theday. I'm standin at the door to the house bent over like an oul hag an coughin. Red as a sprintin pig. Up comes Hilda wantin to know what the secret of peace is. I can smell smoke. I coughs a couple of times an tells her it's not up the Mountain anyhow but soon as I find it I'll tell her.

I'm lookin for the exact same thing Hilda – if ye find it tell me where the fuck it is, I goes. She shuffles away half laughin half not knowin if she should be laughin.

Hilda even feels guilty for thinkin Padre Fabian's a hypocrite for fucksakes. She thanked me this day. *What the fuck're ye thankin me for?* I goes. She says when we arrived we started sayin things she could hardly think about.

Thoughts that would damn her to hell.

She's startin to feel better. When I can straighten up an walk up the stairs I gives her a loan of this book about meditation. It was in Jimmy Brogan's bag that he left me. Even readin it calms ye down.

Dinner's finished. We're sippin coffee an Fabian leans back in his chair an starts another one of his stories. This nun had a wee plastic doll. Like a Tiny Tears. She'd dress it up an talk to it. There was cunts in the Ward for a lot less.

It's when he says the nun became a national heroine when she started to hear the doll talkin back that Pat walks out.

I'm goin for a walk, he goes an gives it the glass to the mouth wiggle. As he's leavin he screws a finger into his temple. I don't know if he means the Monk's nuts or me an Doom for listenin. Probably all it. But I can't move. Ma arse's glued to the seat. I'm tryin not to laugh.

Fabian waits till Pat's shut the door. Ye can hear him laughin all the way down the stairs an the big outside door shuttin. Francie gives it the extra super dooper big white re-start the story father smile.

So this nun's a national heroine for hearin a wee plastic doll talkin. He says. Every day she'd dress it up an talk to it. An whose was the voice? Right. God's. Who else but a baby God wi a wee squeaky voice? She treated this doll like a real wane. Gettin it up in the mornin an puttin it to bed at night. She never went out unless it was tucked up in bed sleepin. For that the doll told her secrets an prophecies an stuff. People came from all over to consult the plastic doll. But this day she goes away wi the rest of the ordinary nuns (ones that couldn't hear lumps of plastic talkin) but she remembered that she forgot to tuck the God\baby\doll\plastic in. She rushes back. But it's in a right huff.

Probably on the altar wi folded arms an tappin the toes

of its left foot on the cold marble. Like Sonic the
Hedgehog. So the God says:

✝ **Ye're lucky ye came back. I
was for the offski there. I was
just goin back to heaven. Fuck
you – puttin yer pals in front of
me. D'you know who I am?**

So she tells the story to the ordinary nuns. An she never
leaves the doll's side ever again. She devotes the rest of
her life to it. The nun dies an the other nuns stick the doll
in a glass case on the altar. Tourists flock to see the talkin
doll every year. Only thing is – it never talks to them.
Christ – our Linda's spoke when ye pulled this wee string
on its back. But it only ever said stuff like,

I want to wear my pink dress.

Or

Why don't you comb my hair.

Or

I want to go out in my pram. Muuuumeeee.

It never said stuff like

✝ *The world's goin to come to a bad end if you don't get yer
act thegether.*

Or

✝ *You're lucky ye came back so ye are. I was offski into the
cosmos there sister so I was. Offski. An I'll tell ye this an tell ye
no more – your jacket's on a shaky nail from now on. One more
slip up. Just one more. Just try it an see.*

Soon as Fabian's finished we explode like a barrel of
sparrows. He's left smug. Smilin. An Francie lookin at
him. Grinnin.

Aye ye're some man Fader, Francie's goin, *ye're di best miracle teller in di world.*

Sometimes I think Francie's in love wi the Monk. An all this time Ball an Chain's just sat there. Not movin. The expression on his face doesn't change. He nods like listenin but he's tryin to figure out where he can get a heavier Ball an Chain – cos we've stopped noticin it. I mean if ye want noticed mibbi a car engine or somethin chained to yer leg. Be creative. A filin cabinet or if ye want to be political the workins of an atom bomb – dud of course. Ball an chains went out wi knights in shinin armour for fucksakes. This's the Millennium – stay wi it man.

THE FIELDS OF ATHENRY

It's night. I'm on the flat roof. Down below Davy's walkin along wi Poppins. Walkin right close. I thinks about shoutin but I leave it out. There's this party goin on in the back garden of one of the big houses. Looks like a weddin. There's big tents an tables all laid out. This stuff of Jimmy Brogan's comes to me. About how he got his first philosophy thegether. The one that done his head in in the end. He was invited to Duffy's weddin. Duffy was marryin a burd from Derry. Well not Derry – that's where he met her. She was from Buncrana.

He's sittin, he says, at this weddin. It's all crack an colourful hats. The starters're gettin laid. So Jimmy Brogan sits down. Chattin wi this oul wummin. Nothin out the ordinary. Just another weddin. It all starts when he looks at his starter. **BOOSH!** Somethin flashes in his head like a photograph. So he jerks up to see if anybody else's noticed. But they're all eatin an chattin away like at the other side of a sheet of glass. He looks up an there's Marion twirlin her curl. She notices him an smiles. Back to the plate in front of him. He says he seen Ireland an its history on the plate. An on plates dotted round the two hunner guests.

Another look up. There's Duffy wi his smile to charm nuns an bankers. Back to the plate. Only some cunt like Jimmy Brogan could've seen this. Only him. What you an me'd see's a flat plate wi a couple of millimetres of green jelly. There's a slice of orange embedded in it. In the middle of the orange's a half a strawberry. Then there's all these thin strips of melon round about one side. But Jimmy Brogan saw somethin else. Somethin completely different. Lookin back now ye could see he was on a journey then. On a journey to the Ward an oblivion.

He sees a green sea of calm jelly. It's Ireland an its altar of fragile peace. A slice of Orange displaced but accepted. Part yet not part. Where would we be without it? On the Orange a wee Red Hand of Ulster strawberry's beautifully defiant. Probably not givin a thought to its Sacred Heart possibilities. It's all mixed thegether. It's all tore apart. An golden waves of melon lap the plate's western shore. Tir Na Nog. The tide's comin in on the white. Fallin on the windin shores of Celtic gilt. At last. At last the tide's comin in.

He looks up waitin for the whole place to be sittin wi long amazed faces.

Eat up son, the oul wummin says. He eats the Red Hand of Ulster. But he's away now. All the threads start comin thegether an everywhere he looks somethin ties a knot in the web. His philosophy's knittin itself out from the fabric of the weddin.

Marion's up dancin. Polite clappin runs through the place like machine-gun fire. Look. She's the Queen of all things Irish. A white tornado spinnin through changin generations. Next thing they're all up doin the same dance. Wanes too. Fat middle-aged cunts that never smile. Geriatrics. Priests an nuns.

Irish Jive! Marion's this way, Duffy's that. Her hair spins into view. Then her smile. Then the hands clasped. Dancin to the beat of one-two-three-spin. Her. Him. The Dance. A truly holy trinity; hearts in sacred grip. An Jimmy Brogan drinks an drinks. An taps his foot to the music. Taps his foot to the music.

It's later. She's in her goin-away clothes. In red an watchin the Irish dancers. To her they're dancin. But to Jimmy Brogan they're paddin lightly on a heavy tradition of love an guns. Four children sit on the stage edge watchin. Amazed. It could be the world's edge.

Reels an jigs. Embryonic circles embroidered on the breast of their dresses.

They'll head

out

an out

an conquer the far lands of the dance floor. That's where they'll go.

That's where I started losin Jimmy Brogan. His metaphors get a bit loose sometimes. But he was good at comin back in. At nailin it. I mind him right in ma eyes. He's tellin me all this. It was like I was starin straight back into a mirror. His eyes were the exact same as mine. Exact same.

We've come a long way to Marion's weddin. From prison ships an universities; abbeys an Armalites. We're the explosion of migration an famine. We're always movin out. We're always pushin up. On buildin sites an mines. On motorways an roads. In steelworks an railways. On drunken corners an jail cells. In asylums an parks. In ghettos an slums. In all them places we sang our songs. Sometimes the walls rang wi laughter. Sometimes they were damp wi tears. There's nothin wrong wi that, Jimmy Brogan says. Tears're for what was. Visions of what will be. Of what should be an what shouldn't.

*That dancer **should** be soarin to the lights. Jumpin heights that make us gasp. Amazed at our own ability to leave mire an bog an starvation. Wanes'll always climb the steps we've made for them. They'll climb wi poems an tears an laughter an guns. An they'll always sing our songs.*

Now some cunt's singin 'Athenry'. First time Jimmy Brogan told me about that weddin he bursts into song.

🎼 *By lonely prison walls I heard a young girl ca aa aa un*
  Michael they have taken you away . . .

It's hard after that to see any other way for him to go. It was all marked out from the weddin forward. All marked out.

I look down at the Italian weddin. An I'm wonderin if there's anybody there in the same frame of mind as Jimmy Brogan. An if there is I want to go an warn them. To tell them to stop right now.

It's a shootin star that goes by overhead. The weddin gasps.

SIX EGGS AN A BOTTLE
OF WINE

It's early in the mornin. Warm. The mist's liftin already an
the houses dotted on the mountainsides're appearin
through it. Rocks in a recedin tide. Me an Davy's finished
the concrete stairs. We're goin to screed the cellar floor.
Concrete. Start plasterin the walls themorra. Or mibbi the
next day.

After breakfast we spend the day takin chances each
bringin the sand an chips up from the Piazza in a bucket.
We take chances each mixin the concrete on the slabs
outside the front door. We take chances each carryin a
bucket of concrete down into the cellar where we're still
workin by candlelight. Not because the electricity's out.
We like the atmosphere. We take chances each screedin the
wet concrete floor to a smoothness. It's called bringin the
fat up. In the darkened candlelight the floor looks like two
inches of black water. As Davy screeds I watch. It's quite
meditative.

We're havin a break about eleven. Poppins made us
some great pieces. Salad. Two mugs of tea. The cellar's
that hypnotisin we're not even talkin. We walk outside in
silence. We know how good we feel. It's goin to be really
hot theday. The inversion's lyin deep into the valley. It's

risin right up to the base of Cucuruzzu. Summits're pokin through liquid fog. Prehistoric. The mist's a vast ocean lappin on rocky islands. A boat in full sail wouldn't surprise me now.

I can hear Italian voices in the streets below. An the singin of birds from the blue sky. The odd hoot or quack of heavier domesticated birds drowned in the sea of clouds. Their cries penetratin this sharp air where swallows spear through flocklets of chirpin sparrows.

Oul wimmin're murmurin by their slow washin lines an somebody's singin an cleanin in the cool shadows of a house. Black figures wander from Cucuruzzu an fade to grey downhill into mist. The day's a meditation on itself an ma breathin's full an cold in ma lungs. Ma temperature drops. Ma steps're easier an slower. The peace Hilda was askin about's here. It's right here. I go to shout on her. But what can I say? What can I tell her?

Me an Davy's back to the screedin. Ye've got to do it for hours so the floor ends up flat an shinin. Otherwise stones stick through. An then one gets kicked out. An the floor starts crackin. Within a year wi frost an heat the new floor's separated from the old. Ye've got to start all over again. So he screeds an I watch. I screed an he watches. We're asleep really. Only the parts of our bodies needed're awake. It really is a peaceful day.

In the afternoon I have a rest in the deck chair at the front door. Davy's inside wi Poppins laughin an gigglin. But that's good.

Down below the Piazza's movin in its usual slowness. Sweat's all over me like baubles of mercury. This oul man meanders by dressed for a Scottish winter. Jumper black jacket hat. The sun glints off the wine bottle. It's swingin wi each stride. The wine inside stays level wi the ground. He's holdin it in the vee of two fingers. An in his left hand there's six loose eggs. He walks away wi the sun on his back. Big hands. I snooze an wake.

Two hours it must be an I'm gazin over the village not thinkin about nothin. Just lookin. If ye seen me ye'd think I was sad. But that's not it. I'm leaned forwards wi ma head restin in ma hands. I'm not smilin. I'm just lettin the place wash over me. That's when he comes back. He comes back unchanged. No different except for the empty wine bottle an the breeze in the fingers of his left hand. There's the shadow of his cap on his forehead cos he's walkin into the sun now. He must've went to a neighbour's. Made a meal wi the eggs. Drank the wine. Mibbi chatted a bit. The Mountain. The fields. The people workin in the Parish House mibbi? But that's nothin. None of that matters. This tremendous feelin of warmth comes over me. First I think it's sweat comin down ma cheek. Or an insect mibbi. But it's a tear. I'm cryin at somethin happy. Somethin good. I'm cryin at the six eggs an a bottle of wine. He nods at the men on the Piazza. *Sera. Sera,* they go back. There's hardly a movement.

The men on Cucuruzzu square've changed position wi the sun. But the same easy talk whistles over the top of the slow swing of the bottle.

Funny thing is – the tears've made me happy. Plus another thing – Padre Fabian's away to Rome theday. Francie says he'll take me to Monte Cassino themorra. It's waitin on me across the valley. It's a quest. Me an Monte Cassino. The Hermitage versus the Opulence. Poor versus rich. Two different parts of the same thing.

MIRACLE OF FISH AN

ROSARY BEADS

We're goin to Alessandra's for plaster. Stucco. But the landscape's sayin relax. Unwind man. Chill.

Davy says try ready-mixed plaster for the cellar. Fabian's happy wi the cellar an amazed at Pat. Pat's a craftsman. What used to be a room of misshapen walls an churned up floor's become an office. Be the envy of any yuppie so it would. He's made cabinets for parish records in mahogany wi gold handles. The shelfs're matchin an shinin – reflectin each other. Smellin of new varnish. Villagers've been in an out all day to see where the paper reminders of their ancestors'll rest. They shake Pat's hand an have a glass of wine from the cellar. It's runnin low. It's Pat's wine now.

Hilda's still got the flu. Pity on a day like this. Suzanne appears in the doorway done up to the nines. WOW she's a babe theday. Bright expensive clothes an this cravat flyin in the slight breeze. I nods at Davy an says *Biggles's burd*. But he doesn't see me. He's starin at her. She smiles an strides off to the hills. Watercolours that's what she's into. Her stuff's great. Except that wi years of negativity from her Ex she thinks she's a housewife painter. But she's captured this place. She's comin out herself a bit. She's

even missin mass. Fabian's gave up convertin us all to
Holy Joes. Things're goin well now. Things're fine so they
are. Just fine.

Poppins disappears round the bend in the tarmac road.
If we keep watchin we'll see her comin out above the
village. On her way up the Mountain. A splodge of calm
on the slopes.

It's a laugh. She tried a practical joke on me yesterday –
threw me a boiled egg kiddin it was raw. *Catch, catch it,*
she says in imitation panic. I step to the side an let it fall.

Later I took an egg she boiled for herself an replaced it
wi a raw one. I dipped it in hot water so she'd not feel the
cold. She swipes the knife an it bursts all over the table
chair an floor. I left her cleanin it up sayin *Damn* an *Golly.*
Davy's creasin hissel on the floor. That's when I decides to
get him too.

Half twelve every day the jeans factory girls eat lunch
on the Piazza. Good weather an foreigners in the Parish
House brings them. They shout up in Italian – *sesso –
sesso – pene . . .*

We shout in Scottish. *Show's yer beard!*

They call me down. I'm sittin on the wall. Doom stays
put in the deck chair. They've learned some English. This
girl starts pointin an sayin,

You like her?

I nod aye all the time.

She points at another one.

You like her?

Yes.

She deliberately picks a right monster.

You like?

I nod yes – *è una bella ragazza* – That made them giggle.
Then she comes away wi:

*What of these Italian women are you thinkin beautiful most?
What one you likeengk most?*

I shouts up an tells Doom what she's sayin. He's

shoutin allsorts in a fast accent. Good job they can't understand. I goes round them one by one. They're all all right. Mostly plump. I walk up an look at one. I lean ma head back an lift ma arm an point. She starts smilin. *No,* I say. I do that to a few along the line. Most of them giggle but one gets all het up. She's learned some English.

Peeg. Urglerly peeg!

But her pals laugh even more an she storms back to the factory. This redhead throws her piece at her laughin.

I come to this babe wi dark eyes. *Giovanna,* she says. I look at her. The most beautiful girl on the Mountain I want to say. But I can't say that.

Giovanna, è una bella ragazza.

They like that. They knew who was best-lookin. Giovanna goes all colours an they start pushin her at me like schoolgirls. There's me an her in the middle of the Piazza lookin at each other. Red-faced. The whole village's laughin an I can't move an I can't stand still. I'm wonderin what the fuck to do. She's standin there wi her head down an her hair hangin in front. Her eyes're stripped into lines like bar codes. The sexiest bar codes in the world. The Jeans Factory girls start clappin.

Clap

clap

clap   clap

clap   clap   clap   clap   clap clap clap clapclapclap

They're gettin faster an faster. I've got to do somethin. Davy's callin me all the daft-lookin cunts. The noise's deafenin. Windies're openin all over. High up in the village walls people're stoppin an lookin down. The church clock bell gives it twenty-six o'clock. I jump forward wi an awkward smile an kiss her on the cheek to an uproar of claps an cheers. But the aftertaste of the

kiss's a vortex of darkness. All these bad things come
into ma head. Bad bad things. There's voices in ma head.
It's somebody else's wife. It's somebody else's wummin.

But she's single. She's not somebody else's wife.
Everythin's blurred an echoin. That's been me since the
Ward. I can get a wummin no bother. But every time I go
to kiss them this fear comes over me. I've got to back off.
Back off. I'm saved by the factory bell an they all run back
laughin an smilin like Christmas. Giovanna turns back an
smiles. Once.

We go for plaster an Doom's slaggin me all the way
down the windy road. Francie's singin some hymns.
Doom won't let up. I don't say nothin. We get the plaster
from Alessandra's an head back up the road. Francie's
doin some Hail Marys now. Doom's still at it. Doin film
scenes in Italian accents.

*Of a all the Piazza's in a all the a places a in all a the world a
you had a to walk into the Armani a forgery a factory a one.*

But I'm not respondin.

Giovaaaaaaaaaaaaaaaaannnnnnnnnnnnnnnnnnaaaaaaaaah, he
says a couple of times. I wait till he's stopped. He's
lookin out the windie. But he's not lookin at the
landscape. I know where he's lookin. He's lookin at the
red an blue speck up near the cross. Suzanne. I let him
stare for a while.

Then I go,
Suuuuuzzzzzzzzzzaaaaannnnnnnnnnaaaaaaaaaah.

He looks at me.
What? he goes.
I say nothin.
What d'ye mean?
I still say nothin.
Tell me what ye're sayin!
Suuuuuuzzzzzzzzzzzaaaaannnnnnnnnnaaaaaaaaaaaaaaaaaaaaaa.

He ignores me. When we get back we plaster all day in
silence. We haven't fell out really. It's just that he doesn't

want to go into it. Yet. He's not ready for friendly banter
on somethin he's not sure about hissel.

In the evenin I'm out walkin. I go downhill this time.
I'm sittin on a rock listenin to the stream. That's when I get
a glimpse of what heaven's like. I'm lookin at this slow
water. Next thing this fish jumps out up to its middle. It
takes a look round an sinks wi a plip back into the pool. I
thinks like the fish. I focus. Right in there where its tiny
brain that runs all along its backbone makes sense of its
submerged world.

I thinks like a fish. I thinks like a fish. I thinks like a fish.
I'm in a deep gouge somewhere downstream. Lettin the
heavy water move over ma scales. I'm tryin to come to
terms wi what I seen up there above the circle of light on
the roof of waterworld. The line of cold water round ma
middle an the warmth of the pressureless air on ma gills.
Breathin it would be like an unquenchable thirst. Sun
makin ma scales shine like metal. The leaves patchin out
the sky so it's just wee bits of waverin light here an there.
An the branches an twigs stretchin out so it all looks like
one big green leaf wi dark veins runnin over its
underbelly. The trunks soarin up to somethin. The hiss of
the wind in the tops of the trees. An the feelin that above
the trees is somethin bigger. More immense even than all
this – I've seen outside ma world. An I dive back under
cover of water wi ma head filled wi bewilderment. An I
had noticed the man standin watchin at the side of the
bank. But I don't think him any different from the rest of
the stuff. No different at all.

So that's it – a micro-acid trip for fish. Meaningless. Not
because it's worthless but because it's beyond explanation.
It moved from its shallow world into the sheer width of
this world. An it kinda knows there's somethin above the
sheer width. But it doesn't know the sky. The sky's a
mystery to the fish. A mystery of light way up through the
truth of the trees.

An in the space between the green canopy of the trees. In the curves an eddies of the air – the mysticism of the fish religion is born. It doesn't know a thing about what's beyond the sky. The Solar System. Or beyond that – the Galaxy. Or beyond that – the vastness of space compared to its six inches of brook. An beyond the whole Universe? Or down into Time? Or out into Movement an Change? An that's the way I am. I can see as far as I can see. An what's just beyond it's a mystery. An I make up religions to bolt onto it. So Science keeps pushin the boundaries out. Shovin the mystery that one step further. Yesterday's mystery is theday's classroom lesson. But no cunt's admittin how connected it all is. Cos they're not really just pushin the boundaries of science out – they're pushin the boundaries of religion out too. The edges of reality where mystery starts are bein pushed out all the time. Science is never killin religion – it's just makin its circumference bigger.

A bell in the church tower goes. It's not the what time's it clock. It's the holy bell. That's a different deep gongin noise. **Gong gong gong** it's goin. An after three ye know it's not goin to stop. It's the rosary bell.

The rosary bell rings an rings. But even if it's loud it's kinda peaceful. Doors start openin an streams of oul wimmin in black make their way along the ribbon of white dusty road. One minute they're a line of oul wimmin equally spaced. Next thing they're a string of rosary beads. Walkin beads. Each one's a walkin Hail Mary, Our Father or Glory Be.

I can't tell if it's prayers or the walk or the bell that brought them from cool shuttered rooms an mosquito nets in spring. They're not talkin to each other. They're only walkin. Up an up to the chapel. Away up the steps some who live closer're already goin in through the door. It's so solemn ye'd think it was a funeral. Below them the Jeans Factory's comin out.

The oul wimmin I'm watchin pass through the gigglin Jeans factory girls like planets in the wrong solar system.

Uphill they float like virgins into the endless space of religion. The thing Hilda was askin about – that silence – it might never touch them either.

They're trapped in the mesh an cages of religion. Mibbi they know somethin we don't.

Mibbi not.

A factory girl gazes at the hills. I think it's Giovanna. I can't tell from this distance.

RADIO CHICKENS

We're plasterin the cellar me an Davy. Radio's on. We
managed to get this oul plastic thing workin.

Radio Chickens, the DJ keeps sayin, *Radio Chickens.* That's
what it sounds like anyway.

We go for more stucco from Alessandra. We're goin
through it. She's got two sisters. Says she's goin to
introduce me an Doom to them. They're married. Her
English's mixed up. She's hardly goin to introduce us to
her married sisters. Last thing we want's shot by the Mafia
for sleepin wi Suzy an Lucy the *Saaar deeee neeee aaahns.*
But it's good Alessandra's tryin to learn some English.
Mibbi we won't end up wi three ton of rocks when we
order a flower pot.

I'm goin to Monte Cassino theday. But first we've got to
find an empty Svelto bottle. Svelto's the Italian Fairy
Liquid.

Davy doesn't like me bein friendly wi Mary Poppins.
Last night me an her were leanin on the wall watchin the
lights in isolated houses. Talkin. I could smell her
perfume. Every time she moved her head the skin
stretched across her neck. I was about to touch her when I
remembered the Memory Lane burd. An somethin else. A
right rotten feelin. So I put sex out ma mind an listened.

Born again experience she had. Nervous breakdown
mibbi more like it. But she read ma thoughts. They were

197

floatin about the surface of ma eyes.

But maybe a nervous breakdown's just another route to God,
she says, *a pathway to Christ.*

I'm thinkin this might be where sufferin does lead to
somethin greater. Mibbi the mad Catholics're not so daft
after all. Nervous breakdown or immersion in God, ye're
still left wi somethin bigger than ye had before. Ye're left
wi a broader understandin of yerself at least. At the worst
it's a psychological breakdown. At best it's an epiphany,
an enlightenment. Then it comes to me. Leonard Cohen
says a nervous breakdown's necessary to get to God. The
song's called 'Suzanne' an all. Serendipity or what?

Cohen sayed Jesus knew only drownin men could see
him. One thing I do know. All the people I've met who've
got God after bein Atheistic've had some cataclysmic
event before it. Two things:

1 Jesus's a safety net invented by neurotics.
2 It's real. He waits – open-armed an compassionate.
Fuck me – imagine it?

Me an Davy's glued feet to the bottom of the Svelto bottle.
We're makin a shrine in our cellar. A Svelto bottle wi feet
an a wee hanky for a shawl. Can't be much more absurd
than what Feed Yer Face goes on about. Him an his crazy
miracles. I light a candle each side of it. Ye should see the
face on Mary Poppins.

♪ *We will kneel now and pray to the Holy Svelto,* I sing

an kneel down.

♪ *We will kneel now and pray to the Holy Svelto,* sings

Davy. Blessin hissel wi the wrong hand.

Suzanne's got to walk away. She's not sure if it's
sacrilege.

Francie peers in not sure what to make of it. We're back
on our feet before he makes us out in the darkness.

Last bus to Monte Cassino, he shouts.

I got flung out for wearin shorts. An a vest. I'm sittin right in the chapel. Up at the altar. It's all darkness an holiness an candles. But there's this dark current runnin under the floor. I can feel it vibratin in ma feet. I ignore it. Blank it. This security guard comes up an starts tellin me I can't stay there wi shorts. I can't make out the words but I can see by his gestures that's what he means. But I kid on I can't even hear him. He crouches down an does it all over again. I kid on I can't understand him. Eventually he goes away.

But he comes back wi this other even bigger guard. They do the same routine an I play daft. It's only when they try to grab me things change. I take a flaky. I even surprise massel. All I can see through ma rage's these two faces backin off an the light of the candles burnin out like solar systems. They've got their hands up an Francie's right over from nowhere tryin to calm me down. I don't know what he's sayin but his voice's soft an soothin. Next thing I know I'm in the bright light of the car park. I don't know how many tourists saw it. Mibbi Francie knew a secret way out. I don't know. I really don't know. It was a blackout.

I'm alright down the hairpin bends to the valley floor. I'm goin on to Francie about it. Chucked out for wearin shorts. As if Jesus had no thighs. All I can see is His holy body. Bare mostly. Sometimes when I'm runnin up the Mountain I see him hangin from the big cross. Well that's what it looks like as I come up over the last hump in the road. By that time I'm so away wi it I could see anythin. But whatever I see he's bare. That's what I'm tryin to say to Francie. He's noddin in agreement an singin. Hymns.

Francie reminds me of superman.

What about dat superman, he says.

That's when I get thinkin about the Chaos Theory that I

read. Jimmy Brogan gave me it on the Ward. Says it can make sense out of things that're mixed up beyond repair. Wi computers we can crunch numbers a zillion times bigger than what we used to. There's this number:

645473927465638238946876481644242424813864546721 64

then it changes to

487317358316856356830165873333665835310757356752 54

then

587457839165783167963872567898989892365763875683 65

But it gets faster an faster till it's a blur an the rattle of numbers changin. An it's letters an symbols an words next:

?\I { sheer mathematical chance *546* anti –
~3556226466336bdfr35235 will hit upon
a☞✆✚①✗☺☕ *et*☝☞✿⑧✝❶➢♗☞✱ structure
☞✆✚①✗☺☕ *et*➢♗☞✱to destroy
particularA\$O/OADCARAO/o* viruses. jksyncfioubye
he+-sees any 6✿☞✆✚①✗☺☕ *et*☝☞✿⑧✝❶➢
♗☞✱✱✱✱✱✱✱✱✱✱✱✱✱✱✱✱✱✱✱✱✱✱✱✱✱✱✱✱
✱✱✝♱✝7t8o37t984unpyt^{349}n ***cv~med**
()()(& wi that theory an the theory
✿☞✆✚①✗☺☕ *et*☝☞✿⑧✝❶➢♗☞✱✱✱✱✱✱
✱✱✱✱✱✱✱✱✱✱✱✱✱✱✱✱✱✱✱✱✱✱✱✱♱✝ I have that if
two men of the ☞✆✚①✗☺☕ *et*☝☞✿⑧✝❶➢☞✆✚①
✗☺☕ *et*☝☞✿⑧✝❶➢♗☞✱ structure ☞✆✚①✗☺☕
et➢♗☞✱to destroy particular A ♗ ☞ ✱

are   put   on

a

()A&VF% A ^xw

3456

eƔ&

man   has

sp874375✿❀3275✳✲✳✳✳✳✳✳@#*✿✳✳✳☞☾↗☺☙ *eƔ*

☖☗☛ ✿⑧✞❶➤♫☞ ✱ ✽ ❋ ✳✴✳✳✳✳❀✿✳✶ ✴✳✞✝✠

(&A%#⊕①&*(&%ent   three   years   workin

☞☾#⊕①↗☺☙☀*eƔ*☖✳✳✳♫☞✿⑧✞❶➤♫☞✳   structure

☞☾#⊕①↗☺☙☀*eƔ*➤♫☞✳to destroy particularA in a carpet

factory   before   goi5   yh   723480970*A#$A **more**

metaphors to #$AV* from. GU′ 1982CY893278 hypothesis

that A&*(VGFY lie in the

jueispugw   an   the   **vast**

complication

I've got it <small>I shouts.</small>

What?

What to do right . . . ye get Superman to mutate right?

Francis's lips're already goin like a fish. Ma hands're up shovin his words back in case they slice through mine an the idea goes the wrong way.

He nods.

He's alright wi that.

But ye don't need him to be intelligent.

He's noddin his head. He'd be lookin over the top of glasses if he had any on.

Ye just need Superman to mutate randomly but that fast that he'd hit on a way to catch anythin by chance.

He looks interested an puzzled. I surfs in on a new metaphor.

Know how everybody's always goin on about livin forever.

Yes.

Well suppose we did. Suppose we all never died. Not even if we got shot or crushed under a bus.

Yessssssssss!?

Well that means – seein as how time'd be infinite – everybody in the world'd do everythin everybody else done. Ye'd be a king an a prostitute, a priest an a trapeze artist. Ye'd be all them things just by chance cos forever's a long time.

He nearly sees what I'm gettin at. I takes a chance an zooms in from another direction.

There's this poet Hugh MacDiarmid – ye heard of him?
No.
No cunt has – it's alright. But it's only academics that read his stuff. I met him . . . I met him in . . . somewhere I used to live. It's in Scots most of it.

Wha kens on whatna Bethlehems
A star shines the nicht...

Who knows on how many Bethlehems a star shines tonight.
Francie looks. His eyes're wide.
In an infinite universe everythin that's possible to happen happens all the time. It's statistically impossible for it not to happen.
And?
If ye treat AIDS wi antibodies that can mutate infinitely fast we might be onto a winner. Applyin an infinite solution to a finite problem.
He's right into it now. If I was a poof I could mibbi fall in love wi the cunt.
Somethin that changes its properties randomly billions of times faster than the AIDS virus. By sheer chance it'll hit upon a structure to destroy particular AIDS mutations.
MMMMMMM, he goes. An he rests on that for ages.
So I gets thinkin. Imagine two men. Same intelligence. Same education. They get put on a research project. But one guy's spent three years in a carpet factory before Uni. He's more likely to hit a creative solution. He's got more metaphors.

Machine metaphors.

Breakdown metaphors.

Work metaphor.

Strike metaphors.

Livin on the fuckin breadline metaphors.

Wool an synthetic metaphors.

He's got the rhythmic trance of long hours in the dusty air watchin patterns appear out a thousand disparate threads. But he's not got the words to concept them. Words're just the ASDA bags to carry the ideas in. But he needs them. That's why he's off to Uni. His metaphors're ready to burst under their own pressure an fill his skull wi the narcotic juices of understandin. *Eu fuckin reeka* he'll say. To the astonishment of his classmates.

I knew it all along, he'll say – *it was in the spinnin not in the pattern. It was in the thread not the machine.*

An mibbi he'll discover his angle of vision has only been ten degrees. An the other ten degrees where the answer lies is directly behind him. A total other ten degrees. An he'll mibbi see wisdom'll not be built by addin a degree now an then to the sides of the ten-degree angle he brung wi him. No sir. He'll have slices of acute angles all over the place. A mad clock that doesn't know how many hands it wants. Fat hands. Thin hands. Hands wi white lines of ignorance runnin up them like a fine lattice. An these'll pivot at the centre point where they'll generate sparks. This electricity'll synthesise hyacinths an biscuits. Or Buckfast an quantum physics.

Francie likes the ideas. He's sayin nothin but I know he likes them. He's not singin. Not even hymns. His mind's racin. It's gettin faster. As it's gettin faster funny thing happens. The van starts slowin down. Eventually we come to a stop by the side of the road. Francie gets out an chips a few stones into the valley. He starts singin opera.

It was his wife's favourite song.

PHOTOGRABBERY

Saturday. We're back. Francie takes me back. I've got the right gear on. This time I can relax an take the place in. Francie goes off hissel an lets me wander. What a place. I get a right lift. St Benedict's tomb. The centre of modern Christianity. The immensity's balanced by the fact I got chucked out yesterday for wearin shorts.

Monte Cassino, I'm sayin over an over to massel as I'm walkin along. Monte Cassino. Monte Cassino. Monte Cassino.

It's a rhythm I'm keepin. An there's a wee fire burnin inside me. I feel protected. I'm walkin the cloisters in the vanishin steps of St Benedict. I don't mean I can hear his steps nor nothin. I mean the waves he made're comin to an end now. One time ye wouldn't get movin in this joint for monks.

An there's somethin else I'm walkin in too. I'm walkin in shattered fragments of pillars an stone rebuilt from the ashes of war. The whole place was flattened. Rubble. The Allies thought it was a German Garrison.

There's two Americans walkin along. Both an almighty fat. They could be twins but they're probably man an wife.

BOOSH

Their camera goes off in my face. Like a pint of radioactive milk. Spiked with glitter an sunlight's been flung into ma face. An I'm kidnapped. An Monte Cassino. Sucked into the wee black box. The Americans walk away. So I'm abducted. An soon I'll live in some Washington suburb sideboard. Foreign soul. Photograbbed.

An steppin from the hot white of the dusty cloisters the chapel's ornate construction starts to appear as ma eyes adjust. Slowly. Exaustless gold patterns start glintin – resurrectin through the darkness in ma eyes.

The simple story repaints itself on the roof. The high dome points to where God should be. Out there somewhere. Or mibbi the high dome covers an protects where God should be. In here somewhere. Not the buildin but me. Us. Who knows? But this place's tellin its story in pictures. The Word in images. The painted Word on the ceilin drenches its colours through the enormous ornament of church an drifts on the melancholy voices of monks chantin out the Sorrow of the Glory. It sounds like they're Glorifyin God but it's sad.

An simple melodies laid over an imperceptible moan of organ conjures more God than the bashful of Angels an trumpet-blowin alabaster boys carved on top of every pillar. Or overcrowded into every corner. This chapel's a letter to God. That's what it is. A love-letter in shapes an pictures. An sound. The Words're curly metals an gold leaf plaster. The sentences're expanses of intricate marble.

But it's not a simple letter. A – *We're here how are you?*

letter. There's a confusion I can't fathom in the hush of
foreign whispers. Can't make it out through the rush of
shapes an colours. A bishop comes up to the pulpit. He
spouts the Word through an Italian microphone. The Word
crackles like little lightnin bolts off the walls. The current
of fear's still wi me. It could be terror if I looked deep
enough. I focus to take it away. A lone monk starts singin.
There's one light that shines in the sanctuary an his simple
melody laces clouds on ma feet. I close ma eyes.

The song carries me at the head of the procession of ma
life – I turn an look back. How many candles've I lit from
the one solitary light? How many've I snuffed? There's a
tear again. I look down at the altar. I look at the candles. I
smell some flutterin out. An even though it's one of the
most beautiful things in ma life – it's disturbin. The monk
sings the same transfixin melody. But I can't stay. I've got
to go. I feel blessed an cursed at the same time. Cursed an
blessed. So through the smoky breath of incense I turn an
walk out into the light outside that's so white it blinds. So
white it blinds.

It was after that day I came across Francie an he's readin
this book. I'd've thought nothin of it but he turns an hides
it like it's a scuddy book. Can't imagine Francie pullin his
wire? Specially wi his room door wide to the wall. I make
out I don't notice. But I double back when he goes to the
bog an there it is on top of his bed. Some textbook for
mega microbiology heads.

GARDEN OF EDEN

We've all got a bit of a tan. I'm feelin fresh an fitter wi
runnin up the Mountain. Mary Poppins's doted on Doom.
They're always sneakin off at night. Into the hills. He's in
love wi her Mary Poppins voice I think. The two of them's
lookin good.

It's Palm Sunday. Locals're bringin parcels of food to the
door. This's the most heavily laden Franciscan house in
the world. It's like ASDA's in here. Instead of little as
possible we're eatin like kings.

All week there's been fires on the Mountain. I don't
know if they're deliberate. Holy Week. Death an
Resurrection. Could be funeral pyres sayin goodbye to
winter. Or beacons heraldin spring.

Every mountain's got its own little infernos burnin in
pagan delight. An spirallin smoke into the warmin air.
Instead of callin an area a village or a town they speak of
mountains. Oh he's from this mountain, or she's from that
mountain. Families're identified by their mountain.

Lookin down from ma Mountain the Gargliano valley's
Lilliput. A flat valley. The river cuttin silver along it. It's a
mad two-piece jigsaw. Each side small houses're dotted
everywhere. Any one of them could be ma home. Wi the
right wummin. I think massel in there – eatin by the
window. Mibbi the light from the river ripplin across her
face. But fuck it! I can't fit in. The wrong-shaped bit of a

jigsaw. But I don't feel wrong-shaped cos there's a bit stickin out that won't fit. It's a big bit missin – a big empty space that nothin outside me can fill.

It's dusk now. Lights're startin to come on an ye can see the Mediterranean shimmerin between the vee of two mountains. I can see Monte Cassino too, in the opposite direction. It's watchin out over the place.

The night's quiet. Davy's away wi Suzanne up the Mountain. He's not been sayin much. First wummin since the Memory Lane burd. Things seem to be comin to an end. Or changin. Mibbi that's it. Mibbi it's time for change.

The wine out the cellar's nearly finished. Pat's been wanderin about wi a permanent glow. Francie's not singin as much hymns. He's singin opera. Some voice he's got an all. Some voice. It floats out the kitchen windies, over the patio, through Cucuruzzu. One fine day it is. Sometimes when ye accept all the stuff that's goin on in yer life – an all the things that's happened – ye feel calm. Serene. It's one of them times. Absolute acceptance. The sun's about to set behind the mountains. There's nowhere else I'd rather be. Nowhere.

One oul wummin I see every night's off to gather wood. I've seen her gatherin sticks. When she picks them up they crackle wi the same noise they'll make when they burn. She's gone into the trees but her voice's singin across the sunset fields. An even though she seems to be answerin Francie she's not singin to nobody. She's not singin even to herself. She's just singin. Expectin no answer. There was this Chinese poet Jimmy Brogan says. He became really famous. An rich. Rich as fuck. But he got to the stage where he never needed the claps an applause an approval of anybody for his poems. He used to write them on round bits of rice paper an twist them into flowers an float them down the river. He used to float them down the river.

It's a while before she returns under the glow of the

Piazza lights. Sensin me there she looks up. I smile an she struggles on unsure wi her sticks. Davy an Suzanne's still on the Mountain.

It's when he comes down he tells me this weird story.

Him an Poppins climb the Mountain. Up an up they go. I know exactly where he is cos he describes all the bits I know. An they're pantin. Breathin heavy. An Davy makes a couple of jokes about that. I don't know if I'm goin or comin an all this stuff. Poppins giggles. She thinks stuff like that's hilarious.

Ye can calm down the now – I'm not even touchin ye yet, Doom's goin. An he grabs her just above the hips – that bit that sends them into squirmin laughter. An cos of the slope he's able to bite her soft on the arse. I think I heard her laughin from the Piazza.

So they get up to the big cross an sit on the grassy knoll. There's nothin to it. Just a man an a wummin up a hill. Lovers. Well not yet lovers. As the sun goes down they can see sheets of shadow move up the Mountain. Takin every crag an contour like silk. There comes a point when all around is dark an it's only them bathed in light at the top of the Mountain. The pinnacle of existence. Doom bumps the gums on her. An this is the first time in years he's had a hard on. Bing! Up it goes. An it's her turn now.

Is that a gun you have in your pocket David or are you just pleased to see me. Giggle giggle. She thinks it's a new joke.

Oh my I didn't know we had planned to pitch a tent tonight, she says before she gives it a wee feel. Davy's not felt like this since stickin the head on Jean. They set about each other on the grassy slope.

After it there's the two of them laughin up the Mountain. The shadow's long since slid over their heads. God's pulled the blanket up an tucked them in. An it's stars now. An somethin of a moon. Nearly half. Owls hootin an all the other stuff of the night. Davy dips in his pocket an pulls out an apple.

Hey little girl – you want an apple? he says in his best Brooklyn accent. The two of them munch in about it an that's when it happens.

The white of the Mountain's shinin here an there in the moonlight. There's a rustle. They shoosht. This black snake slithers across the path right at them. When it gets close it coils its head up. Its eyes glitter. It senses there's somethin unusual. It jerks back down an slithers away into the bushes. Poppins's holdin Davy tight. Tight as fuck.

Do you think that is a sign David? she says.

Naw – fuck off, goes Davy.

An omen? says Poppins.

See the Bible, he says, *it's caused more trouble than drink. Now c'mere!*

They pick their way down the mountain by the light of upturned stones. Stars shinin in their dampness. Doom notices she holds him tighter than ever. But he can't tell if it's the dark or the sex or the snake that's makin her do it. He can't tell at all.

SAY HELLO TO THE PROVOS

Not long after Duffy's weddin Jimmy Brogan was in the Pop. Sunday Afternoon. Two Quid in. Rebel. Pat O'Rourke an the Diddleys. The money was for the Cause so cunts were climbin over each other to stick tenners in the tin.

Jimmy Brogan was a regular. *Alright Jimmy. Alright ma man. Alright -Toichfaidh ar la's,* all ye could hear every time he walked in. Slaps on the back.

The place's mobbed. Can't get movin. Jimmy Brogan's got a good table beside the band. The Diddleys try their fiddles an drums for tune. OK. O'Rourke goes to the microphone. *One two three,* he goes an every right boot an lady's high-gloss shoe in the place's suspended eight inches off the ground. Every right arm's bent an fist held at shoulder level. For three seconds it's like a Madame Tussaud's. All sorts of horrors an grotesqueries froze as wax.

Then:

🎼 *SAY HELLO TO THE PROVOS . . .*

The feet an the fists come crashin down.

An the place's ROCKIN about. The floor's bendin up an down in the middle like a giant drum skin. Then half of them start clappin. So it's fists in the air – stampin feet an the ring of clappin hands. Fiddles. Pipes. Guitars. Flutes.

🎼 *SAY HELLO TO THE BRAVE,* they sing after another

pause. Then it's the same again. 𝄞 *SAY HELLO TO THE*

PROVOS . . .

If ye could see it from the outside it'd be goin in an out like a house-shaped lung. Every now an then it'd stop. Startled crows'd be about to land on the oul slate roof again an 𝄞 *SAY HELLO TO THE PROVOS*'d spurt into

another verse.

Fuck this! says the crows. *We're off to the chapel roof. Worst thing there's 'Bind Us Together Lord'.*

So while the crows fly under the mad emulsion of Sunday clouds Republicanism creeps through the crowd wi the drink. The drink behind the bar's startin to glow like an altar.

That was the day Jimmy Brogan met Liam. An his wife was wi him. Rachel. A right babe. An she's givin Jimmy Brogan the eye all the time.

At the half-hour break O'Rourke an his Diddleys're at the bar gettin claps on the back. Liam's talkin to Jimmy Brogan. He's to come to McDavitt's next he's in Belfast. He looks like the sort of guy Liam an his mates're lookin for. He's heard a lot about Jimmy Brogan. A lot of good stuff. He gives him a big hug. Everycunt clocks it. Jimmy Brogan – toast of the day.

O'Rourke an his Diddleys start the second half by introducin Liam as a special guest.

An here's a special guest from the Falls . . .

They burst into 𝄞 *SAY HELLO TO THE PROVOS* . . .

again. An there's Liam smilin away on the stage. The spotlight's on his big grin an the waft of his cheap aftershave's still on Jimmy Brogan's jumper. Instead of the usual 𝄞 *SAY HELLO TO THE PROVOS* . . . stamp it's a

long polite applause. Liam's searchbeamin the crowd wi his dazzlin grin. Colgate advert he's like. An advert for terror. The mirror ball's runnin dilapidated disco lights in exploded fragments over his face.

The end of the night everybody's pished. Liam's sparkled on the floor. The music's playing. Rachel comes up.

C'mon Jimmy, she goes an trails him out by the hand. An nocunt would ever've found out about it except for one of Liam's mates. He looked up out his stuper for a second. Long enough to see Rachel and Jimmy Brogan disappear. He never remembered it in the mornin. But these images've got a habit of poppin up at the wrong time. Weeks – months later even.

An while he's back sleepin Jimmy Brogan's ridin away goodstyle wi Rachel in the back of an oul burnt-out van.

THE BELL

Eh have a you seen a my bell? goes Fabian at the breakfast table.

Francie keeps noddin over. Smilin. For a minute I think he fancies me. But that's not it. Soon as the Monk's not lookin he leans over an whispers how much he enjoyed the conversation about AIDS. Like to do it again sometime. Very interestin.

Eh have a you seen a my bell? goes Feed Yer Face again.

Everybody's lookin at each other. But me an Davy an Pat's lookin at each other worse than the rest.

My a bell a have a you a seen eet? he says.

Ye should see Pat an Doom's face when I go, *Aye.*

The Monk smiles. Glad at last he's found his bell.

Where ees it? he goes showin me his palms.

In the step Father.

Een een the a stepa?

By this time everybody's lookin. I point down at an angle through the floor.

It's in the step Father. The bell's in the third step down into the cellar.

Een?

Aye, I pat the table, *inside the step.*

He's puzzled. Francie can't believe it.

What you mean een?

I get up out ma chair an take them all down to the cellar.

Davy an Pat's at the back gigglin like school-lassies. I lights up the holy Svelto an bows to it.

🎵 *We kneel an pray to the Holy Svelto,* Davy chants from the back.

The Monk shakes his head an touches one eyebrow. I gets on ma knees on the fourth step down. I slaps the surface of the third step. Hard.

In there Father!

You mean een?

I nods. He shapes a step in thin air an thrusts his hand into it. There's waitin.

Een? he goes, wigglin his fingers, *Een?*

His reaction bubbles up.

An bubbles up. Everybody else's not breathin.

Een the step a?

He smiles.

He grins an walks down pattin his right sandal on the concrete.

He laughs.

An they all laugh.

An I laugh.

🎵 *Our prayers are answered by the Holy Svelto,* Davy chants.

Amen, says I, *Amen.*

An the Monk bellows an says – *You a Scotteesh sens of a humour – I no understand – Francis – go and a get a cakes.*

The Monk shuffles away mutterin all this stuff in Italian an laughin these mini-laughs. Hee hee hee. Ball an Chain lifts his metal ball in case we've got a notion to covet it.

CHANGIN WATER
INTO LAUGHTER

Davy an Suzanne's holdin hands out in the open now. The men on the Piazza smile at them. They smile back. God turns up the sun.

I'm in a pretty zany mood massel theday. Feed Yer Face's off to somewhere holy. I'm plunderin about the rooms see what I can find. Pat's out in the garden wi some wine. He's like a millionaire. Sat at a table under a parasol. Straw hat. Italian bread. Crystal glass. In the cupboard in Francie's room there's this megaphone. The Monk probably uses it for givin out orders to the villagers.

📢 *Evinini a. O a kay a. Time for a your a prayer a sleepy bye byes.*

I press the button an there's this feedback. It's workin great. There's French doors an a wee balcony. I keek outside to see who's down there. It's the usual oul guys on the Piazza. Pat's talkin to Doom. The sun's shinin on Pat's wine glass an he's sippin away. Sip sip sippin away. Davy's leant back in a deck chair. They stop talkin an both of them's lookin right along the valley to the vee where the Mediterranean shines. They're sharin the peace. The only noise is the murmur of the oul men on the benches. That's why it's a bit of a shock when I burst onto the wee balcony like the Pope an start blessin the place.

🔊 *Cucuruzzu – I bless you in de name of de father and of de son and of de holee speereet!*

I'm blessin away goodstyle. The oul men're astonished. Doom looks up so he's just a big mouth an two swivelled eyes. Pat shakes his head an pours another wine. I do it all another time.

🔊 *Cucuruzzu – I bless you in de name of de father and of de son and of de holee speereet.* But there's hardly any reaction.

Doom shouts up. *Are you off yer fuckin head? These people take all that dead serious.*

I shout through the megaphone, 🔊 *Where's Suzanne?*

He shakes his head. *Put the thing away.*

🔊 *Tell me where Suzanne is first.*

He tries to ignore me. But that's a bit hard wi all the village starin up.

🔊 ♪ *Suzanne takes you down to her place by the river . . .*

I starts singin.

In the chapel, he shouts, *in the fuckin chapel.*

I'm just about to shout **B**RUTTO ASINO when Pat grabs the thing an rips the batteries out.

Are you fuckin crazy? he says. Then he looks at me. He looks at me like he's said somethin wrong.

Doom's lookin up. *Can I go back to sleep now he says?* He snuggles his head into his shoulder an closes his eyes.

He's fifteen feet below me an ten feet to ma right.

Pat's away. I'm getting quite manic now. I go in the scullery an fill a bucket of water. It's heavy. I humph it over to the balcony. But I've got to empty some out. It's too heavy for what I want to do. I check an Doom's still sleepin. There's a sink in Francie's room. A wee wash handbasin. I pour half of the water down it. That's when I notice another packet of megaphone batteries. I snaffle them an stick them in the big cone. Off I pops down the stair.

In the dark lobby beside the chapel I can see nothin. Ma eyes're adjustin but there's low prayer comin out the cracks in the chapel door. I get on the belly an commando over to the door. Squeak. I shove the big electric snout in there.

Thees ees a God a speakin. A you a better pray a lota better than a that a or I am a comin down there to a sort you out.

I'm pishin massel. I'm on ma back. I'm waitin on Suzanne comin out all flustered. But it's a big fat Italian wummin. Then Giovanna – the old not the babe. Then another two. They're blessin theirselfs as they step over me. Kissin their crosses like I'm the devil. I peek in when they're gone an there's no Suzanne. Fuck! I bolt up the stairs an I'm about to plank the megaphone back where I got it. Then I see the half bucket of water.

I'm out on the balcony again. Doom's snoozin. I get the bucket up on the railin. I throw it. *Doom*, I shouts.

This is exactly what happened. I throws the water. It's halfway through the air.

I shouts. He turns. The water splooshes into his face. He's not even got that micro-second where ye can flinch an avoid the brunt of somethin.

He comes tearin up the stairs. He runs into the room but I'm facin him wi the megaphone.

📢 *Davy Doom Davy Doom,* I'm singin – the exact same way we sing the Daddy Doom song. The water's drippin off him. He crashes me onto the balcony an he's layin in about me wi the megaphone. It's hissin an howlin. Sometimes his shoutin's comin out it an sometimes ma screams. The men on the Piazza don't know what to make of it.

It ends up wi Davy stormin off.

When Feed Yer Face comes back we're at the dinner. He sits the bashed megaphone in the middle of the table. He sits down and folds his arms starin at each one of us in turn. Then he stands up again an holds the thing in the air. It's a sorry sight of a megaphone now. A right sad sorry sight.

Noatouch eh? He goes. *Noatouch!*

An at that he stamps off. I don't know what's up wi me.
I'm getting crazier by the minute. But I'll make some
ground up themorra. I'll go wi Francie an the Monk to
Santa Maria Goretti's glass coffin. That'll turn the heat
down.

DRIVIN PARADISE

On the way out of Cucuruzzu this parishioner flags the van down an gives Fabian a Viennetta ice cream. Raspberry. She hands him it like it's the millionth Viennetta she's gave him. He accepts it like he's never even seen one before. So we drive off wi the Monk cuttin it into sections. Me Francie Suzanne Hilda Ball an Chain an Hissel. Six bits.

Francie can't eat his cos he's drivin. So Fabian sits it on the seat. Even in the front it's a padded plank right across. Fabian does his usual – goin on an on about how he's not supposed to eat this kind of luxurious food. How his vocation demands livin simply off the land like St Francis if he can. But he's droolin. He's starin at this bit of Viennetta like it's a curly eighteen-year-oul Italian burd an he's infatuated.

Eeef eet was a slice of a bread a. Or a piece of a fruit a . . .

I'll eat it for ye Father, I goes, reachin over the padded plank. He snaps it to his chest.

No no, he gives it the big cheezy grin, *I'll be a leetle martyr*, he says an scoffs the lot in three bites.

GULP

GULP

GULP

Des Dillon

Fabian says the trip's a lesson in humility. An a beeg reminder of what sacrifice is. He's right about sacrifice. Ma arse's killin me. Wild. Miles away. Santa Maria Goretti's tomb for fucksakes. We'd be as well visitin the pyramids the time it took us. Five hours there an five hours back.

An that's wi Francie drivin like a maniac. He's throwin us about the compartment – the fuckin box wi planks as seats. He's takin corners like a man wi involuntary spasms. He jerks the wheel right. Bang we're all crushin into the left of the van. Ball an Chain's ball's makin dents in the panels. Then he jerks left an we're across the other side. Star Trek.

Only good thing's it's crushin me into Mary Poppins. She smells nice. But even that's soon cancelled out wi Ball an Chain.

He   is   fuckin   boggin. Boggin.

After half an hour I've slid all the windies open so as the smell'll at least get span round. There's a brown pong trailin behind us all through the windin roads. Like a comet of sewage. An there's mad Francie grinnin an singin

𝄞 *Sweet Heart Of Jee-sus Fount of Love and Mer-sea . . .*

An the Monk's batterin out the Hail Marys. But these're not yer normal Hail Marys. They're deformed. Usually the Priest says the first bit an the rest say the last bit. An the thing is, to get them done quick we should join in an drown out his last line an he should drown out our last line wi his next first line. They've not got a clue.

228

It should go

> PRIEST: Hail Mary fulla grace
> the lord is withee
> blessedarthou among
> wimmin anblessed is
> the fruit
>
>> US: Holy Mary
>> motherofgod prayfrus
>> sinners
>
> PRIEST: of thy womb Jesus
>
>> now an at thehour
>
> PRIEST: Hail Mary fulla
> grace
>
>> US: of ourdeathamen
>
> the lord is withee
> blessed artthou
> among wimmin . . .

But Fabian's havin none of that. An I think I know
why. He's got these big mother fuckers of rosary beads.
Size of golf balls but they're made out pebbles. An
they're smooth. An they're shiny. But it's not varnish. It's
cos he's rubbed them to fuck wi all the prayers. I can see
Francie's big grin reflected in the one Fabian's rubbin.
They're heavy the beads. If ye were the American
halfway up the mountain an ye wanted to make some
cunt sleep wi the fishes ye can forget about concrete
wellies. Just wrap a pair of these fuckers round them an
chuck them in. They're that heavy they're makin him say
the prayers dead slow. Like the way ye get taught them
at primary.

*Yessss Miiiiiiiiiissssssss Bosssssssssswellllllllllllllll
Slowwwwwwwwwwwww Miiiiiiiissssssss
Bosssssssssswelllllllli
Haiiiiiiiiiiiiiiiiiiiiiiiiiiiiiiiiiiiiiiiiiiiiiiiiiiiiiiiiiiiiiiiiiiiiiiiiiil*

Maaaaaaaaaaaaaaaaaaaaaaaaaaaaaaaaaaaaaaaaaaaaaaary
full   of
       grace   the   Lorrrrrrrrrrrrrrrrrrrrrrd
                             issssssssssss

with thththththttheeeeeeeeeeeee

That's the way he's goin. An these daft cunts've joined
in. An Ball an Chain's eyein the beads wi envy. An he's
lookin at his iron ball. Ye can tell he thinkin about outdoin
Fabian wi a pair of rosary beads made out iron balls. An
mibbi he'll lump about Italy wearin them slung over his
shoulder. There's a penance. So I'm the only one not doin
anythin. They don't even lose the rhythm as Francie
throws the microbus into corner after corner. Even wi
death whisperin in the tyres I don't want to pray. I'm
bored stiff an ma arse's buzzin wi pins n needles. The only
thing missin's a nun wi a guitar singin happy songs about
how it doesn't matter cos we're all in the hands of Jesus
anyhow. But right now I'm in the hands of the maddest
cunts I ever met. Not countin the Ward.

Fabian's probably sayin the prayers on automatic pilot
an lettin his head wander over the big secret dinners an
cream cakes he gets off parishioners. An then he martyrs
hissel to starvation when he comes back to the house.
Refusin dinner so we feel bad for eatin. But Francie's
not on automatic pilot. I wish he was. I wish he fuckin
was.

At five to three we cross the Gargliano river headin
north. The mountains're big shoulders over hilltop towns
an hamlets hangin on to terraced green an red an brown
fields. An that's a man sowin seeds. He's minuscule but
it's the wave of his arm. Even at distances some things're
unmistakable. He's castin them into the ruts an furrows
where the seeds that fall will grow or die.

There's beggars along the sides of the roads. We stop
in this wee village. Franciscans don't even need to beg.
They're charity magnets. People come up an give them

stuff. Sometimes they need to sneak through places like
the SAS to avoid free cookies buns an rock cakes.

The Hail Marys've stopped. Everybody's in a dwam
brought on by the
hummmmmmmmmmmmmmmmmmmmmmmmmmmmmmmmmm
of the wee wheels on the road. Italy rolls back like a film.
It's movin past outside. In front. To the other side an to the
back. I'm surrounded by it. But it doesn't really feel like
Italy. It's like watchin a film or readin a book. I need to
shove massel into it. I need to rip away the gauze between
me an the pastel country we're trundlin over. Francie's
grinnin his Cheshire at the passin trees. Fabian's smilin wi
his hands up his sleeves an his arms restin on his belly.
Hilda's bitin her bottom lip. She looks like she's watchin a
horror film. An she is. She's watchin a horror film. She's
watchin the horror film that's inside her head. An it's
called:

hilda

It's her life. An if we seen it we'd go – that wasn't a
horror, that was fuckin bo-rin. But it's the feelins she's
glued to her film that makes it a horror. It's a horror for
one. Ordinary things horrify her. Did she do the right
thing all them years ago when the Priest arrived for tea in
Newcastle? Did her family think she was stupid? Does she
apologise too much? An right there. Right where the
corner of her tooth touches her lip. There's more goin on
there than at the centre of the atom. More forces pullin an
pushin. More pulsars an quasars an black holes than the
universe. An she looks an she looks an she looks. An Italy
speeds by. No cure here. She probably thought this trip on

her own'd cure her. The last gasp – she leaves her familiar kitchen. Leavin all his things that're still hangin in the Wardrobe. Leavin the routine wi the black hole of a missin man to walk round. But it's not goin to work. She's transferred all her insecurities to the Monk an the routine here. Sure when she goes back her sons an daughters'll've cleared the last remnants of big Hughie out. The bowlin balls. The outsize suits. The hats that used to deflect his loud voice. The voice that bent her over an sent her scurryin into the kitchen to worry about the state of the scones. The Diary of a busy man. A man that runs the workin man's club. But he's been dead seven years. Seven years wi a dead person's a bit much. Aye. Dead right. It is a horror. Only we can't see the ghosts.

An there's Mary Poppins. The inside of her cheeks're pressin against the outside of her teeth. Her palms're thegether an shoveled between her legs. Her cravat's hangin down an catchin the wind now an then. Her hair's blacker than it should be but her body's younger. A lot younger come to think of it. A lot younger. Christ wi this lot I could be back on the Ward wi Jimmy Brogan.

BRSHSHSHSHSHSHSHSHSHS BUMP BUMP TOOT TOOT GRIN DON'T GO AWAY SANTA MARIA GORETTI WEEZ A COMIN AT YA HIGH BUZZ LOW SPEED PRAYIN PRAYIN PRAYIN FLINGIN THE HAIL MARYS OUT THE WINDIES LIKE CONFETTI

Time goes by. Nobody's sayin nothin. Bein stuck thegether's separated us. We're trailin our worlds up the valley leavin a multi-coloured smear on the landscape now.

Francie's still got a bit of Viennetta on the seat next to him. Meltin. Fabian grabs it an starts eatin it. We all do another Star Trek. Francie's fizzin. He goes to grab it back off Fabian but remembers just in time that he's supposed to be the picture of serenity. So he grins at trees. Fabian sees he's angry. He's a bit taken aback.

Francis. Francis. It a saves you from a breakin a your vow of a poverty.

MUNCH SLABBER

But Francie's not wearin that one. He's got faster. The hard seats're bumpin on ma arse bone an Mary Poppins's findin it hard to keep the brush pole up her arse in position. It's only Francie's teeth that're grinnin. His eyes're flickin about in the rear-view mirror like a mass murderer. Fabian has another go at placatin him.

I'll a be a little a martyr Francis. I'll a break a ma a vow of a poverty for a you a.

The van takes a wee wander up onto the verge. An it's no ordinary verge. It's rough volcanic ash. White porous stones. An we're all over the road. There's stones zingin pingin an shoomin all over the place. An thirty feet below in a tin roofed village this wummin jerks like a fish an falls over. Stunned by a stone. We leave the verge for the relative safety of the tarmac.

Sorry Fader, says Francie an bursts into song.

233

𝄞Fai-aith of our Fathe-ers holy

faith . . .

Jesus H Christ. These two guys're mad. An that's the point when I start to like Fabian. That's the point I start to really like him. He's great. Mad as fuck. They say all poets're mad. Well so's all monks. He's a master at lyin to hissel an an apprentice at lyin to every other cunt.

It's ages of Hail Marys, Our Fathers an Glory Bes. I'm brainwashed by the lot. Next thing this fanny hits me right in the face. It's a beach. Pure babes wall to wall. An the sun's lightin them up like catalogue models.

The monk breaks into a sweat an prays faster an faster. Francie revs an revs but he can't get away from it. Smell of petrol an fumes. There's too much cruisin traffic an peachy arses stridin up the boulevard. Ball an Chain moans an drops his head. I think he came in his cassock. But it's infatuation stations for me. I don't care if the Monk's prayers're directed right at me. Hilda's starin into the rainbows in her cheap imitation crystal beads. I'm clearin the steam on the windie. I feels ma elbow touchin Poppins's tit. It's good. I don't move it. An neither does she. Neither does she. There's too much points of lust on this beach. Ohhh ma sex's on fast forward. Fast fast forward. Ma hard on's shovin ma joggers out like a tent. But I don't give a fuck. I'm takin wi it all. I don't know what to do wi ma hands but ma fingers're twitchin to touch the blur of colour. The smear of sex. Poppins's eyes're poppin in horror at the oul tent pole. Ma eyes don't know where to settle. This arse. That belly. Them tits. That beautiful face. Mona Lisa. Mona fuckin Lisa. It's a Babel of babble. Ma ears're assailed wi sweet voices. Screams an squeals an the odd fleshy slap reverberatin up the beach. An the water lappin on the shore. **Sniff sniff. Sniff sniff.** The water lappin on the shore. It's a carnival of smells. Ma nose's stuffed wi hormones. Sex sex sex. Oh God forgive the bumps an dips that drive ma blood.

The rubbin bodies bulge an groove against the social membrane that stops this beach, an me, an every cunt in this van probably, from shaggin theirselfs into dusty exhaustion. I'm desperate for the tide to rush in an them to rise an dress into the anonymity of clothes. I try to take ma mind off it. I try for a gap through the bodies but always some perfectly shaped fanny bulge comes straddlin into view an I'm transfixed. Transfigured. I set ma focus on the horizon. There's satisfaction out there in the cooler waters. The sky of heaven's meetin the waters of the earth. An they never mingle. They keep pressin each other away. A pressure rests on a line that must never be broken.

There's a softness seepin into ma hard on. Poppins's prayin wi the rest of them. Ball an Chain's red-faced an guilty stoppin his ball rollin about the van by wrappin his bare foot over it.

It's no use. The Mediterranean pulse beats. The sun's scorin into the roof of the van. The sweat's runnin from ma face. Ma armpits. I close ma eyes but it's like the way ma mind went in the Ward. Ma mind's dartin through breast after breast. I get a few smiles. Curious looks really seein as how there's a mad monk spoutin prayers out the side of his mouth. The prayers're flyin out the windie an wrappin like clingfilm smack in faces walkin along. An they walk along alright. An infinite Miss World. Luminous green an yella an red right on – almost off really – costumes shaped like arrows pointin the way to paradise. An I'm followin the arrows. Followin. An every time ma head's lost in little nooks of curvin thighs.

The walkways glitter wi black African skins sellin fake watches. But they're all glisters an no gold. Next thing a schoolgirl. Sixteen if she's a day. She sees me lookin an Presents Breasts. Nipples Up! I feels like shoutin. She doesn't look sixteen now. They're too fifteen flat wi nothin to hold them up. Pancakes fallin off ladders of ribs. She sees I'm too guilty to look. Nipples down an she walks off to tempt somewhere else.

The traffic clears an we're off in a cloud of dust. Gettin closer to the relic.

I persuade Feed Yer Face to stop at this secluded bit of beach far up the coast. Well away from the sex. Poppins an Hilda're in paddlin but I'm down to ma boxers an right in the water. Mad thing is there's two swans swimmin. I never knew they could live in salt water. I need to cool down. I need to wash the sex away.

It's great. It's easy to float in salt water. I'm that buoyant I could laugh. I'm a shape in the sea. The Mediterranean's a fine clingfilm cold on ma skin. I lick ma lips. They're salt. I can only hear the silence water makes pressin in yer ears. The sky? That's a tub of gel stuck on ma face. Takin every contour. Ordnance survey. Each hair strand is submerged. Fibre optics searchin the water for anythin that might creep up. I float. I undulate wi the waves. I'm dead. An I like it. Death is blue. It's the noiselessness of water. The depths of the sky. An far down the coast the beach is a squirmin world of sounds an colour beckonin me. Callin me like a lighthouse. An ma lust's a moth. But I can't fly there till I rise from this little death.

When I get out I sit an meditate on this rock. An who comes into ma vision but Jimmy Brogan. I open ma eyes to get rid of him cos I don't like the feelins he's brung. The swans dip an weave on ripples of sunlight punctuated by troughs of dark. Jimmy Brogan's face appears again broken on the surface. I look to the side of it into the water. Below the swans' webbed feet trundle. Below that crazed fish eyes glare an dart one beat away from piercin bird beaks. An lie-in-wait-predators-Pike. The teethy guys hover over slugs an leeches hidden by the mire of settled dust. Everythin seems still. Nothin movin down here really. But Jimmy Brogan looms out of the murk. Things flurry an burst out the dust headin for the surface – away from him. He pushes up glad to be floatin. He surfaces like the wrong barrel. A million swans move over the surface reflectin in every wave. .

I concentrate on the whiteness an when I look again he's gone.

SANTA MARIA GORETTI

We arrive. It's a busy town. All that's goin through ma head by this time's Snow White an the glass coffin. Maria Goretti's supposed to've not decayed. I'm expectin white skin an long black hair.

There's a massive chapel but ye go down the stairs to an even bigger space. Concrete. It looks like it's been excavated an concreted. A very modern tomb. The size of a football pitch. It's mobbed. I'm amazed. Not just cos it's mobbed but because most of the mobees are Japanese. Cameras're clickin everywhere. An every click's a micro-tut. Tuttin against its own audacity an irreverence. Treatin this hushed tomb like Blackpool tower.

There's a queue. An I mean a queue. Three lines. Up at the altar the coffin's laid out on the edge of the marble. The distorted images of the crowd's reflected on its surface so it looks alive. Like a fire's burnin inside it. A fire of blacks an browns an milky white flashes. The queue's in three lines. The three at the front kneel down in unison. They bless theirselfs even though they're probably not Christian. About thirty seconds an they're up an away an the next three kneel down. It's a slow movin line. But when ye're in it ye're part of it. Nothin could stop any of us pushin an pushin. Shufflin to the altar an kneelin an sayin a prayer. Bein humble. But it's givin me a black feelin. I don't want to kneel. A black forebodin thrums

through me every time I imagine massel there. A dark
repulsion. I'm shakin. Not so as ye can see but I'm shakin.
There's a panic attack inside me. Waitin. It's mibbi been
sittin in its comfy chair smokin a pipe an readin a paper.
The *Terrorgraph* probably. Now it sees it might have work
to do an it's starin over the half-lenses of its glasses
through the windie in its room an out at ma eyes. He can't
see what's makin me tick faster. All he can see's the crowd
but he knows there's work to be done. He scans the inside
of ma skull in case I'm projectin it up there but I'm onto
him. I think of good things. I think of good things. I think
of good things.

I've got one. The queue's movin down. The end's fallin
off onto the altar like the edge of a glacier. I lock onto
somethin in ma past. It's pickin brambles. The sunshine's
wiltin on our late-September shoulders. The queue's
movin on an breakin off. I remember burns an rivers
rubbin dark water on the brownin backs of me an Jimmy
Brogan. I try to hold onto it. I try to hold onto it. The cold
water on ma back. The warm sun everywhere above the
water line. An the smooth pebbles under the skin of ma
feet. Hard silk. It was beautiful. I never thought at the time
it was beautiful. But it was. It certainly was. The most
beautiful thing ever. An clean. It was clean. I'll never be
that clean again. I'm tryin to hold onto it. The queue's
movin forward an the end's snappin off, pausin at the
coffin an shearin like bits of broken metal to the left an
right. It's me an Jimmy Brogan but. We're in the water.
What're we doin? We're laughin. That's it we're laughin
like fuck. But then this other wedge comes drivin down.
It's the Ward. An Jimmy Brogan's shakin his head side to
side. An tuttin. He's tuttin loud an wet. An he's sayin ma
name over an over like I'm a wane an he's caught me
stealin the biscuits. Then he starts tellin the same story
about him an me in the water. He's sayin it's his memory.
I've stole it. He wants it back. Fuck you Jimmy Brogan.

Fuck you. Get out ma imagination. Get yerself to fuck out ma head. Cunt.

Panic Attack's up out his chair an peerin out ma eyes now. That alarm's been raised. I'm tryin to hold onto the memory but all I can see's the ripples as Jimmy Brogan's makin for the banks an the white foam's trailin behind him like blankets. He climbs out. He slaps across the grass. He's laughin. I don't know if I'm in the water or out it. But I look up the sky an the rain falls. It falls loud on the water like a curtain call – people clappin. Clappin Jimmy Brogan for such a great show. The sun ships between clouds an this amazin rainbow roars across the sky an Jimmy Brogan's movin away. Movin away.

An the queue's nearly down to us. I go back to Jimmy Brogan splashin in movin memory. But it doesn't work. I go back to me pickin brambles. Pickin brambles. I'm keepin the panic at bay. I focus on each individual bramble. Pressin wi a pressure that almost bursts but doesn't. But I press too hard between ma finger an thumb an the juices run down ma fingers like purple blood. The colour of Lent. I don't want to kneel down. I don't want to kneel down. Kneelin down's not what I want to do.

It's me an Fabian an Francie. We kneel at the glass an make the sign of the cross. There's a complete darkness tryin to push its way into me up through the floor. But ma knees're on the holy altar. Insulated against evil. It's only ma toes that's on the concrete.

I can feel the reinforcin bar inside the floor tightenin. It's hummin like a buzzbar – electric. But nobody can hear it. The floor's about to crack. Like an eggshell. Somethin's goin to burst through. It's tryin to thrust itself into me. But I'm fightin it. The panic's under all ma skin an I'm about to give into vibrations an floods of tears. There's somethin on the surface of glass. I flick round an Francie can't see it. The other way an Fabian he can't see it either.

This place appears inside ma head. An Jimmy Brogan's

there. I can't see who he's wi. Looks like people he knows. There's nothin but burnin candles an murmurin voices. It's a chapel in fact.

I flick twice again but they're prayin away Francie an Fabian. The back of ma neck's on fire.

A man in ma head turns an grins at me. I can smell him. He smells like Brut. I shake ma head like a horse an break the focus.

I concentrate on what's in the glass coffin. The figures're still surgin silently about the glass but I'm lookin right through them. They don't exist. They don't exist. They don't exist.

But I'm manic now. I can't tell why but the ghosts in the glass've churned me up wi adrenaline. But I'm saved. It's like a miracle. I look in hopin for the snow white skin of Santa Maria. A skin I could touch. Dry silk. That's when I start smilin. I really want to laugh but I can only smile cos of the crowd. Their queue's standin still but their minds're pushin forwards. Pushin forwards.

Santa Maria Goretti'd have a hard time decomposin. She's plastic. Fuckin plastic! Ma vibratin from terror switches to vibratin wi laughter. Ma shoulders're goin up an down. The queue'll think it's tears. Passion. Religious fervour. But it's plain laughin. It's the king's gold clothes. It's halfway across Italy to see plastic feet. The good thing is the terror's gone. I hold ma laughin in. Even if she is plastic. An even if I am laughin like a hyena wi its nose tied wi sellotape there's still this awesome feelin in the place. An it likes me. It likes me laughin. It thinks it's OK. *It's OK*, it says. *Go ahead and laugh. That's good. Laughing's like God*, it says, *laughing's what He wants you to do. Laughing's the best medicine for you. The best medicine of all.*

Thanks, is what I say. But I say it too loud an there's a micro-pause in Fabian's prayers. Francie prays on regardless. The crowd turn to each other unsure to be angry or sorry. Because by now there's tears rollin out like beach-balls on the sides of ma face. Lashins. I shake ma head an flick one onto the coffin. It's a fairy tale. A fuckin fairytale. An I want to lift Maria Goretti an cuddle her. Even if she is plastic. I want to tell her it's goin to be alright. Everythin's goin to be fine. There's nothin to worry about now Maria ma wee darlin nothin to worry about now at all.

An that's when this feelin rushes through ma middle. I know I'm talkin about this like it was ages but it's seconds. There's no time at all hardly since we knelt down. The Gospel of the stars an the mountains that I was on ages ago's down in this concrete cavern. Travellin right through ma middle. Like somebody's draggin a tinsel Christmas tree through ma heart. I take a deep breath. But quick. Then everythin goes . . .

I come to up the back. Everythin looks like nothin's happened. Francie an Fabian's talkin to some holy people an Ball an Chain's draggin his ball up the side to the approval of a bunch of fanatic nuns. I read the story again. I read it upstairs earlier. *Bambini per Peternita*. Child of eternity. That's what she's called. I'm lookin about for the feelin that went through me. I can't understand. But the main thing is I knelt down in Santa Maria Goretti's tomb. The main thing is – I knelt down. At the altar.

She's encased in glass. It's glass encased in interbuzzin tourists. They're in turn encased in air. An that's encased in cold concrete. Far from the coffin there's the low buzz of foreign voices. A polite acknowledgement of Babel.

But there's another buzz that's gettin me in the neck an I can't talk about it. Not because I don't want to. It's because there's no words for it. Ye're as well tryin to prove the world's round wi music as provin the existence of God wi Science. An that's the kind of thing I'm tryin to talk about here. I'm tryin to say somethin about a feelin in this place.

Through the reinforced steel bars. Through the hard concrete. Through the easy air of tourists the message's missed. Save the odd priest or nun dotted here an there listenin wi more than the sum of their senses.

The queue's a morbid mixture of love. Of hope for somethin after death. An awe of death itself. A curiosity. An where better cos there's death live in a glass box. An I'm awesome wi love.

Ye shouldn't've been raped Sleepin Beauty. Ye should've been kissed an squeezed an walked through fields. So I kiss ye in the name of the fathers an the sons an crush the spectre of men who will not kiss.

It's concrete winds blowin down the draughts of words from the upstairs church where mass has started. The words're clashin wi Maria Goretti's simple chapel of forgiveness an silence. He's a monk now. The guy that raped her. The guy she forgave a day before she died. The guy that would not kiss's kissin now.

GOOD FRIDAY

I'm addin a bit onto the run now. I wind through the streets before headin up the Mountain. The different angles an turns an strains loosens me up before tacklin the hill. Down the twistin alleys of Cucuruzzu orange an lemon trees grow. Simple things. Really vibrant colours. If ye painted them the way they are ye'd be accused of misrepresentation. Happy trees – that's what they are. Orange an yella.

Along the alleys successive generations've built house after house. Houses stuck onto houses at crazy angles. All colours of reds an tans. White walls mostly. The odd dilapidated buildin faded to grey. Looks like the whole buildin's been plugged out. Or the occupants died an so did the house. There's houses on top of houses in the steep hillside. There's houses hangin onto the mountain by God knows what. In every street ye can reach out an touch the opposite walls wi yer fingertips. Ye turn a corner an there's a wummin inches from yer face washin the dishes by a windie. She nods an ye move on an there's an Italian babe blushin in her underwear. Turn again an ye're blinded by oranges an lemons. Turn again an ye're knocked over by a rush of barkin dogs chasin a bitch on heat. Sometimes ye feel ye're walkin through houses. Most locals're intrigued an smile or wave. But the odd suspicious oul wummin'll glare ye all the way to the end of her alley.

It's real. It's really really really real. That's what I'm sayin over an over to keep the rhythm theday. It's the heart of Italy. The heart of Italy an birds whistlin. We're right in the thick of the people. Intermingled wi their lives.

I'm springin up the Mountain now. On the last bend I see the figure again. Crucified to the cross. But movin. Still alive. All the other times I thought it was dead. I thought it was Christ. But that's not who it is. It looks familiar but I can't tell. I keep runnin but the figure looks more flesh than illusion. It looks like Jimmy Brogan. That's who it looks like. It's only the high that's doin it. It's only the run. Endorphins. That's what it is. Endorphins.

When I get there he's gone. Only the flat hardness of the wood. I'm sat on a rock an beads of sweat're tricklin down ma face. Ma breathin slows to an even pace an I hear animals scurryin around me an flappin back to the space I invaded. I look out over the mountains. They fade in tonal perspective away an away an ma spirit goes out an out wi them. An the further ma spirit goes the more cleansed an free I feel. The more cleansed an free I feel the more part of the Mountain I become. Suddenly I understand why Italians're so close to their mountain.

All around the birds're singin. I think of St Francis talker wi animals – feeder of the poor – enlightenment on the side of a mountain. But I'm happy to listen to their multitudinous words. Sounds webbin the mountain wi peace. Calm comes over me like a drug. I look down an see the fires. Burnin the brush of last year's crops mibbi.

But the scene's gatecrashed by what happened at the bank this mornin. Me an Davy went there wi Francie. There's this cylindrical door made of thick steel an plate glass. Once ye're in one side it closes. After a pause the other side opens to let ye in. One at a time. Inside there's an armed guard. Bank robberies're a way of life here, Francie says. Outside there's a sign – NO GUNS. It's legal to carry guns. The sight of the sign makes me shiver. An the sight of the real thing on the guard's holster makes me shiver more. I can't wait to get out. Every cunt's lookin at me. I'm that nervous I'm makin the guard edgy. There's sweat runnin off me. That's probably how I jogged up the Mountain theday no problem. Adrenaline. It's like I'm tryin to run away from massel.

Dere's family feuds, says Francie, *mountain against mountain. For generations,* he says. Last year one family travelled to a neighbourin mountain an shot eight of another family dead. He pointed at the mountain where it happened. Ye can't imagine it. It's all slow an easy. An I think I can make out a horse an cart meanderin up the hillside. It's not Belfast. It's not where ye'd picture the savage nuzzle of guns.

Families carry the feuds on. Histories of resentment. Passed on. Feuds run through generations like eye colours.

Romeo an Juliet for fucksakes! Davy says, *there might be more to that than meets the eye. Feuds tend to be the strongest family from one mountain tryin to wipe out the strongest family from another. If one's wiped out the genes of the victors're assured supremacy without competition for the immediate future.*

As Doom's bumpin his scientific gums – on the surface, this country looks peaceful an calm. Yet beneath it's Ireland all over the back. I push it all into darkness. Into the loch that's in ma head for drownin things. Its surface is black. An it's deep. I re-focus on below. The people of Cucuruzzu're walkin slowly in the Piazza an little streets. That's the chapel bell I hear in the distance. Ye get used to that. The more ye fade into the life the more the Chapel bell fades. I'm fadin into the Mountain. The resonance of the bell's risin up.

I think of kissin Giovanna on the Piazza the other day. I imagine her sittin here next to me. What would it be like to stay here. To be in love. To sit on the hill on Sundays wi a picnic. Some wine mibbi? Me an her. The world shinin in her eyes. Me learnin Italian an her learnin English. I look about an imagine her walkin through the trees towards me. The pear tree blossoms hangin against the blue sky. Movin up an down in small movements. Undulatin in the sun. Up an down, side to side sometimes cos there's hardly any breeze. They're like little weddin dresses. I shake the tree an the petals shower us. We're laughin in a crazy snow.

The white blooms fallin in her dark hair. Behind her the trees scribbled out against the sky. Somethin old – the trees an the land. Somethin new – me an her on the Mountain. Somethin borrowed – her. Time. Somethin blue – the sky an the melancholy silence watchin me. Tellin me ma dream's a dream. An the meanin? What's it all about Alfie? The big

It's only all manner of spring things meetin. Life focusin on itself. Regeneration. Resurrection. Just another way of lookin at things.

Before Jimmy Brogan died he says he was tryin to find a way of lookin at things. A way of lookin at the world he could live wi. I never knew what he was on about at the time. It was only after he was gone I started to remember some of the things he talked about. He made me promise I'd find a way of lookin at it that was OK. An answer. I said, *Aye Jimmy no bother ma man. I'll do it.*

He left Jig-a-Jig his paintbrush.

He seemed happy wi that. It was only a long time after I started to understand what he meant. If he'd've found a way of lookin at it that was OK he'd still be here.

One mornin I woke up wi Jimmy Brogan's voice in ma head. He's tellin me to look for an answer. I started. I was on Prozac at the time. The Ward was goin really slow. I had all the time in the world to think. All the time in the world.

So that's what I done. At first I was doin it more for Jimmy Brogan than me. But then I started enjoyin it. I could see that I could find a way of lookin at it I'd be OK. Everythin'd turn out fine. The doctors thought I was goin catatonic. But that's not what it was. I was goin inwards. I was swimmin that dark loch I was tellin ye about.

There's a mountain in everybody's head, Jimmy Brogan sayed. He was tryin to climb it when he fell off. One of the last things he sayed was, *Wee bits at a time – wee bits at a time.* I learned a lot from him.

By the inch it's a cinch, he sayed, *but by the yard it's hard.*

Nothin I think about now's original. It's all just a synthesis of what Jimmy Brogan taught me an all the stuff I've read. That's how I decided to search for what he was lookin for. I never wanted to let him down.

Down from the Ward's a glen. Two streams meet there. There's an ancient dovecote. Monks used to live in the Ward. It used to be a monastery. The grass is Holy. It gives off micro-volts when ye touch it.

Jimmy Brogan's dead. I sat down beside the stream. I'm lookin at the dovecote through the trees. It's a nice shape. A nice satisfyin shape. I think – there must be millions of objects in the universe wi satisfyin shape. But if ye put the dovecote onto a busy main street the satisfyin shape disappears. Diminishes anyway. It becomes harder an colder. But it's warm an invitin now. Like it's sayin, *Come in – I'll give ye shelter from the storm.* I'm lookin. I'm lookin.

I'm tryin to figure out what's so invitin about it. Then I thinks I sees somethin. It's Jimmy Brogan. An he pulls this branch down an waves it about. Winks an he's gone. The trees. The trees're breakin up the satisfyin shape. Obscurin the view a bit. Crackin across like slow lightnin. Breakin the symmetry. Jimmy Brogan's directin ma thinkin.

An symmetry bein broke's what stops things stayin the same. Mibbi it's the breakin of symmetry that leads to beauty. Mibbi beauty's not somethin that's fixed. Somethin ye can reference. Mibbi it's dynamic. Mibbi somethin's only beautiful cos it's movin on. Changin all the time. Mibbi change's what it's all about. Things constantly resurrectin theirselfs out of theirselfs. Re-invention.

Change is a constant. Wow – there's a fuckin laugh.

Change = Constant.

I should've knew that. It's pretty obvious when ye think about it. Change. That's the thing alright. The body's tuned into it. Made to detect any change an adapt to it. We're built round the concept of change. Measure slight changes in temperature wi our skin an adjust. Light. Measure slight changes in noise wi our ears an adjust. Movement wi our eyes an ears. Texture wi our skin. Taste. Smell. On an on we're geared up to live in change. Dark. Change is our reality. An we treat every day like it's the same as the one that went before. Every minute. Seconds even. That's where things change. In the seconds not the days or weeks.

Wait till I tell Doom that one.

There's allsorts birds whistlin an chuck chuckin on the Mountain. Sometimes, for seconds, there's silence. But even the absolute symmetry of silence's better for bein broke now an again by the idiosyncratic whirl of birds. But not all breaks in symmetry're good. A lorry in the silence's horrible. Loud an clanky. Mibbi symmetry's got to be broke natural. Poets an artists can break symmetry wi the poise of a humminbird or the Knowin of God. I'm not mistakin inventiveness for creation. There's nothin original. There's nothin new under the sun. Synthesis creates the illusion of creation. Ye get to kid yerself on ye're a tiny wee bit like God – or whoever the fuck created the universe. Since that big bang or big whoosh or whatever it was there's only ever been synthesis. There's only ever been change.

Jimmy Brogan wasn't tryin to create a new way to see the world. He was tryin to put thegether a collection of imperfect ways he could handle. A world he could believe in.

Even the whistlin birds've got their own individual imperfectness. Our voices're different as fingerprints. The engines of creation deliberately misfire so that the engines can evolve as they revolve. Creation's timeless. It's not the product. It's not the raw materials that synthesise to make the product. Creation is intervention. An intervention was in the beginnin, is now, an ever shall be, world without end. A fuckin men. I always hated stagnant water. Even if it wasn't stinkin. It might be fresh but not goin anywhere. But I love runnin water. An waves. With or without lacy frills. Always goin out or comin in. Without intervention of this creative force the world stagnates. The question is – who the fuck controls the creative force?

SALVE REGINA

I'm in the cellar this mornin. We're not workin. I want to get away from every cunt. Pat's goin spare cos the cat's pished his bed last night an he had to sleep on the floor in a sleepin bag. The room stinks of cat. I feel like a pressure inside me. Even daylight's hard to take. The sunlight's pressin on ma skin like fathoms of water. So I'm in the cellar. There's shufflin above. An low murmurin voices. The everyday prayers of conversation as we try to eke what we want out of each other wi words. I've got no candles. I'm takin a small refuge in darkness.

If they look in I can see them but they can't see me. Darkness's where Jimmy Brogan took refuge. After he came back from Belfast. A terrible darkness filled his head. The elastic band that had snapped in his head gave way to a million snappins. They snapped wi an amazin rapidity. Nothin could be done till it was all over. He was powerless – even over his own mind. When the chain reaction was over he was left wi the silence of a beach an the recedin sea's the distant hiss of reality. It was like rebuildin a street after an earthquake. An all the time there's this image of Our Lady of the Poor. An the pigeons. An the guns an grunts of what happened beneath the altar. He told no cunt.

He started takin long walks wi his personal stereo.
Monk music. *Miserere Mei*. Two – three – four in the
mornin he left his Maw's. Long walks up the Lochs.
Leavin the orange street lights on Blairhill for the silvery
darkness of the canal was good. Yip – definitely good. He
made his way under owls an stars protected by the
plainsong's spell. Near the Lochs he padded over the
woodchip paths that wind through marshes an birch
trees.

The owl's lookin down. A chunk of fluff wi two big
bike reflectors blinkin away. Tawit tawoo they're goin.
Who's this fat cunt bumpin off the grey bars of birch? If you
were the owl an ye floated above Jimmy Brogan ye'd
understand how the owl's angry. Right round about
him's a circumference of nothin. Nothin's stirrin from his
epicentre of gloom to the arcs of scurryin mice an insects
way on the periphery of vision. An birds prefer to hop in
the grass an brush rather than let the starlight catch their
feathers under the watchful eyes of the owl.

An the music plays on. ♪ *Ooh aah ahh Saaa al vay ray ay*

ay ay gee ee ee nah mater misericordi ay ay aya ay . . .

An the owl waits for planet Brogan to move through the
black void an the migratin circle of animals to pass
randomly over the forest floor again. For night-time
normality to return. The crack an swish of branches moves
off an the owl ruffles its shoulders an blink blink resets its
eyes.

Jimmy Brogan wanders listenin to the chants. But it's
not like you an me listenin to music. He thinks it's just for
him. Personal. The monks're in the trees. The pressure of
the headphone's gone. The wind pushes lightly over
Jimmy Brogan's ears. The chants're comin from the trees.
He's put that much weight on since Belfast he's puffin. He
sits on a rock an watches. In lines, the ghostly barcode of
the loch beams its silver strips through the horizontal edge

of trees. The music plays on. Louder an louder. The monks must be gettin closer. The epicentre of the music's in Jimmy Brogan's head. Dead centre. ♪ *Aaaa vay Ma ah ah ree ee ee ee ahah . . .*

Jimmy Brogan breathes deep. It seems like he's never goin to stop breathin in. His chest's risin. Jimmy Brogan breathes out. Endless mist pours from his mouth an

falls

an falls

an falls

fillin the floor wi milky turbulence. Pushin around roots of trees. Ahead the dark shapes of cowls're movin through the barcode in lines. Singin. Chantin. Heads bowed. They're everywhere. He's encircled. They've walked round about him. The incense burner's click click clickin. Its brass chain sparkles in the moonlight. A trail of dark smoke rises. He breathes in again deep an out again long. He melts into the rock. He is the rock. Jimmy Brogan – Holy Rock. The monks pray to him. Kneelin in circles far as he can see. Their knees're lost in mist an the smoke trails up from the incense. Up where the owl flies off – a black speck against the sky. *Fuck this!* it's sayin, *I'm offski.*

When the sun comes up Jimmy Brogan's in his bed. He's a fuckin vampire. Stays in his room all the time now. His Maw brings him six rolls on sausage an a mug of tea every three hours. That's all he'll eat. Tomato sauce on them. He's gettin fatter all the time. The doctor's got him on Prozac. Even goin to the toilet's an expedition. He carries a knife. Ye never know who ye might meet in the lobby.

Anyway. I'm fed up wi the cellar now. I've tried meditatin but it's no use. Ma mind can't concentrate. There's somethin happenin away far away in ma head. Like a film projected through the wrong end of a telescope. I come up into the light. I go into the wee chapel an try some prayers. Hail Marys Our Fathers an all that. But they don't do nothin. On the Ward they worked. I was readin a prayer book at breakfast this time an Jimmy Brogan started goin on about religion. He thought he was nearly onto an answer. It was just before he died.

Jimmy Brogan was goin to start a new religion. *I'm on ma way now,* he says. He was on a right up. High as a kite. The whole table of loppin tongues an missin teeth's munchin wet sugar puffs at him. Dribblin tea. Except me an the Chief. *No amounts of lagagto can stop me,* he says. *Ma new religion's goin to take over the world.*

It's not Atheist, he goes.

Big pause for effect. Munchity munch go the sugar puff eaters. All their eyes're on Jimmy Brogan's lips.

Not Pan Theist . . .

Wee pause.

. . . nor this theist nor that theist.

Me an the Chief's transfixed. If any cunt could get an answer Jimmy Brogan's yer man. He's the kiddie that told them to let the tyres down. He's the boy that got the trapped lorry out from under the bridge. Jimmy Brogan toast of the land.

Ma new religion's based on changin every day. Every time I learn an experience more. Ma mind'll change a wee bit. I'll not stagnate any more in oul beliefs. It's goin to be dynamic. Change change change. Dyna Theistic. The name of ma new religion's DYNA THEISM – God is Change.

It's warm in the wee chapel. I feel the radiators but they're not on. It's just me an the wee red sanctuary light burnin away on the altar. It's a laugh. Well it would be a laugh if it wasn't so sad. The way Jimmy Brogan ended up. Not long before the Ward.

Jimmy Brogan kept goin up the Lochs an conjurin up his monks. But after a while he couldn't even go out at night. But that was OK cos his monks surrounded him in his room. Singin. Chantin. Prayin. He'd conduct them. Now an then his wee Maw'd appear through them like a spectre wi his rolls an tea. By this time he's eighteen stone. Eighteen stone!

Duffy was amazed the size of him. He'd been away in London. Marion's flung him out cos of the things he does in Ireland. An London. An Manchester.

Fuck sake Jimmy ye've got an arse like a side of beef, Duffy says.

Jimmy Brogan chomps away on his rolls sayin nothin. Duffy's lost a lot of hair in London. An his leather coat's wore away to grey an some white patches. Under the arms's cracked. Jimmy Brogan keeps lookin at the door. He looks worried. Still says nothin. Duffy's footerin about the room. Jimmy Brogan's lookin out the side of his eyes. Followin Duffy about the place. Suspicious at everythin he touches. Jumpin at sharp moves. Duffy wades through the jeans an y-fronts an empty roll-up packets. He crushes a few cassette boxes on the way to the windie. He crunches over some rolled up socks.

It's fuckin stinkin in here Jimmy . . .

Duffy goes to lift the snib.

LEAVE IT

FUCKIN LEAVE IT

OK OK, goes Duffy palms in the air. The door handle swings down.

Are ye OK son? the wee Maw shouts in. Jimmy Brogan grunts an the door handle swings back up.

What's the matter big man?

Bring them in, goes Jimmy Brogan.

Eh?

Why don't ye just bring the cunts in the fuckin door?

What're you on about?

Ye think I'm fuckin daft? By this time he's tryin to get up out the bed. He points three times hard to the middle of his forehead. *Put it right there . . .*

. . . right in there.

BCHCHRRRRCHCRR Toichfaidh ar La . . . I'm no feart. Right there goin right there!

Duffy doesn't know what the fuck's goin on. Next thing Jimmy Brogan rips a pillowcase off an shoves it over his head. His muffled voice fills the room.

C'mon shoot me.

Silence.

Shoot me.

Silence.

If you can't do it get they cunts out there to do it!

Silence.
More silence.
What cunts out where Jimmy?
Jimmy Brogan shouts so the cunts outside can hear him.

The fuckin Provies that's who. Yese can do yer own dirty work . . .

Duffy can't make head nor tail of it. Jimmy Brogan shouts again.

Come in ya bastards!!!!!!

Duffy opens the windie. Jimmy Brogan whips the flowery pillowcase off an stares wi big bulgin owl eyes. The street's empty. Nothin. Only a lonely dog howlin streets away an an ice cream van chimin.

There's no cunt out there Jimmy, Duffy goes. *No cunt. Look for fucksakes!*

An he waves his hand under the ledge outside. Jimmy Brogan shoves up to sittin position an cranes his neck to see. His eyes're tryin to climb out an down behind the sill. In case the cunts're on their hunkers. Waitin to spring up an riddle the place.

See – nothin, Duffy says. He smiles. Jimmy Brogan lies back a bit in the bed an grins. Unsure but grinnin anyhow. But in that silence there's this loud click from the radiator.

He crashes out the bed an climbs under so's the bed's a steep hill to the Pink Floyd poster. Dark Side Of The Moon.

They're in the radiators. They're in the fuckin radiators, he's screamin

from under the shakin bed. *The Provies're in the fuckin radiators.*

Even Duffy's feart now. He doesn't know what the fuck to do.

The door flings open an in walks the wee Maw. She looks at the tilt of bed. She can see her boy from there. She looks at Duffy.

I'll leave this here, she goes an puts down this tray wi twelve rolls on sausage an two mugs of tea.

I'm not sure what you take son so there's the milk an there's the sugar there. When she goes out Duffy sits on the only corner of the bed that's on the floor an nibbles at a roll. Slurps at the tea. Nibbles at the roll.

It was a last-gasp attempt to save him. Duffy took Jimmy Brogan to a monastery.

Nunraw Abbey. Middle of nowhere. Perfect. Jimmy Brogan was breakin up an tryin to find an answer. He was wanderin about the grounds. He's in the middle of this deep pine forest. The two feet of needles're swallowin all sounds so the only thing's the delicate hiss of the wind passin over the tree tops. Animals scurryin sometimes. He's tryin to find a way out an he comes across a path. An there's this tree. It's got a statue of Our Lady in a recess in the trunk. It's one of them holes in a tree ye see in Disney films – usually wi a hootin owl in it he says.

He stopped. He thought he was an atheist. But somethin made him stop. He looks about. Down below the burn rushes below a curtain of birds. An he sees that through a gauze of trees. Nothin's clear. Nothin's clear at all. Beside the trees a wall an a field of cows watch him. He does the strangest thing. He kneels down. Knelt there he waits for the bad things to come into his head. Like the space left by a comet. A black gap where light should be. But nothin. Nothin at all. An even that wee thing's good. That nothin. An the birds soarin through the trees like Star Wars pilots're surprised at such a bulk.

He prays on the off-chance it might help his pain. Mibbi his subconscious never stopped believin in miracles. The miracles ye get drummed into ye at primary. Who knows? But Jimmy Brogan knelt there in the middle of the forest's somethin I can tell ye. Really somethin.

He needed to believe in somethin – fast. But there's nothin so special about the tree or the statue. The tree's a birch an the statue's fifty pence worth of Taiwanese plastic. He says somethin happened. A new web was put in place for his subconscious mind. A web made from parts of his oul net of tradition an his new threads of pain. Every knot that had to be tied transmitted electromagnetic pain in an evergoin sphere along the wires. Every knot that had to be untied left a black hole. It's black gravity tuggin always. Tuggin. An shook the web's structure so much he thought it was goin to reach resonant frequency an rip apart. But same time as bits're rippin apart other bits're tyin thegether. What happens's his history gets married to his misery. A new net of things he knew an things he knows now.

That's how he found a path to travel. That day. That was his wee miracle. He starts thinkin about some cunt sayin God never made Man. Man made God. He hoped it wasn't true. He needed God to exist. Somethin in the wee plastic statue. An it comes to him. Mibbi the sayin's right. Mibbi prayin's puttin spiritual power in somethin. An icon. A real thing mibbi. Who knows. A place? Mibbi we bank our power like dollars. Deposited so it can be withdrawn by anybody that needs it? The thought encourages him. He thinks he sees the pink face smile an wink. He prays some more.

Hailmaryfullagracethelordiswiththeeblessedartthouamong wimminanblessedisthefruitofthywombjesus

holymarymotherofgodprayfrussinnersnowanatthehourofour deathamen

Funny thing is he can remember the prayers. Ingrained. An he's kneelin. That's a thing he thought he'd never do again. Kneel beside a statue.

Well that's what happened that day. It never stopped him goin into the Ward. But he says it saved his life.

That first time it was only the tree an the statue. That's all. He'd've missed it if a bird flew by an his head swivelled. Years after Jimmy Brogan was first there the doctors took us on a two-day visit. His face was gleamin an his eyes were two blue stars in the void of space. Hope an Faith. That's what I called them. In the constellation of See Saw. See Saw so that when one's down the other one's up. An when they're level? They're exactly in harmony. Absolute peace. There's an electricity about Jimmy Brogan this day. His high's spreadin out in all directions like a Messiah. Touchin everythin an everybody. It's **the tree,** he's shoutin.

The tree!!!

Turns out the tree's saturated wi mementoes an holy thank yous for miracles received. People's been comin from everywhere to see it. To pray. Jimmy Brogan started somethin rollin all they years ago. Somethin rollin.

Jimmy Brogan's walkin to the tree. But he slows an he's bent forwards like there's a gale – but there's no wind. No wind at all. He's got to penetrate the surface of love that's growin out from it daily. Even the doctors are still. Still as mice. Then his eyebrows near hit the clouds. He starts shoutin out. Crows take to the sky like a sudden umbrella.

JEESUS JEESUS CHRIST – Imagine hydrogen right? Imagine hydrogen's the first note in the melody of creation.

I'm silent. I'm lookin over a wall at these cows. The whole ward's listenin. Fegan shakes his head.

If hydrogen's the first note of creation . . . the first note . . . well . . . well . . . all the other elements must be the other notes. If we find out the order we'll hear the tune. We'll hear the fuckin tune! Da da da da daa daa daaa. An if we hear the fuckin tune . . . if we hear the fuckin tune . . .

But he trails off. Ordinary day trippers smile. Jimmy Brogan's kneelin. Spoutin Hail Marys. An in the sky the crows whirl round in their crazy umbrella waitin for stillness.

EASTER SUNDAY

We're all at mass this time. Even Davy's there. He's two in front holdin hands wi Poppins. Pat's right at the back. I recognise his cough now an then. I'm concentratin on the sanctuary candle. It keeps draggin me in. I keep thinkin of that freaky stuff at Santa Maria Goretti's. It's the worst I've been since the Ward. I never told nocunt. But I'm in a foreign country. Out ma routine.

Ball an Chain even manages a smile across. I give him a polite bow. An there's Giovanna. The babe not the cook. She's squintin across at me. Smilin. It's good here. It's a good place. So I'm wonderin how I want to burst out cryin. There's this lump of nothin the size of a football risin inside me. It's givin me the bends. Same time this sweet air filled wi blossom's blowin in the side doors. Even the Italian men're happy theday. Standin at the back. The altar's all flowers an through the open door I see the Mountain. An the outline of the cross. An there's a figure on it. I crush ma eyes an look again but it's still there. Hangin like Jesus. But it's not far away. It's close up I see it. The figure. Well not the figure – the hand. The hand an it's tryin to rip the nail right through his skin. At each stretch there's an indentation in the palm. An more blood squirts out an runs down. Then I'm back in the chapel again starin at the varnished hand of a wooden Jesus. Probably the light in ma eyes. Probably the light. I decides to take one last run up the Mountain before the dinner thenight. The Last Supper, Francie's callin it. We're all goin home themorra.

On the way down from mass Francie catches up wi me. It's the last supper right enough. He's decided his vocation lies back in scientific investigation. Somewhere he can do somethin about the human race. Somethin practical he says. He thinks he's thought out a few procedures that might shed some light on the AIDS virus. He owes it to his Marie. I asked him how come if he was that sure about the monk stuff. But he couldn't explain. *Marie*, he says like that explained everythin. *Marie*. I look at him. In his eyes I see the hand again pullin itself off the nail. Freein itself an clenchin. An the blood runnin out the fist. An when it's far away from the wood an the nail it comes to me – things're always changin. Even the unchangeable changes.

When I pass the cellar Davy an Suzanne's down there on their knees prayin to the Holy Svelto.

The hill's pushin me back theday. More than any other day. I'm fit. Fitter than ever. Ma muscles're ripplin under ma skin. Tryin to burst free. Ma legs're shovin against the path – the Mountain – the country – the whole fuckin planet! But the force that doesn't want me up the hill's shovin harder. The more it resists the harder I push into the ground. The fields're empty. Olive trees're wavin about wi their leaves clickin. Birds're walkin on the main road. It's Hitchcock. There's not the roar nor the distant hum of any cars movin. Down the village the sun's shinin bright on empty streets. Everyone's indoors preparin meals.

I'm the only man in the world. But on I go.

The Mountain doesn't want me. On an on. Up an up. I've got the makins of this force that's holdin me back. Jesus I have. By fuck I'm the man for it.

When I gets to the dip before the top I get a wee leap in ma heart. It feels like a heart attack but it's only adrenaline. It's only fear. I know what it is on the cross. Well – part of me knows. But the part that knows's not tellin me exactly what. But it's tellin me it knows. *I know,* it's sayin, *I know alright!*

But I don't want to see anythin on the cross. I want a good clean sharp edge. The white of the Mountain an the blue sky. That's what I want. The Mountain an the sky.

But that's not what I get. This time there's some cunt there. Not the ethereal figure it usually is. It's real. Thick as soup. I just walk. The fear's gone. It's hard to explain. I'm gettin the same feelin like as if I'm walkin towards a gigantic mirror. But it's not reflectin exactly what's behind me. Whatever it is on the cross's the epicentre of that world. I'm the epicentre of mine. An I'm walkin.

It's him. The Mountain. The sky. But there's somethin else. They're all invested wi these feelins. Feelins I've not had since the Ward. All the objects're buzzin wi emotions. An the main thrum's emanatin from him on the cross.

An me – I'm the epicentre of ma world. The other Mountain. The other sky. The path windin down. The valley. The village. They're all permeated wi ma feelins.

An the two worlds're headin towards each other like folded space. I get there an stand on the grassy knoll. I'm eye level wi the apparition. First it's not movin. It looks dead. Then it turns its head an lights a fag.

Can ye fuckin believe it!? he says.

That's when I know who it is fully.

I'm thinkin I'll be back on the Ward in no time at this rate. No fuckin time at all. *Oh hello,* they'll say. *We've kept yer bed warm. Did ye really think ye'd make it out there on yer tod?*

I sit on a rock. He smiles.

I thought you were dead! I says. But he laughs. An shakes his head.

Des Dillon

*Ye're some man. Did ye think they could kill me off easy as all
that?* Jimmy Brogan goes.

I thought ye were dead!? I says again. Same time I'm
lookin about makin sure nocunt's watchin.

I thought ye were dead?

I was only hidin. To get us out. Only hidin.

I go to say somethin but all this stuff starts surgin
through ma head. It's the same stuff that was trapped in
Santa Maria Goretti's glass coffin.

Let it in! Jimmy Brogan says, *It's me. It's us. It's you! Let it
in.*

So I let it in. It's the riots. It's night after the gun incident
in McDavitt's. Jimmy Brogan knew he was quids in wi
Liam. Quids in wi the Provies. The Brits're dressed up like
robots an they're firin plastic bullets. The crowd surges
forward an rains bricks an bottles an petrol bombs down
on the Saracens. An Jimmy Brogan's amazed how far the
crowd can chuck stuff. Then the pop pop pop of the
guns again.

CrzzzzzzzzzzzzzzzzzzZZZZZiiiiD

the crazy cylinders whizz through the crowd. There's the
dull smack of flesh an a scream. Some lassie's gettin
dragged up an alley by some toothless wimmin howlin at
the soldiers. The crowd pours into the thin alleys waitin
for a silent break. Jimmy Brogan's grinnin like half a bin
lid. There's breath in the air an adrenaline runnin down
the walls. It could be blood. Ye could lick it off. All these
bodies pressed thegether. Boys an girls men an wimmin.
There's sex in the violence. Somewhere. The Brits're
rumblin up an down the street but they can't break
through the barricades of burnin cars an concrete blocks.
In the dark gaps of the inferno there's a song playin on a
scratchy oul stereo, something about armoured cars and
tanks and guns . . .

It's the anniversary of Internment. Ten years. A lot of these cunts've been locked up. Jimmy Brogan's joinin in the song cos he can't throw so far. Next thing there's a breath on Jimmy Brogan's neck. Then a voice.

Ever fired an Armalite Jimmy Boy?

It's Liam. Jimmy Brogan turns his head. The crowd's startin to move out the alley again. Crates of petrol bombs're bein shifted forward. Mostly by wimmin. Wimmin like yer Maw. Like yer Auntie. Yer Granny even. Ordinary wimmin. Liam grins into Jimmy's face. The crowd's bumpin by them. He shoves a pistol up the crack of Jimmy's arse.

Ever fired an Armalite? This is a peashooter compared tell ye that.

Get that to fuck out ma arse, Jimmy Brogan says an squeezes Liam's neck. But he lets go when Liam's eyes darken. By this time the riot's goin on in the street an it's only Liam an Jimmy an two other cunts. An a couple of oul wimmin at their back gates ready to let people through their houses. Funny thing is the stars're out an a shootin star goes over Belfast.

The main thing Jimmy Brogan remembered about that night wasn't the riot or the crowd. It was Liam's cheap aftershave. **Sniff! Sniff!** Brut. Yer nose's yer memory. That's what it is. For sure.

Jimmy Brogan sneaks off wi Liam an two Provies he's not met before. There's a Sierra parked a few streets back. The only one that speaks's Liam. The other two get in the back. An Jimmy Brogan's feart. Still reelin from the reality of the gun in McDavitt's. But he's kiddin on it's OK. No bother. Take it in his stride.

Toichfaidh Ar La Jimmy Boy, goes Liam.

Toichfaidh Ar La, Jimmy says back. Liam's twistin round all sorts of corners. Goin over the same streets twice an three times. Make sure nocunt's at them probably. But the

voice keeps comin through. No matter how Jimmy Brogan
tries to block it out. He thinks the two in the back snort out
a laugh but he's not sure. He's not sure at all. No sir. It's
Liam's wife's voice he hears in his head.

*Get out of this while ye still can Jimmy – It's not for the likes
of you. Not for you at all.*

An for a second ye could see the somethin between
them in her eyes. An his. An there was somecunt else
watchin too. Liam. He could see the somethin in their eyes
an all.

She'd said that cos Jimmy Brogan'd patted Liam on the
side in McDavitt's. But he'd patted him on the gun. Liam
thought Jimmy Brogan done that on purpose but he never.
He was shocked when he felt the gun. It'd brung it all
home to him. Compressed all his years of romantic
republicanism into a tiny sphere. A black hole. The snout
of a gun. Jimmy Brogan became a singularity of fear.
Liam's wife saw it. Liam laughed. He thought Jimmy
Brogan'd deliberately patted the gun.

*Ye're some man Jimmy ye shouldn't go round pattin folks on
the gun like that – they might go off in yer face. Ye don't know
who's watchin,* says Liam. An Jimmy Brogan doesn't know
if Liam's smilin or grinnin. Or if he's laughin or cryin
hissel.

So the terror's buildin in the car for Jimmy Brogan. He
doesn't know what's happenin. But it's as if Liam can read
his thoughts.

You're the fellah for us Jimmy Boy, nat right lads? he goes to
the two in the back. They snort again. Jimmy Brogan's
hidin it well. He's hidin it well. In the wee mirror ye use
for puttin on yer lipstick he can see their dark eyes an
wide grins. They're grinnin wi their mouths shut. Two
pink faces. Like satanic ventriloquist dummies. Evil as
fuck. The car swooshes on an on.

The faces grin.

Liam smiles.

Jimmy Brogan's losin it.

The faces grin.

Liam takes another bend.

The faces grin.

Jimmy Brogan can't take much more.

Liam swishes round another corner.

He can't take any more. His pressure bursts.

Whe . . . where're we goin Liam?

Chapel. Mass.

The two in the back burst out laughin. They're like two drunk cunts on the way home from a disco. But they're not that. They're not that at all. One's got hardly any teeth an in passin headlights they're like wooden children.

We're goin to chapel Jimmy Boy. Do our duties.

Maybe pray for that RUC man we done Jimmy!

The car's turned

left

an right

that many times Jimmy Brogan doesn't have a clue where he is. The guys in the back're quiet now. The radio's playin some sad music. Sounds like a cello. He jumps when Liam puts his hand on his thigh. Mibbi he senses how feart he is.

Ye'll be alright Jimmy boy. Ye'll be alright, Liam goes.

The eyes of the two in the back. Jimmy Brogan's seen that look before. Lights're trailin over the surface of their eyeballs. Sometimes it's like fire an sometimes it's like ice. The car heads on an leaves the glow of the city behind. The eerie green of the dashboard an the red flare of a fag lights up Liam's skin. For a minute in the sheer black of the windscreen he looks like the Devil. Satan. Beelzebub.

It's a chapel right enough. Jimmy Brogan's relieved at the loose way they get out the car. For a while he thought they were goin to shoot him. Mibbi get him to run an shoot him in the back. Trees – that's where to go. Into the trees. He couldn't figure out what he done. He's gettin worse. He's losin it. Fast. The arches're three dark shapes. Somethin like a wound-up elastic band snapped inside his head as they opened the door. Not loud. Not so as anybody else'd notice. A light snap an some reverberations that's all. Blue sparks feedin outwards from one brain cell to another until eventually his hair lifts.

In here Jimmy Boy, says Liam. It takes a while for the interior to form through the darkness cos the headlights on the car were blindin. Still on. He hears movement. This oul crone wi a face like a pile of rocks's wakin up on one of the pews. She coughs away. Her tattered blankets fall to the floor. Liam laughs. But the other two're somewhere in the dark. There's hunners of candles lit an the wax on the floor's icebergs pokin through a sea of marble. Next thing's a shadow. Somethin grotesque tryin to push its way up out the floor. Hell tryin to burrow into Heaven. But it's the oul crone.

Jimmy Brogan thinks it's a gun bein cocked but it's the bolt on the door. The oul crone coughs some more. *Right y'are Liam. Right y'are.* She walks towards them again. Her gums shine in the flickerin lights.

Ye'll be wantin yer stuff? she goes.

Liam nods. The other two're movin about on the altar. Jimmy Brogan can just make out Our Lady of the Poor – covered in pigeons. Her face looms through shadow. Mother of Christ – lost at sea. Paint's flakin from her. She looks like she's gave in. The oul wummin shuffles off excited. She's mutterin.

D'ye ever pray Jimmy Boy? Liam goes.

Jimmy Brogan looks at him like he never heard the question. He did hear it. Liam asks again.

Pray, he blesses hissel, *d'ye ever say prayers?*

Jimmy Brogan's puzzled. Liam nods to the altar. Below the good ship Mary lost at sea two black figures move.

Let's say a wee decade for the Cause Jimmy Boy. Liam kneels down. The yella light of candles fills every crack on his face. He looks plastic. Made up. Jimmy Brogan kneels beside him. They're spoutin out the Hail Marys goodstyle. Jimmy Brogan hears the shuffle behind but keeps prayin. He's scared. Really scared. The other two're on the altar prayin an all. But what's Liam up to?

The nuzzle of a gun presses under his nose. *Know what this is Jimmy Boy?*

Jimmy nods. His eyes're swivelled so they look like white holes in the blackness. There's no prayers now. Our Lady's dejected. The pigeons warble about cooin an gigglin at each other. The two Provies stand up an move behind him. The oul wummin cackles. Jimmy Brogan turns an Liam puts the Armalite at the centre of his forehead. He turns him like it's connected to him. Like it's a lever connected to his head. Liam walks back round so Jimmy Brogan's facin the altar. The rifle's makin a wee O in the middle of Jimmy Brogan's forehead.

You've been a bad boy Jimmy, says Liam, *an bad boys've got to be punished.*

They drape Jimmy Brogan over the barrier. First thing is he pishes hissel wi fear.

I hope ye enjoyed yer ride Jimmy, Liam goes, *she's a rare wee ride ma Rachel – is she not?*

Get yer fuckin head down. Liam keeps pushin his head down an the other two slap him. Punch him. An nocunt can hear him. Not unless there is a God. It's big bells ringin an blue flashes. He's prayin now.

Take his strides off, he hears Liam sayin to the two Provies. *Get the knickers off him.*

They rip his boxers off. Jimmy Brogan's cryin as he feels a cock up him. The oul crone laughs an claps like a schoolgirl. Claps wi glee. Liam walks forwards an Jimmy

Brogan smells the Brut. The crone kicks Jimmy Brogan any chance she gets. An spits on him. An her spit smells of Buckfast.

For a blackness the three men rape him. Sometimes it's blow jobs at gunpoint. Sometimes it's the stingin hiss as they put candles out on his flesh. Sometimes it's the scratch of the crone's nails down his rump. Like she's tryin to tear him to shreds. It's all spinnin.

He's numb. The door's bangin in the wind. Only the candles at the far end of the altar're lit. There's a shadow above him. He focuses. Too weak to move. There's the oul crone. She's rumpled her dress up an she's pishin on him. Pishin an laughin. Pishin an laughin. Her mouth's broken by her pointed tongue. A crazy Q. An she laughs an she laughs. The oul bastard. Oul cunt. But he can't move. An even wi all that he's glad to be alive. Grateful they never killed him. He falls into the dark again wi the last of her pish runnin off his face. Baptised into hell.

On the way across the Piazza there's Pat an Davy watchin me. They can see there's somethin different. An there is. I'm Jimmy Brogan. I'm fuckin Jimmy Brogan. Pat an Davy come runnin down the stairs onto the Piazza.

I'm Jimmy Brogan – I'm fuckin Jimmy Brogan, I'm shoutin. Pat comes across an gives me this hug.

How did yees not tell me? I'm shoutin. *Yee haa! How did yees not tell me who I was?* But I'm laughin when I'm sayin that. I'm laughin an they're laughin. I'm laughin ma fuckin head off. Or I'm laughin ma fuckin head on. Or I should say – I'm laughin ma head an Jimmy Brogan's thegether.

Ye're beamin son, Pat says, *was the Mountain good to ye theday?*

Aye Da, I goes. *The Mountain was good to me theday.* He gives me this big hug. Him an Davy smile at each other.

It's good to have ye back son. Good to have ye back, ma Da says. Davy smiles an shakes ma hand.

Welcome back, Jimmy, he says.

TWO STARS SKIMMIN

I'm lyin on the flat roof. I'm lookin out to the stars thinkin
about all the things that's happened. The washin flaps
now an then an blocks out the sky. There's no moon.

This music's goin through ma head. A wummin sings i
a high voice. A crystal voice. It's clear an ma eyes're
wanderin about in the stars. I'm thinkin there's a purpos

The patio's cold an hard on ma back but the universe
domed about me like I've been transported to a little
hillock in heaven.

It's all simple an awful. The truth. He's resurrected.
been carryin him wi me all the time. I thought when I
came down off the Mountain theday I'd feel bad. I wai
on it. But it never came. From one point in space time
another point in space time everythin's changin. Alwa
Change change change. At one end of change there wa
universe. At the other end of that change there's a new
universe. Continued resurrection. Me. Us right now. Y

At the bottom of the Mountain there was me. At the
of the Mountain there was Jimmy Brogan. Nailed to a
cross. But he's not there now. Cos I am Jimmy Brogan.
was his plan all along. That's how he escaped the War
He found a way of lookin at it he could live wi. The w
He folded inside-out in his own head. He showed **the**
the good side an kept all the bad things locked away.
Locked away till his outfolded self – me – could look ;

them. Locked away till he could resurrect. That's how ma Da an Davy brung me here. I'm startin to realise. They brung me here cos I'd started bein strange again. Thought it might help me. Keep me out the Ward. The two of them's havin a party in the room. Cheerin an laughin thegether. The prodigal son an the pal back from the dead.

An as I look out two stars're skimmin the atmosphere. When they touch the surface they light up an leave a sprinkle of who they are. But then I notices they're startin to look like they'll pass close to each other. An more an more they come thegether. They're like two edges of an arrow blade, but the angle's gettin thinner an thinner. They're goin to crash I'm thinkin. I'm expectin them to explode. At least collide. But they don't. They come thegether. One minute there's two. Next minute there's one.

On they go off on a new course. Hurtlin over the curve of the earth.

I take a deep breath. I smile. The stars an the moon're reflected in ma eyes. My face is wrinkled by happiness. An I'll tell ye this for nothin – I believe in the magnificence of man.

The divided self
RD laing

*If you enjoyed this book here is a selection of
other bestselling titles from Review*

MY FIRST SONY	Benny Barbash	£6.99	☐
THE CATASTROPHIST	Ronan Bennett	£6.99	☐
WRACK	James Bradley	£6.99	☐
IT COULD HAPPEN TO YOU	Isla Dewar	£6.99	☐
ITCHYCOOBLUE	Des Dillon	£6.99	☐
MAN OR MANGO	Lucy Ellmann	£6.99	☐
THE JOURNAL OF MRS PEPYS	Sara George	£6.99	☐
THE MANY LIVES & SECRET SORROWS OF JOSÉPHINE B.	Sandra Gulland	£6.99	☐
TWO MOONS	Jennifer Johnston	£6.99	☐
NOISE	Jonathan Myerson	£6.99	☐
UNDERTOW	Emlyn Rees	£6.99	☐
THE SILVER RIVER	Ben Richards	£6.99	☐
BREAKUP	Catherine Texier	£6.99	☐

Headline books are available at your local bookshop or newsagent.
Alternatively, books can be ordered direct from the publisher. Just tick
the titles you want and fill in the form below. Prices and availability subject
to change without notice.

Buy four books from the selection above and get free postage and
packaging and delivery within 48 hours. Just send a cheque or postal order
made payable to Bookpoint Ltd to the value of the total cover price of the
four books. Alternatively, if you wish to buy fewer than four books the
following postage and packaging applies:

UK and BFPO £4.30 for one book; £6.30 for two books; £8.30 for three
books.

Overseas and Eire: £4.80 for one book; £7.10 for 2 or 3 books (surface
mail).

Please enclose a cheque or postal order made payable to *Bookpoint Limited*,
and send to: Headline Publishing Ltd, 39 Milton Park, Abingdon, OXON
OX14 4TD, UK.
Email Address: orders@bookpoint.co.uk

If you would prefer to pay by credit card, our call team would be delighted
to take your order by telephone. Our direct line is 01235 400 414 (lines
open 9.00 am–6.00 pm Monday to Saturday 24 hour message answering
service). Alternatively you can send a fax on 01235 400 454.

Name ....

Address ....

....

....

If you would prefer to pay by credit card, please complete:
Please debit my Visa/Access/Diner's Card/American Express (delete as
applicable) card number:

Signature .... Expiry Date..............